They were staring at each other, his silver eyes going dark. Was he interested? His previous actions indicated not, but at that precise moment he looked as though he might be contemplating kissing her. She was considering pressing her lips to his, but he didn't strike her as the sort who would stop with only a kiss. She already knew she would be unable to resist him, so if she did as she yearned to do, they might end up in this tub together. Most certainly they'd end up in that large, enticing bed.

Marlowe's breath caught, held, until finally like the air in a balloon, it slowly leaked out. The way he'd looked at her that night—no other man had ever regarded her with so much heat in his eyes, like a fire slowly simmering until it was smoldering. Oh, certainly, she'd seen want, lust, and yearning. She'd reveled in her ability to bring it to the fore, to be able to create such desire. But it had been different with him. Terrifyingly so.

By Lorraine Heath

LORRAINE HEATH

A Tempest of Desire

AVON

An Imprint of HarperCollinsPublishers

A TEMPEST OF DESIRE. Copyright © 2024 by Jan Nowasky. All rights reserved. Printed in the United States of America. No part of this book may be used or reproduced in any manner whatsoever without written permission except in the case of brief quotations embodied in critical articles and reviews. For information, address HarperCollins Publishers, 195 Broadway, New York, NY 10007.

First Avon Books mass market printing: December 2024

Print Edition ISBN: 978-0-06-338445-3
Digital Edition ISBN: 978-0-06-338446-0

Cover design by Amy Halperin
Cover illustration by Victor Gadino
Cover photographs © Getty Images

Avon, Avon & logo, and Avon Books & logo are registered trademarks of HarperCollins Publishers in the United States of America and other countries.

HarperCollins is a registered trademark of HarperCollins Publishers in the United States of America and other countries.

FIRST EDITION

24 25 26 27 28   BVGM   10 9 8 7 6 5 4 3 2 1

This book is dedicated to
Dr. Ryan Mooney, who calmed my fears and used his surgical skills to send the cancer into oblivion.
Dr. Deepna Jaiswal, who used her oncological expertise to ensure it stays there.
All the nurses, NPs, PAs, technicians, and staff who always have a ready smile, a kind word, and provide incredible care during a challenging time in a cancer patient's life.

And last but not least . . .
Nathan, who refused to believe this chapter in our story wouldn't have a happy ending and held my hand through it all.
I love you, babe, more than words can ever express.

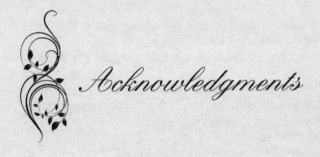

Acknowledgments

When I began working on this book, I was recovering from having a heart valve replaced and was also dealing with a cancer diagnosis, which resulted in another surgery and immunotherapy treatments. As of this writing, the heart is doing well and the cancer appears to be gone. However, during the past several months, I had days when I was in a fog, times when I would think one word but type another, occasions when my fingers were confused by the keyboard, and moments when nothing in the story made sense.

However, it takes a village to produce a book and I had an incredibly supportive village.

First and foremost, I want to thank May Chen, my amazing editor, who insisted I focus on my health first and not worry about my deadline. The book would get written when it got written. Working with May has always been a delight. She has a way of helping me to make the stories more than they were when I drafted them. In addition, she is a lovely person to hang out with.

I also want to thank my agent, Robin Rue, who checked in often and kept my spirits up. She assured me I'd get through this to write many more books.

And to the wonderful Avon Books team who worked their magic to get this book ready for publication. I'm grateful this story came to life in their talented hands.

My deep appreciation to Meg Cabot, who had posted on social media that she'd had heart surgery and, soon after, became my commiseration buddy. Her insights, honest sharing of her experiences, and humor made the journey toward healing not quite so isolating or baffling.

And finally, to my awesome readers, who may not have even known how much I needed and appreciated them. You kept me going, inspired me to get this story finished, and brought me to tears on numerous occasions.

Without you, dear readers, none of the words of this story would have mattered.

With love and gratitude,
Lorraine

A Tempest of Desire

Prologue

From the Journal of Viscount Langdon

It was not an easy thing to be born the son of the Earl of Claybourne—the Devil Earl, as those of influence referred to him in whispers. My mother worked diligently to redeem his unsavory reputation in order to ensure he and his children were accepted by those who mattered. But few could forget, or were willing to overlook, the fact that he'd once killed a man.

I found it difficult to reconcile that facet of his past, as I knew him to be a kind and protective father. Although he taught me things that few sons of noblemen knew. How to secretly pull a card from the bottom of a deck. How to deftly pick a pocket. How to accurately measure a man's worth.

But of most import, he taught me to wholly embrace and enjoy my passions.

I was six years of age the first time he took me on a journey via the railway. I fell instantly in love with the motions of the coach, the speed. I marveled at how this machine could unite the world, equalize the masses, and quickly take me on adventures. I could spend the day at the seaside and be back home in time for dinner. I could travel places with hardly any bother at all.

And I did. Often. Whenever I had the chance.

Then on a dark and stormy June night, in the year of our Lord 1878, the railway that I loved taught me that, with no warning whatsoever, life could drastically change between one heartbeat and the next.

Chapter 1

*W*hile the howling wind tore around him and the rain lashed at his upturned face, he staggered to the edge of the cliff, braced himself against nature's wrath, and hurled the empty whisky bottle into the blackened abyss that contained monstrous waves thrashing against the rocky, sandy shore.

His harsh laughter was carried out to sea as his black greatcoat whipped around his calves, and he wondered why he'd even bothered to wear it. The brutal rain had drenched him. The wind threatened to shove him right over the edge. But he stood his ground.

And trembled.

Just as he'd trembled uncontrollably that fateful night when his world changed completely. There had been a storm then as well, as harsh and unforgiving as the one he faced now on his tiny, secluded isle. Where he came to escape the horrific memories.

Only they refused to leave him in peace. They

battered him as vehemently and with as much fury as the tempest that surrounded him. And if he couldn't escape them, he could at least teach himself to ignore them, to send them into the darkest recesses of his mind where they might lose the power to plague him.

Consequently, he stood there stoically and refused to allow them victory, to force him into scurrying back to the residence where a warm fire and another bottle of scotch waited. Where he could hide from the unfortunate truth that he'd gone mad.

Stark raving mad.

Oh, he did a bang-up job of giving the appearance of being the same as those who surrounded him. Moving among the *ton*, as he had in the before time, with a lackadaisical confidence, an easy smile, and a bold laugh. He flirted with the ladies, danced with them, even charmed them. Many were hopeful of becoming wife to the Earl of Claybourne's heir, of bearing him children. None knew he was no longer worthy of inheriting his father's title, of carrying his own courtesy one.

However, he thought his family was beginning to suspect the truth.

In a few days, he would see them and pretend that he was again as he'd once been.

They'd pretend as well. Pretend to believe him when he told them that he came to this island to study the stars. That he required the isolation and solitude in order to devote himself to his new passion for the sky—since he'd abandoned his passion for the railway.

As soon as the Season had concluded the previous August, while everyone else had departed for their country estates, he'd come here—where a small stone castle had withstood the rigors of time and, with diligent devotion and his own hands, had become once again inhabitable. He had no companionship, no one with whom to break the monotony. No one visited him without an invitation—and he issued no invitations.

And if there were nights when the loneliness devoured him, he would endure it. He would do whatever was required to protect his secret. For the sake of his family. He would do nothing to bring his parents shame when it had taken so long for them to be accepted by their peers. He would not undo all their efforts to belong by revealing the truth that he no longer did.

But of late, the loneliness was worse than ever. Insatiable. Strengthening. Like the tempest, until it possessed the power to destroy all in its wake. To destroy him.

Yet what he yearned for most desperately at the moment was not within reach: the warmth of a woman's soft body, the flowery fragrance of a woman's flesh, the gentle lullaby of a woman's sighs, the sweet taste of a woman's lips. Still, dropping his head back and glaring at the black and fathomless star-hidden sky, he bellowed, "A woman! A woman! My kingdom for a woman!"

Lightning flashed with such brilliance, turning night into day, he had to avert his gaze, look away . . . look down.

And that was when he saw *her*.

Lying face down and motionless on the beach,

bare arms outstretched as though she'd been reaching for salvation, but fallen short, waves ebbing and flowing around her, trying to lure her back into the dangerous depths. With naked legs clearly visible, appearing to be absent her frock, she was unmoving, her moonbeam hair—like tendrils of seaweed—spread Medusa-like over and around her. Had the Fates answered his cry? Or was his drunken and demented mind even more lost than he'd surmised, conjuring an apparition that appeared real enough to steal his breath?

Blackness swooped back in to conceal her. She'd been detectible for only a second, maybe two. Surely it had been a sea creature of some sort, a dolphin or an infant whale, washed upon the shore, and he'd seen only what he wanted to see: a mermaid, a siren, Neptune's daughter. What he was suddenly desperate to find: someone to ease the wretched ache of loneliness that had taken up residence in his soul.

He raised his lantern, but the light it provided was not enough to conquer the darkened abyss where she lay crumpled. The low glow strictly adhered to its purpose of ensuring he knew where to place his foot when he took his next step.

Then lightning again defiantly zigged across the sky, and it was as though every speck of illumination in the heavens touched her as he wanted to. She was no apparition but flesh and blood. How the hell had she ended up marooned on his shore?

She moved not at all. Had she drowned?

Pivoting, his greatcoat flaring out, he raced toward the path that would lead him down to her.

Perhaps she'd been a passenger on a ship. In this storm, it would have been destroyed. He imagined her flailing about in the rough seas, desperate to reach land, her sodden clothing and hair dragging her down. The salty swells filling her mouth, her lungs, until she no longer had space for air. What a ghastly way to go.

He was far too familiar with ghastly ways to die.

Shoving back the gruesome thoughts that thrived among his horrid memories, he focused on her. The trail was muddy and slick. Scrambling along it, he lost his footing time and again. But finally, he reached the narrow shore that the sea was striving to capture.

Again, lightning flashed, serving as a beacon to direct him toward her. He rushed over, dropped to his knees beside the inert form, and set down the lantern. Gently he rolled her over. She wore little more than a chemise and drawers. Placing his hand on her ribs, he felt the movement of her drawing in air as well as her almost violent shivering.

Not dead, not dead. Thank God.

Slowly, gingerly, his fingers brushing lightly over her cold skin, he swept aside her hair to reveal her pale sand-dotted face. "Miss? Madam?"

Nothing. No response. Not even a whisper of a stirring.

His curse rivaled the storm in its intensity. Using the lantern as his guide, with an impartiality he'd been forced to master on another night such as this, he swept one hand over her, searching for wounds, signs of bleeding. He could detect a few scratches and dark splotches that probably signaled the beginning of bruises. What concerned him the most, however, was that she was as frigid as a block of ice.

A small woman, she wasn't going to survive much longer if he didn't get her warm.

He shrugged out of his greatcoat and wrapped it around her as though she was a gift from the Fates who could easily break if not handled with care. He feared that somewhere she was indeed broken, and he simply couldn't determine where precisely she might be hurt.

In spite of her drenched undergarments, he easily lifted her into his arms, her head lolling into the nook of his shoulder, as if that part of him had been designed specifically for her. He would have preferred to have kept her positioned like that so she might be a bit more comfortable, but he needed to be able to carry the lantern. Therefore, he maneuvered her until she was draped over his shoulder, her backside resting beside his head.

Reaching down, he grabbed the lantern before shoving himself, with a great deal of effort, to his feet. Staggered, caught his balance. Straightened further against the blinding onslaught of the storm.

The path he'd followed to get to her was slick with mud. However, in the opposite direction was another trail, rocky and firmer, that led up to the residence. He would have steadier footing along that route, even if it was somewhat slippery. He wanted to ensure he wouldn't drop his precious cargo.

How she'd come to be in so few garments was a bit puzzling. Perhaps she'd sensed that the ship was not destined to reach land and had unburdened herself of anything that would have prevented her from doing the same. He couldn't imagine a lady of quality being so bold or practical. Heaven forfend, they should be caught not properly attired—regardless of any precarious circumstances that required not being so. While something about her teased at the edge of his memory, he couldn't recall meeting her at a ball or any other Societal affair. Which meant she was, in all likelihood, not a lady of the highest caliber.

Was she some man's fancy piece, fallen from his yacht? Being engaged in a bit of naughtiness might explain her reduction in clothing. But the mystery of her was for sorting another time.

It worried him that she was exceptionally quiet and inert, that his uneven and jarring movements over the rough terrain did nothing to bring her out of her lethargic state. He'd seen people who hadn't moved because of the sudden shock of the situation. He'd known some to survive catastrophe only to succumb to death a few days later. Whether from disbelief, fright, or sorrow. The mind, he was discovering, could be a powerful influence over the body. But he would do all in his power, limited though it was, to ensure she didn't die.

Finally, the soft, welcoming glow from the windows of his ancestors' fortification came into view. According to family legend, ages ago, this isle had served as the first defense against any invaders. Later, a lookout spot so smugglers—who used the coves and caves on the distant shore—could be warned with torches lit on high when trouble was arriving via ships. Not everything in which his forebears had engaged had fallen within the boundaries of the law. His family's estate edged up against the sea in Cornwall, a few miles across the water from this narrow strip of land that his ancestors had long ago claimed. On a clear night, he could see a faint glow from their far-off manor that occupied the top of a rise. On a moonless night, when smugglers usually dealt with their contraband, they would have easily seen flames flickering from lighted torches atop the walls of a walkway that stretched between the towers of his present dwelling.

He knew that to be true, because it was how he communicated with his family. But not tonight. Tonight, the storm would not allow unprotected torches to remain alight. Not that he would have summoned his family to traverse the dangerous swells that the tempest had roused from slumber.

He rushed up the dwelling's steps, hung the lantern on a peg beside the door, grabbed the latch, and shoved open the heavy oak. He stepped into the warmth of a large living area. So much bloody wonderful warmth provided by the fire on the hearth.

He'd left lamps burning in this room, his bedchamber, and at the bottom as well as the top of the stairs. He'd known before the night was done, with his belly filled with booze, he'd be in no state to light them.

He shifted his burden until she was settled in his arms. She emitted the tiniest soft mewling that he could have sworn burrowed its way through the layers of his armor to settle within his chest. It felt as though his heart had released an erratic beat to accommodate the unexpected arrival. He wouldn't soften toward her, wouldn't soften at all, because anything that was not rock-hard could break. Even steel and iron could shatter with enough force. The only way to protect a heart was not to have one at all.

He turned for the stairs and his lower back protested. It plagued him since that fateful night when his world—when he—had changed. He ignored the pain as he did most of the reminders that his life was no longer as it had once been. He started up the steps. The woman made another whimpering sound.

"It's all right," he murmured. "You're safe now."

"Bawl . . . une," she muttered. "Lost."

Christ, she'd been traveling with someone. He'd known there would probably be others but had dearly hoped none had been close to her. He couldn't quite make out the name, not that it mattered. All that mattered was that she didn't succumb to the horrors she'd endured before washing ashore.

"We will find them," he tried to reassure her. He didn't need sorrow weighing her down. He often wondered how many people involved in catastrophes died from the heartbreak of losing someone rather than any physical wounds sustained. "Any and all of your companions."

"No . . . one . . . else," she mumbled.

"You were alone?"

Silence greeted him. Did she know what she was saying? Had she been the only one to fall over the side in the rough seas? Yet he'd seen no evidence of anyone else or of a ship torn apart by nature's wrath. No masts, no sails, no splinters of wood. No barrels, no cargo.

He didn't want to contemplate that perhaps she'd been tossed over the side, that someone had deliberately attempted to do away with her. He couldn't discount the possibility. He'd grown up on the tales of how murder had played a role in bringing his parents together.

Finally, he reached the top of the stairs and turned into the only bedchamber with a bed. He'd not bothered to replace the rotting, decaying furniture he'd tossed out from the other three bedchambers, because he'd anticipated never having guests.

Gently, he maneuvered his coat from her person, allowing it to hit the floor, before he lowered the soaked woman to a settee near the fire. Quickly he added additional logs to set the flames to roaring rather than being lazy as he preferred. Then he dragged a blanket from the bed and draped it over her, tucking it in around her.

While drawing his shirt over his head, he dashed over to a small cupboard and snatched two thick towels from a shelf, running one of the linens rapidly over his drenched hair and torso as he made his way back to his guest, grateful for the heat of the fire.

The woman was shivering with more force, her teeth clattering louder. He wanted to wrap her in his embrace so the warmth of his skin could ease away her chill. Wanted to do all within his power to ensure she didn't die. She couldn't die on him. Not another to burden his conscience.

But first he had to get her dry. He knelt beside the settee, uncovered one of her arms, and began to briskly rub a towel along its length, all the while studying what was visible of her, searching for other injuries. A lump marred her forehead, scratches and bruises her face. "Miss? Miss?"

She didn't respond except to shiver more violently.

Working diligently, he moved to the other arm and then to her legs, striving to ensure her modesty so as not to alarm her should she awaken. But soon modesty be damned. He had to get her out of the wet clothing. He would do it impersonally, paying no attention to what he was uncovering.

He'd do as he'd done once before and focus on the task, not the person. It would make it less painful if his efforts failed. He fought not to recall a time when he hadn't been such a pessimist, when he hadn't realized how innocent he'd been. How foolish. How naive. How childish. Before he'd discovered how cruel life could be.

He wouldn't even consider that he'd find corpses, that anyone on board hadn't safely escaped the thrashing water. He pushed back the memories of others he'd been unable to help. Most had perished before he got to them, but some had died in his arms, calling out for their mothers. They haunted him still.

It had been far too long since he'd divested a woman of her clothing. His fingers fumbled with the buttons, ribbons, and laces as he fought not to notice the hint of warmth striving to burst through the chill of her skin, like a seedling emerging through the soil come spring. He tried to prevent his knuckles from making contact with her flesh, but it was an impossible task when her clothing was plastered against her as though it were desperately searching for whatever solace she could provide.

He needed to tend to her quickly so he could search the shore for others. Her companions, friends, family. Anyone for whom she might have a care. Even a husband. Although she wore no ring, so perhaps a suitor.

But why were any of them out on the water when there had been signs of a storm brewing?

Finally, finally, he managed to drag off what remained of her clothing. He ordered himself to forget the lovely bits he'd been forced to view because doing so had been the only way to remove what needed to be removed. Gathering up her tangled strands of hair, he draped them over the arm of the settee to prevent the wetness from touching her and making her uncomfortable. Then he grabbed another blanket and replaced the damp one, gently tucking the dry one in around her.

Although her skin was still cold to the touch, she was shivering less. Clumps of sand clung to her face. He considered leaving her to deal with the granules later, but imagined her rubbing them into her eyes, the damage they might cause. Having spotted no one near her, he'd have to circle the island, might be gone for hours. He dared not leave her until he knew she wouldn't need him, that she was out of danger.

He went to the wash bowl, dipped a cloth into the cool water, and then squeezed out the excess.

Returning to her side, he knelt on the floor and tenderly began to wipe away the grit, careful to keep his touch light so as not to scratch her. She had finely arched brows. He was fairly certain the cut at the edge of one was going to leave a minute scar. He wondered if she was vain enough to be bothered by a marring of her skin.

Her lashes were long, thick, golden. Her cheekbones high and sharp. A lump on her cheek was going to cause her some discomfort. As would her nose, swollen and bloody, a gash going down one side of it. Fortunately, it was no longer bleeding. And he realized much of what he was wiping away was blood. Her chin reminded him of the bottom of a heart his sister often drew on her correspondence. Not quite pointed, but fanciful all the same. It was her mouth, however, that drew him.

A wide and crimson cut marred one corner of her lower lip, causing a bit of swelling, but even without that puffiness, there was a plumpness to her lips that he suspected would provide a man with a great deal of pleasure if he were to indulge in tasting her.

Removing most of the sand revealed that she'd been badly battered by the sea.

Leaning back slightly, he took in the whole of her features—and he felt a kick to the gut. He was struck once again with the familiarity of her. He was fairly certain he had seen her before, but the circumstances remained a mystery. Something about her seemed off, but he couldn't quite determine what aspect of her didn't appear to be particularly right.

He tried to envision her without the bruising, scrapes, swelling—

Her hair was the incorrect shade, but if it were black—

He shoved himself to his feet to take in all of her. By God, he knew her.

Not that they'd ever been properly introduced because nothing about her was proper. But on a few occasions, he'd seen her, studied her. Had even lusted after her—like half the men of his acquaintance.

He came close to bursting with ribald laughter. He'd cried out for a woman and fate had seen fit to deliver to his shore London's most infamous courtesan.

Chapter 2

Early May 1878

The secret rooms at the Twin Dragons catered to men and women with certain needs. For the most part, the women needed a benefactor. The men, as men were wont to do, were in need of a dependable fuck. Not that the purpose of the rooms was advertised as such.

But it was a place where men could openly escort their mistresses about and enjoy various entertainments. Dancing in the ballroom. Gambling in a nearby parlor. And a few private bedchambers that were let by the hour for couples testing the waters of compatibility for a lengthier alliance.

Although gents did sometimes regret their decision to bring their paramours here, because it was not unusual for a wanton woman to catch someone else's eye and decide she wanted to be wanton with him for a while, and thusly let her regular go. Of course, there was the occasional unattached female who had already left her lover and was searching for more virile pastures. And naturally there were the free-roaming gents who were weary of the chase and wanted a bit more permanence when it came to who warmed their bed or engaged in the naughtiness one wouldn't ask of their wives.

Langdon fell somewhere in between. He'd never had a wife nor a mistress, but the thought of having the latter was beginning to appeal to him. If he wasn't continually on the prowl, he would free up time for other pursuits. It just made sense to have a lady who was there whenever she was needed. And if he was on occasion seen with her, maybe the mamas would leave him in peace.

"I don't know why I came," Jamie Swindler muttered. "I can't afford to keep a woman on a constable's salary."

While Jamie's family was not of the nobility, his father and Langdon's had grown up together and were more brothers to each other than some men who shared the same blood. As a result, Langdon and Jamie considered each other cousins—*of the heart rather than the blood*, both their mothers were fond of saying.

"But you can look at one and tell me if she appears . . . shifty. If she might steal from me."

"None of these are upstanding women, Langdon. I think you can assume they look out for themselves first, above all else."

"Your occupation is making you a bit of a cynic."

"Prove me wrong."

How he wouldn't half like to. He was considering even making a wager on it, but then he saw *her*. On Hollingsworth's arm, gazing around as though walking through her dominion and owning every breath of air within it, doling it out and stealing it where she could.

"Good Lord," Langdon murmured in awe. "I'd heard Hollingsworth's woman was the fairest in London, but still I'd not expected her to be so incredibly breathtaking."

"And damned well knows it, she does."

"She'd be a fool not to." And even from this distance, several feet away from her, the sharpness in her gaze as she scrutinized her surroundings—the inanimate as well as the animate—indicated she was no fool.

Unlike the low neckline of the gowns of most of the women in the room—a neckline that in some rare instances revealed the shadow of a nipple—hers offered only the barest shadow of her cleavage. Holding so much of herself secret made her all the more alluring.

The vibrant red silk, hugging her torso before flaring out with the aid of a bustle, went well with the onyx shade of her hair. But it was the manner in which her eyes sparkled whenever Hollingsworth spoke to her that made her truly striking.

Then she smiled, and it was the most mesmerizing, intoxicating arrangement of lips, teeth, and features he'd ever seen. It encompassed the whole of her face, making her cheeks appear fuller, her chin less pointed. Not that any aspect of her needed rearranging. But it was a revelation to note she could look even more beautiful—not because of her physical aspects, but because something extraordinary seemed to burst forth from the depths of her soul.

For the past couple of years, young swells with an artistic bent had begun sketching her and, more than once at various clubs, arguments had broken out regarding who had managed to capture her likeness in its truest form. But how could lead, charcoal, watercolors, or oils reveal the *experience* of her?

A book might show an image of a lioness, but it wasn't until a person was confronted by the reality of the beast that he could truly appreciate its magnificence.

"She looks rather attached to Hollingsworth," Jamie said, "to be enjoying his company. I doubt she's looking for a new benefactor."

"No. You have the right of it." He'd heard no whispers of discontentment on her part or on the earl's.

The discontentment flourishing was all within himself—that he'd not enticed her into his arms before Hollingsworth had. But then she didn't move about within his social circles, and, before tonight, he hadn't move about outside of them. Hence, he'd only heard rumors of her after she became entangled with Hollingsworth. As the months went by, so the rumors had grown into epic proportions.

He was incredibly aware that members of his family were always under scrutiny by the *ton*. While he was well-liked and considered quite the catch—after all he was heir to an earldom—he knew how easily, quickly, and irrevocably one's reputation could become tarnished with one unfortunate decision.

While Hollingsworth was known to escort his

paramour to the theater and the occasional symphony or exhibition, he'd never brought her into any noble's residence. Having seen her at last, Langdon was under the impression that he flaunted her as a means to raise his own self-esteem as the man wasn't particularly handsome and had yet to take a wife. Hence Hollingsworth having such a confident beauty on his arm was certainly no hardship and could do his reputation little harm. As a matter of fact, it no doubt enhanced it.

"What is it you want in a mistress?" Jamie asked.

Her, he almost said. "Ah, someone entertaining, I think."

Jamie furrowed his brow. "In what manner?"

The answer should have jumped from his mouth: *How do you think? Bed sport.*

That's what mistresses were for and yet . . . the way she moved, the manner in which she interacted with those approaching and leaving the couple—confidently, appearing interested, giving the impression she found them far more fascinating than she expected they'd ever find her—made him realize that even a mistress should be wanted for more than what she could deliver between the sheets.

"I can't put it into words, but I'll know her when I see her."

The problem was, he suspected he already had, and she wasn't available.

Chapter 3

Off the Cornish Coast
April 1879

$\mathcal{U}$pon opening her eyes, Marlowe's first thought was that demons—for surely her sins would prevent her from being welcomed into heaven—had the most gorgeous bare buttocks. Firm, round, and . . . begging to be squeezed. Or at least the devil standing near the wardrobe with his back to her did. A quick image raced through her mind of how his butt cheeks would flex, tighten, and loosen with each powerful thrust he delivered. He would move with such grace and beauty that she would be mesmerized.

Her second thought as she watched him cover up that lovely backside with a pair of black trousers was that she might not be dead. For surely, once released from this mortal coil she would experience no pain. However, she ached in places she didn't even know a person could ache. Her face hurt most of all. And her head. Now she knew how a piece of iron felt when the blacksmith's hammer banged away, forging it into something useful.

Just as she'd been forged.

As the devil drew on a shirt, she couldn't help but admire his broad shoulders as well as the way his back tapered down to a narrow waist and slim hips. He really was lovely, should pose for a statue. Then he turned and silently she cursed. *Damn it all to hell.*

She knew him. Indeed, he was the very last person she wanted to set eyes upon, much less be in his lofty and irritating presence in such close quarters. Her hands tightened on a blanket draped over her, and she was hit with the sudden realization that she was naked beneath it. How she had come to be in that revealing state was cause for some consternation. She remembered divesting herself of her pelisse, frock, and shoes when the prospect of going into the water was looming before her. But the remainder of her clothing . . . Oh, Lord. She had her suspicions, and she drew the warm woolen blanket more closely around her, even as she pushed herself upright to a sitting position so she wouldn't be at a disadvantage for what was certain to become a confrontation.

He lifted a dark brow that rested over incredible silver eyes, eyes she'd always feared saw far too much. "Back to the land of the living, I see. Marlowe, as I recall."

Irritated with the snide tone of his voice, she saw no point in confirming what she suspected he knew to be true. All of London identified her by only a single name, so famous was she. Whether it was her first or her last remained a mystery, and she preferred it that way. It prevented her from being truly known, even though she was a regular in the gossip columns, disliked by wives, unmarried lasses, and widows who feared she might snatch away their husbands, betrotheds, or lovers. Although why in the world she would want a disloyal scapegrace in her bed was beyond her reckoning. "Viscount Langdon, *as I recall*."

A muscle in his cheek ticked. Apparently, he didn't like her haughtily using his words or his tone. Neither did he fancy her any more than she fancied him. As though she gave a tinker's curse regarding his opinion of her. He was not hers to please. She could irritate him as much as she liked, and she was going to *like* doing so very much. She glanced around. "How did I come to be in what is apparently a bedchamber?"

"You washed up on my shore."

Ah, that would explain the gritty sand that clung to her the way some men wanted to. But she had a protector who didn't tolerate any such foolishness. Although she'd never had a problem putting a man in his place when his hands wandered to where they ought not. But then she'd never had to deal with anyone who bothered her as much as Langdon did, in ways she didn't quite understand. From the moment she'd first seen him—

She shook off the thought. Now was not the time to let the past intrude. Now was for dealing with the present, and a lord who believed he could own pieces of the earth that were impossible to cordon off. God, the arrogance. "*Your* shore?"

"This tiny island is part of my family's holdings. The main estate is across the way, along the Cornish coast. You muttered that there were no others." With his brow deeply furrowed, he looked to the window. Blinding lightning briefly blocked the darkness beyond. A second or so later, the thunder roared its anger.

A shudder of fear rolled through her with the reminder she'd been out in it. She tightened her arms around herself, knowing she'd been blessed to survive. In all of her twenty-two years, she'd never been caught in a tempest such as the one she'd encountered earlier. While being tossed madly about, she had believed down to the depths of her soul that she was doomed. Had anyone else, even a drunk, odorous stranger been standing there, she might have asked to be held so she could weep for a few seconds and bask in the knowledge that she was alive to do so. But she wanted Langdon no nearer than he already was. Besides, she very much doubted he'd offer any sort of comfort.

"Are you certain no one else went overboard from the ship?" he asked, suspiciously, as though she'd have no interest in saving anyone who had. As though she was selfish, thinking only of herself and her own needs. Although she really couldn't blame him for having that opinion when she'd spent the past few years cultivating such a persona, when in truth she was no more than a sow's ear determined to be mistaken for a silk purse.

"I wasn't on a ship." Not a classic one anyway, not what she suspected he was envisioning. She shouldn't take any sort of pleasure in proving that he had the wrong of things, and yet she did. He thought he knew her. All of London thought they knew her but all they truly knew was what the ink in the gossip columns revealed and it was shaped by those who resented her.

He swung his gaze back to her. "Hollingsworth's yacht, then."

With that, it became evident he knew her protector quite well. Not that she was surprised. It certainly wasn't a secret that the Earl of Hollingsworth saw to her care. Nor was it a secret that he possessed a yacht. "I wasn't in any sort of boat."

"Then how the devil did you get here? You're certainly no angel with wings."

She smiled, or tried to, but her mouth protested and when she touched her tongue to the corner of her lower lip, she felt the small laceration and tasted the slightest tang of blood. "But I am an angel with a hot-air balloon."

He looked as if he wanted to protest at her daring to refer to herself as an angel. A bit of sarcasm had threaded through the word when he'd used it. Before he could object or say something else to irritate her, she rushed to continue. "Hung on for dear life. Swells took it under, me with it. I don't remember much after that, I'm afraid." Which she suspected, all in all, might be a blessing.

He narrowed his eyes and a deep crease appeared in his forehead. "But you wouldn't have been alone. A pilot would have been flying it. I should be out looking for him."

His assumption annoyed her beyond reason. She thought him young enough to be more enlightened. On the other hand, it wasn't uncommon for people to believe the worst of a woman in her position—or her inability to do anything except lie on her back. "I was flying the thing myself. I'm an aeronaut."

"You're a woman."

"I've always heard you're brilliant, and it's a challenge to get anything past you." Inwardly, she cursed. She was accustomed to flirting, but now was not the time and he most certainly was not the man. "Ballooning is a rather common hobby among women." And had been for almost a century now. The sky was the one place where a woman could be completely free of societal constraints. Where she wasn't chattel. Where she wasn't dependent upon the kindness—or in most cases the tolerance—of men. Where she could go her own way, do as she damned well pleased. Not that she felt a need to educate him regarding the craft's history. In fact, she wanted as little conversation between them as possible.

"Daft women apparently," he stated succinctly. "Did you not notice a storm was afoot?"

He stared at her as if she hadn't a sharp knife in her cutlery drawer. Perhaps she hadn't. She'd seen the darkening sky but hadn't cared. She'd wanted to be someplace where she had more control. Where she was the mistress, the queen, the ruler. Where she could think. Where perhaps she could recapture those dreams she'd clung to when she was a young girl and her father would take her up in his balloon. She longed to reclaim the peace and absence of doubts she'd held then. When she'd believed her future was hers for the taking, could be anything she desired. Instead, it had been fashioned by circumstances beyond her control. And of late, she was simply so damned weary of disappointments.

"Sometimes battling it out with a storm is the better choice." It looked as though he was going to make another point about her dunderheadedness, but she cut him off before he could form a word. "I appreciate the rescue, Lord Langdon, but I'm certain I've been enough of a bother. Perhaps you'd be good enough to direct me to the village where I might be able to secure a room in a tavern until the storm passes."

"There is no village. No tavern." He spread his arms wide. "This is the only dwelling on this small stretch of rock, so until the storm passes, madam, I am afraid you are quite trapped here."

He didn't say *with me*, but then he didn't have to. She blinked three times, studying him intently, striving to determine if he was having a laugh at her expense or outright lying in an attempt to keep her within easy reach. He wouldn't be the first man to do so, although he had been the first to indicate he had no interest in her whatsoever. The cur. It had come as a blow to her pride. Utter nonsense. The man obviously had questionable taste when it came to women. Or perhaps he objected to fallen women being out in public instead of hidden away.

Obviously, someone had removed her clothing, which was presently draped over a short screen and drying near the fire. As no woman was in the room, serving as chaperone and seeing to her needs, she did hope it hadn't been him, hating that a tiny part of her was hoping that it had been him. Teach him to reject her, would she? God, pride was an awful thing, responsible for her current predicament. However, if he had done the honors of stripping her bare and meant her ill, he probably wouldn't have taken such care with her camisole and drawers.

He must have noted where she was looking because he asked, "You always travel in the sky in only your underclothes?"

She was so tempted to reply in the affirmative, to fuel whatever fantasies he might harbor about women in balloons, but she didn't want to add to his less than favorable opinion of her. "When I realized I was in a spot of bother, I began shedding what I could because I knew if I did indeed land in the water, the weight of the drenched clothing would drag me under. I don't suppose you noticed if anything made it to shore."

"My attention was on you." He didn't seem comfortable admitting that, as if he found fault with himself for focusing on her.

"Don't fret. I shan't send word to the *Illustrated London News* announcing your devotion to me."

He grimaced, after which his eyes narrowed, and she wondered if he was considering tossing her back out into the storm. She didn't know why she was striving to taunt him.

While they'd had few interactions, she knew his reputation. The *ton* viewed him as trustworthy and, according to gossips rags, mamas were always shoving their daughters in front of him. Debutantes no doubt swooned if he gave them so much as a passing glance. Not that she blamed them. He was truly too deuced gorgeous.

Especially as he stood there in a shirt he had yet to button or tuck. Such a lovely and wide V of smooth skin was visible. Around his neck he wore a pewter chain. Attached to it and dangling a few inches below his throat was a pewter disk she couldn't quite make out. She'd never seen a man wearing a necklace. Somehow it made him look all the more masculine, made her want to get up, cross over to him, and slide her fingers between the pewter and his skin. She was convinced both would be equally warm.

Needing a distraction from those disturbing thoughts, she glanced about at her surroundings. Nearby was an incredibly large bed that had to have been custom-made. A wardrobe across from it. A cupboard. A washbowl on a stand. A small square mirror hanging above it. The settee upon which she reclined. Beside it, a narrow table that sported several remnants from glasses, the contents of which had, on multiple occasions, spilled over and dried into messy rings. Something a servant wouldn't be allowed to let stand, which left her with suspicions regarding his staff. That perhaps it was minimal at best, nonexistent at worst. Scattered throughout the room, hither and yon, were stacks of books, many of them appearing ready to topple over at any minute. She cleared her throat. "Am I to assume then that this is the guest bedchamber?"

"The only bedchamber."

His, then. Where he slept. In that massive bed. Which she'd suspected, considering she'd watched him draw on his trousers and shirt.

"And staff?"

"You're looking at him."

She nearly laughed. No respectable lord would refer to himself as staff. Perhaps he was more disreputable than she—or the gossips—had been led to believe. "No spare servants' quarters languishing about in case they might be needed?" He leveled a stare at her. She nodded, with the understanding that her options for escaping him were becoming quite limited. "Am I to assume, then, that you had no assistance in getting me out of my clothing?"

In spite of the distance separating them, she could have sworn he was blushing. "You were like ice, trembling. I dared not leave you in it. Are you still cold?"

She couldn't quite stop quaking, tiny little tremors, but irritating all the same. Perhaps the frigid sea had worked its way into her very core, and she'd never know warmth again. She drew the blanket more closely around her. "The fire's helping. Pity you don't have servants. I think a bath would do me wonders."

"Then a bath you shall have." Abruptly, he headed for the door.

"Wait! What? No."

He stopped and turned back toward her.

She shook her head. "I've inconvenienced you enough already."

"I'll be more inconvenienced if you die."

She batted her eyelashes at him. "The gossips whisper you're a silver-tongued devil, able to charm even the most cantankerous of women. I'm teetering on the edge of swooning at your concern for my health."

One corner of his mouth eased up and the motion did strange things to her stomach, caused it to tighten and tumble. The same way it had felt just before her balloon began hurtling toward the sea. It would be best not to tease him, not to give any aspect of her person a reason to be more aware of him.

Crossing his arms over his chest, he leaned against the doorjamb. "I once saw two young girls fanning you while you were spread over a chaise longue."

It had been at a scandalous soiree attended by men and their paramours. The theme had been ancient Greece. For the two hours the young women had been with her, she'd paid them more than most servants earned in a month. She lifted a shoulder. "I enjoy being spoiled. Rather deserve it, I think."

"Yet, you don't want me warming water?"

"I don't want you deciding I'm too much of a bother and tossing me back out into the storm."

"It would just toss you back, and I'd once more have to deal with a drenched female."

She didn't want to consider that she might enjoy sparring with him. Most men fawned over her, hoping to receive favors, or to be considered for the position of her next paramour.

"Marlowe is an unusual name," he said slowly, in a manner that reminded her of savoring a bit of chocolate.

What had prompted his statement? And what did it matter? "My father admired the writings of Christopher Marlowe." That much was true. As a matter of fact, he'd gone about boasting he was a descendent of the Elizabethan playwright. That tale, however, she'd never believed. A pity she and her mother had believed others.

"So you admit Marlowe is your first name. I shall collect my winnings at White's."

She couldn't imagine him caring enough about her to place a bet on her name. No doubt he simply enjoyed wagering. With the lifting of a shoulder, she gave him a sly look. "I admit nothing, my lord, except that my father admired the writings of Christopher Marlowe."

She couldn't decide if the sound he made was a scoff or a bitter laugh, but regardless, she felt as though she'd somehow won.

With a nod, he unfolded his arms and took a step into the hallway. "You're welcome to make use of anything here."

With that, he disappeared.

To her everlasting disappointment, she rather wished she'd been awake to enjoy his hands roaming over her as he'd swept away the cotton, silk, and lace. Wouldn't she have a story to tell, then? She'd elaborate, of course. Embellish. After all, in her circles, many a woman took pride in boasting about having her attire removed by Lord Langdon. And much to her chagrin, on occasion, he dwelled in her fantasies.

It was more than his handsome features. It was the manner in which he looked at a woman as though, if given the chance, he'd devour her and leave her ever so grateful he had.

Chapter 4

London
Late May 1878

Sitting beside Hollie at the round table where cards were being dealt and wagers made, Marlowe was bored. Bored. Bored. Perhaps it was time to find a new paramour. Or retire completely from the courtesan business. Even if she'd had only one devotee. And being with him had made her notorious. He'd taught her so much and she was grateful for his tutelage. Ah, but she was bored.

Because Hollie was mostly interested in boring things. Cards mainly. Cards, cards, cards. Nearly every night. Here at the Twin Dragons in a room where the lighting was dim and the cigar smoke thick. A secretive chamber to which men didn't bring their wives, but instead on their arm, they often sported a woman of ill repute. One who dressed so tawdry she would be forbidden entry to the main gaming floor of this establishment.

But Marlowe never looked or acted tawdry. She could stroll into the palatial ballroom of the Duke and Duchess of Lovingdon, and no one would blink an eye in surprise or drop their jaw in horror. Because she had also mastered the art of appearing to belong, even when she didn't. She knew all about the power of deception and how to best use it to her advantage. She'd been tutored by an expert: her father, who had successfully perpetrated a fraud for years. And she'd been an unknowing accomplice.

But she'd never again be taken for a fool. Never again would she fall for another man's ruse. She was in complete control.

Even if at that particular moment it appeared she was under the thumb of the Earl of Hollingsworth, that he dictated her actions. He didn't, but men feared women with power and so she pretended to be at his beck and call, when in truth, he was at hers. But she'd learned the most powerful kept their power hidden in the shadows. When one possessed something of exorbitant worth, one didn't need to boast about it. As a matter of fact, it was best not to. When discovered by the doubters, it made victories so much more rewarding, especially when everyone was expecting her to lose.

And if there were times when her position made her feel like rubbish discarded by the *ton*, she had but to review her accomplishments to know it was all worth it.

These men who might dine with the Queen knew Marlowe. As did their wives, who sometimes strolled the hallowed halls of Buckingham Palace. While they might never invite her into their parlor or allow her to wed one of their precious sons, they couldn't prevent her from flirting with the heirs, teasing them, giving them hope that they might learn the exact shade and pattern of the wallpaper in her boudoir.

Tonight, as always, she wasn't involved in the game, but merely served as an elegant and expensive ornament. She didn't mind. It was the role she played in his life. In exchange, he provided her with a very nice town house on Mistress Row—the unofficial name of a street in London where many lords provided accommodations for their indulgences—as well as a more than satisfactory allowance, which was hers to do with as she pleased because anything she needed she purchased on credit and he paid the amount owed at the end of the month. And while she often felt like a valuable piece of pottery to be gazed upon but not touched . . . well, she'd managed to be perceived as being an exquisite bit of art few men could afford to possess.

Hadn't Hollie told her often enough that her beauty was beyond compare and a gift to the eye of the beholder? Then he'd taught her that aloofness would increase her value. Even if at times, it also increased her loneliness.

For some strange reason, tonight the loneliness seemed particularly present and cut a little deeper than usual. She had the uncomfortable sensation that it was because of the man sitting almost directly across from her. He was far too handsome, his gaze too intense as it seldom left her. While the other men at the table concentrated on their cards, every aspect of him seemed to be focused on her. Although maybe it was merely the strange color of his eyes that made it seem so. A silver, such as she'd never seen. She was left with the impression he was uncovering her secrets, one by one. She had a strong urge to fetch her pelisse and use it to cover her bare chest, shoulders, and upper arms. She was grateful to be wearing gloves that went past her elbows, even if they caused her to have visions of him slowly removing them, kissing the exposed skin as he went.

Hollie had taken her to the most risqué parties—and on a couple of instances to an orgy—and yet on none of those occasions had she felt that her clothing revealed more than it hid. This man wasn't leering. No, no, it wasn't anything with which she could feel truly insulted. The appreciation in his eyes, however, was still a bit unsettling.

She'd never had a fellow peer at her as though he'd like to slowly take complete possession of her.

Chaps had looked at her with greed, lust, and blatant lasciviousness, but this man was scrutinizing her with sensual carnality. Whenever he slowly lifted his glass of scotch and took a sip, studying her over its rim, she dearly wished he was sipping her.

During the years she'd been with Hollie, she'd never truly experienced desire. To discover herself now yearning with such desperation was somewhat frightening. She felt nearly completely out of control. It was absurd. She'd not even been properly introduced to the man. However, she had managed, based on those nearby speaking to him, to determine who he was: Viscount Langdon.

While the other gents were animated, shifting in their chairs, puffing on their cheroots, occasionally braying with laughter, Langdon was nearly still, not really part and parcel of the gathering. Except for the infrequent times when he drank his scotch, he was like a panther that had sighted its prey and was striving to determine precisely when to leap forward and conquer it.

Each time after the cards were dealt, his hand whispered over the baize as he lifted the edges of his cards and barely gave them a cursory glance, and yet he had incredibly good fortune, taking nearly every hand. However, he gave the impression that the win was expected and brought with it no sense of satisfaction. He was simply whiling away his time in anticipation of something more important, more . . . rewarding.

Watching him, she suddenly realized she was no longer bored. She could recall reading nothing untoward about him in the gossip rags or in the Society columns she scoured. She'd always had an interest in the happenings among the nobility, mainly because she'd always believed she'd be part of it. It had been a shock to discover she wouldn't—not the proper part at least. However, she had managed to secure herself a spot along its edge.

And she'd turned that small spot into a kingdom, surrounded by high walls and a moat.

Yet she didn't know if it was enough to protect her from Langdon—or the way he made her feel. As she'd once dreamed of feeling: precious and special. Desired. Appreciated. Cherished.

"Fetch me a scotch, will you, love?" Hollie asked quietly, snapping her attention away from Langdon.

She took a quick assessing glance around the table. Only Hollie and Langdon still had cards in front of them. It was her job to pay attention to the play, and she'd not been doing so. "Yes, of course."

She caught Langdon's eye and gave him the smallest of smiles before sultrily getting to her feet. Hollie had taught her how to move so men would follow the sway of her hips, and while she normally enjoyed being on display, for some reason she didn't want Langdon watching her performance. He didn't strike her as the sort to be trifled with. She reached the sideboard, surprised to find her hand shaking when she lifted the decanter.

Situating herself so she could see over Langdon's shoulder, she slowly poured, waiting and watching, until he finally lifted his cards. Although he was incredibly guarded with them, she managed to catch a glimpse.

After setting down the decanter, she returned to her chair beside Hollie and placed the drink beside his hand. Then she slipped her own hand beneath the table, slid it along his thigh, and squeezed his knee. The signal that he couldn't beat Langdon.

She watched as Langdon tossed more coins into the center of the table, his gaze never leaving her. "Twenty quid."

Hollie leaned back, sighed. "You've cleaned me out, old chap. I don't suppose you'd take my vowels."

"No."

"I thought not. However, I do have something to offer that's worth much more than twenty quid."

"I'm not interested in baubles."

"But based on the way you've been watching her, I'd say you are interested in my mistress."

Marlowe's stomach lurched as she swung her head around to stare at Hollie. "What?"

"You can have the remainder of the night with her in a private room here," Hollie continued.

"I don't bed unwilling women."

"Oh, I think she's more than willing. I've also seen the way she's been looking at you. You don't mind, do you, love?"

"Hollie, this is ridiculous."

Leaning near her ear, he whispered, "Of late, you've complained of being bored. I suspect he is anything but."

She hadn't complained. She'd mentioned wanting to go ballooning. She shook her head.

"Let him give you what I, of late, have failed to deliver." He pressed a kiss to a spot just below her ear. "Consider it a gift, a new experience. A broadening of your education."

He was risking losing her. What was that about? However, it wasn't as though she had a reputation to protect. Well, unless she considered living up to the title associated with her: London's most notorious courtesan. Still, none of this sat well with her. "I'm your paramour, not your whore. I'll not be bartered. I choose with whom I lie."

"Fair point." He turned his attention back to Langdon. "You can take only what she is willing to give, although I suspect she won't object to a kiss. Beyond that, you'll have to entice her into wanting more. I suspect you're up to it."

Good God! Why was he doing this when she'd already signaled he'd lose? What was in it for him? They'd always had an understanding, and he'd treated her so well. Was this his way of showing he was done with her? "Hollie—"

"I'll accept those terms," Langdon drawled.

She couldn't have been more stunned if he'd suddenly stood and removed his clothing. Words failed her as the fury bolted through her. Men always thought they were in charge, but in this matter they were not. She simply had to determine how best to deliver the message that made that fact crystal clear when they were alone in that room together. That she was intrigued by that perfectly shaped mouth was beside the point. That Hollie was striving to gift her with a kiss from another man might be the oddest gift he'd ever given to her and he'd given her some unusual, unforgettable ones.

"In that case," Hollie began, "I call."

With a negligent flipping of his wrist, his gaze never leaving her, Langdon revealed his cards. And she fought with every last bit of weaponry within her arsenal to not let the shock—or disappointment—be revealed on her face. They were not the cards he'd been holding, not the ones she'd glimpsed. Not the cards that would have ensured he won.

Not the ones that would have seen them together until dawn.

No. The assortment of random suits and numbers that formed no meaningful pattern whatsoever ensured he lost. He'd had a chance to win her—and he hadn't taken it. She was being a complete dunderhead because she was insulted. Hurt. He didn't want her. When had any man not desired her? Accustomed to sloughing off men's advances, she was unprepared for responding to a rebuff. She had a strong urge to pick up the glass she'd refilled and toss its contents at that handsome visage. The bastard. No man had never not wanted her. Good Lord. There were even women who had expressed a desire for her.

"I thought perhaps you were bluffing," Hollie said, as he tossed down his pair of jacks.

Only Langdon hadn't been. He'd been holding four aces. She was certain she'd seen four aces.

Tapping a finger on the table, Langdon continued to look at her. "Fortune doesn't seem to be with me tonight." Then he stood and presented her with a shallow bow, that almost came across as a salute. She simply couldn't determine if he was mocking her. "Madam, enjoy the remainder of your evening."

He ambled away, leaving her with a riot of emotions roiling through her. Anger, hurt, doubt, confusion. Her value resided in being wanted, desired, craved. And she'd never felt so discarded in her entire life. God, she wished she'd one day have an opportunity to make him feel the same.

Chapter 5

*L*angdon had needed to escape the bedchamber. More specifically the nearness of Marlowe. Stretched out on his settee with nothing adorning her except a blanket, while the glow from the nearby flames danced over her, lighting upon and caressing her skin. He'd wanted to march over, take her in his arms, and warm every inch of her with his own flesh gliding over hers.

While initially the thought had been innocent enough, a result of taking pity on her because of her bloodless pallor and her minute trembling, her tart tongue had soon shifted his musings toward the direction of a more sensual basking in heat, one that would keep cauldrons burning for centuries, oil continually boiling for defense. More than once with acerbic wit she'd made him want to laugh, and it had been far too long since he'd been amused by anything.

He'd heard her speak on fewer than half a dozen occasions, but he'd always been taken with her confidence. Not to mention the slow manner in which words rolled out of her mouth in the same lethargic way that a sated woman rolled out of bed. Nothing about her didn't scream with sexuality, wasn't calculated to arouse the senses to their maximum heights.

Even now with her bruises, scrapes, and tangled mess of hair, she appealed. God help him for viewing her as anything other than an injured woman in need of care. Hell's teeth. She'd crashed into the sea, for bloody sake. What did it say of a man's character if he was the least bit enticed when he should be focused only on bringing about an end to her torment?

Even if it added to his.

He'd wanted her from the moment he'd first laid eyes on her, and his desire had only increased that evening nearly a year ago when she'd been offered to him. He'd actually admired her for the horror that had crossed her lovely features when Hollingsworth had made the inappropriate risqué suggestion. That her protector would share her as though she were a bottle of scotch to be enjoyed between friends had sickened Langdon. Her reaction had assured him that it was the first time Hollingsworth had ever made such a dastardly proposal. Still he hadn't been of a mind to take advantage of it because to do so would have made him no better than a thief. Stealing what wasn't rightfully his to take, no matter that permission was being granted by Hollingsworth. But it wasn't being granted by her, and that was all that had mattered to him.

That night he'd been unable to take his gaze

from her because he'd found every aspect of her intriguing. She didn't walk through a room. She glided in a sensual manner that involved the entirety of her body. She looked at a man straight on as though her power was equal to his. In any situation she could hold her own against him. When she studied a man, she left the impression that all his secrets had become hers, and she would guard them with her life.

And now having her here, knowing she belonged to another, was pure torture. Being stretched out on a medieval rack would have been preferable.

His mood souring, he stomped the rest of the way down the stairs. Not that he made much noise since he had failed to put on his boots. When he'd been drawing on his trousers, he'd felt a strange sensation of being watched—no, of being admired—traveling up and down his spine. After dragging on his shirt, when he'd turned and caught her staring at him, he'd had the absurd need to puff out his chest, like some randy peacock. He hadn't, but then neither had he secured any buttons. He knew women found no fault with his physique.

It was ridiculous to want to preen for her. She was spoken for. Had been for a few years now. He liked Hollingsworth. He certainly had no intention of cuckolding her benefactor. He didn't think she would either. He'd never heard a whisper of her being unfaithful to him. As a matter of fact, her loyalty was one of her more redeeming qualities.

With a resounding curse as he finally reached the kitchen and began warming water, he wondered if perhaps he should dump a pot of cold water over his head in an effort to douse the fever striving to take hold of him and convince him to surrender to his animalistic desires. He needed to turn his thoughts elsewhere.

He walked over to the large wooden table he used more for preparing food than eating it, pulled what remained of the loaf of bread his mother had brought over a few days earlier, and sliced off some pieces. He began slathering butter on them. She had to be starving after her ordeal. He could take her something to eat while she waited for the tub to be filled.

The weather was fierce, demanded that a body remain indoors. Earlier, he should have stayed confined, but he'd been fighting his demons and had thought that, somehow, he could face them in the storm. He didn't want to contemplate what might have happened to her if he'd not been out there—if he hadn't spotted her. Deuced silly woman. To go off on her own, into the sky.

He didn't find fault with that sort of independence. He'd grown up surrounded by strong-minded women who never hesitated to voice their opinions or preferences. He had a feeling Marlowe would fit right in with them—if not for her . . . unusual choices in life. To not hide the fact she was having relations with a man out of wedlock, her actions unsanctioned by the church. Most people considered her sort of indulgences sordid. But he wasn't so much of a hypocrite as to enjoy the pleasure a woman provided and then judge her poorly for delivering it.

But she wouldn't be delivering anything to him. As long as the storm raged, she'd be his guest. With her bruised and swollen bottom lip, she should probably limit speaking, which shouldn't be a problem because he couldn't imagine they would have much of anything to say to each other.

Fortunately, the first things he always packed when planning his journey here were books. An avid reader, he enjoyed a wide assortment of material: philosophy, history, mystery, even the occasional romantic tale. He wondered how Marlowe's tastes in reading ran. But at least reading could occupy her. Although he suspected she was skilled at occupying herself.

He was in awe of her fortitude. And her not backing down from verbally sparring with him was actually more thrilling and enjoyable then he cared to admit. Few women had ever dared to be anything other than incredibly polite and congenial where he was concerned. Marriage to him would one day make some lucky woman a countess. Even if she wasn't interested in marriage, a lady never seemed to want to do anything that would make her fall out of his favor. Marlowe Whatever-the-Deuce-Her-Surname-Was didn't seem to care one way or the other. He respected her speaking her mind.

Even more, he admired that after the ordeal she'd survived, she wasn't cowering or weeping or giving the tempest any sort of victory over her. He'd once attended an afternoon soiree in a garden, where a woman, screeching as she was being chased by one of the owner's peacocks, had swooned into Langdon's arms once she was safe from attack when another gent distracted the fowl. He couldn't imagine Marlowe screeching as the storm had tossed her about. Good Lord, she'd maintained the presence of mind to discard any clothing that might have dragged her beneath the waves. She'd sacrificed her modesty, and he suspected she'd done it with nary a thought except for survival.

He wondered if survival had been at the root of her decision to become a courtesan. She struck him as being willing to do whatever necessary when faced with difficult choices, even if it meant traveling the more difficult path.

After placing the bread on a plate, he filled a pail with the water he'd warmed and put more on to boil. With sustenance in one hand and the handle of the pail in the other, he headed up the stairs.

Strange how it felt as though it had been eons since he'd seen her, how his legs picked up their tempo as though delivering him to her in haste was of prime importance. As though each moment not in her presence was intolerable for them both. Which was utter poppycock. Based on the way she'd looked at him in horror with the realization she might be spending the remainder of the night with him if his hand had been better than Hollingsworth's, he suspected even now she was dreading his return. He could well imagine that if he so much as glided a finger along her cheek, she'd scratch out his eyes.

He would just have to convince her that she appealed to him not in the least and was perfectly safe from his advances—poor girl. Not to experience what he could deliver.

He strode into the bedchamber, came to an abrupt halt, and felt the agony of air backing up in his lungs. She'd donned one of his shirts. It fairly swallowed her arms and torso.

Gazing in the mirror hanging above his washbasin, she was standing on an uneven heap of books. He had no shelves in here, but always piled his books around the chamber because he loved being surrounded by them, and no matter where he alighted, one was always near, within easy reach. Her calves, so lovely and unblemished by her ordeal, were clearly visible because his shirt left a good bit of leg exposed—so much leg. Small feet, tiny toes, lovely, lovely calves. The sort deserving of a hundred kisses. While he tried not to look, he was, after all, a man and possessed some sort of instinct when it came to noticing when a woman was enticingly revealed.

With eyes wide and filled with dismay, she quickly turned toward him, which threw off not only her balance but that of her support. Books began shifting, sliding out of place. Her arms began windmilling—

He dropped what he was carrying and rushed forward.

During one heart-stopping second, Marlowe knew with certainty that she was going to land on her backside or worse, crack open her skull.

Instead, she found herself pressed up against a firm chest, her feet dangling over the floor, and strong arms locked around her waist, holding her in place, while hers circled broad shoulders. The shirt she was wearing had ridden up her thighs and was very close to revealing her bum, but she could hardly care. She'd never known anyone to move with such swiftness. She'd certainly never seen so much worry and concern directed her way. He'd looked as if he might die if any harm came to her.

His brow was furrowed, his breaths were rushing in and out fast and hard, and those silver eyes had gone a darker pewter. "What the devil were you doing standing on something so unsteady? Did you not think to simply take the mirror off the wall?"

The storm had stolen her ability to think any rational thought. Which was evident because at that precise moment, she should be shoving against him and demanding he unhand her. Instead, she wanted him to carry her to that huge bed and slip beneath the blankets with her so his body could cover hers, return her to a place of safety and protection and so much heavenly warmth.

Ever since she'd opened her eyes to the sight of his backside, she'd been fighting not to remember the terror that had gripped her when she'd been plummeting back to earth. How she'd screamed even though no one was about to hear or to help or to save her.

She'd been completely and absolutely alone and had realized, at that most inopportune time, that she'd been alone for a good long while now.

But somehow, by some miracle, she'd been spared death, and she wanted to get on with living. Hence, while he'd been gone, she'd decided to at least brush the tangles from her hair. But within this chamber was no cheval glass or dressing table with a mirror. Only the small mirror on the wall that she was certain he used when he took a razor to his square jaw—which he hadn't done for several days based on the thick stubble he was now sporting. She hadn't been certain he'd appreciate her making herself quite so much at home as to take the mirror down. She'd been unable to locate anything to give her the height she required to gaze into it, anything she could easily move, other than the books piled around the room. But when she'd finally managed to view her reflection—

She was surprised he recognized her because she barely recognized herself. "Is my nose broken?"

Sympathy touched his eyes. "I don't think so."

"But all the swelling." On either side of her red nose and beneath her eye. A gash also marred her nose. A huge scraped and discolored lump rested on the upper curve of her right cheek. It hurt like the very devil. Then there was the gash at the corner of her lower lip and a bump on her skull near her hairline.

"The sea definitely battered you. I suspect it bashed you against rocks a few times as it delivered you to shore."

"*Delivered me to shore?* You say that as though it had been benevolent."

"To be honest, it could have killed you."

For a while she'd thought it would. She had no memory of it kindly *delivering* her anywhere. She did recall being dashed against a rock, pain ricocheting through her head as she fought to find purchase, just before being sucked back out into the unforgiving waves.

"How long will I look like this?"

He shook his head. "I'm no physician but I've

had experience with bumps and bruises. In a few days, the swelling should lessen. The bruises will no doubt darken and then fade."

And hopefully all the injuries elsewhere would simply go away. She'd been so comforted by his holding her and his attentions that she'd barely noticed the discomfort in her ribs, but they were beginning to protest. "You can put me down now."

She was surprised by how slowly he did it, like setting down a fragile raw egg. Inch by inch, as though he drew as much solace from holding her as she did from being held.

Suddenly, he fairly leapt back. "Ah, Christ, the water."

"It shouldn't have cooled too much."

"I was referring to that which I left heating in the kitchen."

Then he was gone.

And she couldn't help but think that while a storm raged, they were going to be locked in a strange sort of fellowship.

Chapter 6

$\mathcal{U}$pon his first return to the bedchamber, much to his surprise, he'd discovered she'd tidied up the mess—shattered plate, butter smeared on the stone floor—placed the copper tub, which had been against a wall, in front of the fireplace and dumped the pail of water he'd left behind into it. He'd brought another plate of buttered bread along with another bucket. After that, numerous times he'd lumbered up the stairs carrying a pail in each hand. The current trip would be his last.

Like the times before it, returning to the chamber was pure torment . . . and absolute heaven.

With his shirt hiked up just below her hip, she sat on the bed, one leg curled beneath her, the other dangling off the edge of the mattress, her gaze focused on the windowpane where raindrops sluggishly answered gravity's call. Beyond, the stars were still obscured, and the sea, visible only when lightning struck, continued to churn in protest of nature's foul mood.

Holding a handful of her hair, she attacked the

ends of the tresses with his brush, striving to rid herself of the tangles. She appeared lost in thought.

Perhaps her musings kept her occupied to such a degree that she didn't notice his arrivals or departures, didn't notice the *splash* as he poured the heated water into the tub. He'd never known a woman to show such a lack of interest in modesty.

He couldn't help but think there would be no games with her. A man would always know where he stood. No coyness, no pretense of shyness. No devious flirtation hinting at promises that never would be delivered. No false protests or insincere teasing.

He wondered why, while wearing little clothing, she appeared so comfortable around him. Not that he'd given her any reason to fear him—or at least he hoped not. The females in his family would have his head if he ever treated a woman poorly. Not only the females. Every last member.

Perhaps because he'd had such a rough youth, his father had taught him and his siblings to treat others as they wished to be treated. Although at the moment what he wanted was to be treated to those lush lips moving provocatively over his.

He cleared his throat. "I believe you have enough water for a nice bath now. I'll leave you to it."

Quickly she twisted around. "Don't go, please. I know it's silly, but I don't like the howling of the wind, the way it screeches."

"It makes that noise because this building is centuries old and not everything is as firm as it once was. But its foundation is sturdy, dependable. It'll not carry you back out to sea."

"I didn't think it would. I just . . . I can't really explain it. I'd just rather you not go."

He wished she didn't look so worried. With all her injuries, the deep furrow in her brow, caused by the depth of her concern, had to be painful. If she weren't ruined but were a lady with a pristine reputation, he wouldn't remain in the residence, much less consider staying within the bedchamber with her. He'd be huddled outside in his greatcoat, battling the storm rather than his fascination with her boldness and lack of decorum. No proper lady would dare ask of him what she just had. However, he was far too familiar with how the horror of a traumatic event—and a tumble from the sky had to be a harrowing experience—could linger and make a person feel surrounded by and immersed in danger. Even when encircled by friends in a familiar environment. Here she had neither friend nor the familiar. While he'd prefer to be elsewhere, because the last thing he wanted to see was her actually bathing, he felt a measure of responsibility for her since she was in his domain. "I'll stand in the doorway, my back to the room."

"No need." She slid off the bed and he fought not to envision her sliding over him. "Simply turn around. It'll take me only a tick to discard your shirt. Then you can make yourself comfortable on the settee."

Every word she'd uttered was dangerous. But the water wasn't going to remain hot forever. She needed to make use of it while it was.

After swinging around without further argument, he closed his eyes to ensure he caught no glimpses of her. Unfortunately, without his vision to distract him, his hearing heightened until his ears absorbed the rasp of his shirt traveling over her skin. Although she kept her promise and moved quickly, it still seemed that eons passed before the sound faded away. In its place came the soft splash as her foot disturbed the water. To be liquid, to have the ability to close around her—

It was lust, all lust. Just a need that had come upon him because he'd been too long without the comfort offered by a woman's body. Then he heard the other foot going in.

Following that came her soft satisfied moan as she lowered herself. Quite suddenly his trousers were far too tight. Jesus. He might die right there. He should journey out into the storm so nature could squelch all these rampaging thoughts and desires.

"You are free to turn around," she said.

No, he bloody well wasn't. After inhaling deeply, he slowly released the air that had filled his lungs. It didn't help. He could hear the water stirring, imagined her leaning back, lifting her arms, and the water droplets sliding over her skin as the rain did the glass pane. She would be that smooth, that taut.

"Langdon?"

He shook his head, knowing he had no need to explain the inappropriateness of the situation and yet some comment was called for. "You are the least modest woman I've ever met."

"Not so immodest. Turn around."

He glanced over his shoulder and released a

huff of air that could have passed for a laugh. A blanket was draped over the tub. Only her bare shoulders and above were visible. He'd seen more skin in ballrooms. He faced her.

"I thought it would allow the water to remain warm longer," she said with a small smile that involved her eyes more than her mouth, the sort that would bring men to their knees. It almost did him. It was teasing and fully come-hither.

Good Lord but he was tempted to strip down and climb in there with her. But that required an invitation. He wondered what it might entail to secure one. On the other hand, she belonged to another—although not by law or before God. She had an arrangement that could be broken in a heartbeat.

Before she could detect where his thoughts were wandering, he cast a glance toward the bed, easily finding that for which he was searching: his brush. She'd had little success taming her hair. It reminded him of a rat's nest he'd once come across in the stables at the family's estate across the way. He'd been a young lad at the time and fascinated by it. Strange how as a man he was now fascinated by another sort of tangled mess.

After retrieving the brush, he sat on the floor by the tub and took hold of a section of her hair. She was the one who had established the atmosphere for setting aside all societal norms. He certainly had no intention of coming across as a timorous schoolboy.

"What are you doing?" she asked.

"I'm going to see if I can work more of these tangles out."

"It's a slow, tedious process. Probably best to simply chop it all off."

It would be a sin to do so when it appeared to be gloriously thick and full. He wanted to see the golden strands glistening after a good brushing and cascading around her shoulders and down her back.

"My sister, Poppy, once wanted to cut off all her hair. She thought it unfair that her brothers didn't have to spend as much time caring for theirs. My mother tried to dissuade her by telling her that hair was a woman's crowning glory. Poppy responded, 'Must be why men are always at war, seeking to obtain that crown that comes to women naturally.'"

She made a sound in her throat that might have been a subdued laugh. No doubt she'd discovered her injured lip didn't tolerate well being stretched into a smile. "Therefore, she didn't cut her hair," she stated.

"Came to dinner that evening with all her tresses sheared off." He chuckled low, remembering how all the members of his family had tried to ignore the sight of her and to pretend all was as it should be.

Just as he was pretending now that having a woman in his tub was not unusual—even if his body was determined to continually remind him that it was.

*M*arlowe liked his laugh, titillatingly hushed as though he was sharing a secret or engaged in an act of a far deeper intimacy. But what she liked more was the affection reflected in his voice when he spoke of his sister. "Brave girl," she said, filling her tone with admiration.

"That's our Poppy. Don't think she ever again took scissors to her hair, not even for a bit of a snip." He applied the brush several times to the end of the strands he held. Finally a few of the knots gave way. He was positioned near the middle of the tub's side, facing her, so she had a clear view of the triumph that lit his face before he advanced to the next set of tangles and began another battle.

While she had truly considered taking scissors or a knife to her hair, she was grateful he was attempting to save it. Even if she was convinced it would turn out to be a fruitless endeavor. It would require an abundance of patience. And yet, she couldn't deny how much it warmed her to watch him taking such care and working so diligently. She couldn't recall the last time anyone—other than Hollie or a paid servant—had sought to do something for her, to please her.

"Strange," he said reflectively, quietly. "I remember you as having black hair."

In spite of the notoriety being with the earl had brought her, she was surprised the viscount remembered such inconsequential details regarding her. She had assumed, when he'd walked away from the table that night, he wouldn't be bothered to retain much, if anything, about her at all. "Hollie prefers dark hair so most mornings I mix a concoction of wine and a few other ingredients to pour over the strands."

"You waste wine on your hair?" He glared at her, sounding truly offended.

"It's not wasteful if the manner in which I use it brings someone else pleasure. Besides, I don't use my best wine." No, she saved that for when she was alone. It was her comfort, her indulgence.

"Not much wine here. I prefer scotch." He turned his attention back to her hair, and she was grateful for some reason that it was its natural shade of blond. It was only when the Season was fully underway and London was swelling with nobs that she colored it for Hollie. Although that time would be upon them soon.

She was a bit disappointed that at some point between the minute he'd gone to fetch the first pail of water and the last, he'd secured most of the buttons on his shirt, save a couple at his throat. She really shouldn't be enticed by a man who obviously had no interest in her. Who had cheated at cards to prevent her from being alone with him and to ensure he kept her out of his bed.

Although she did wonder if she'd be sleeping in it tonight. After all, there was only one bed. Perhaps she'd curl up on the settee. He was too tall to be comfortable on it. Yesterday she wouldn't have cared if he experienced any discomfort at all. But today, tonight, he'd saved her life. She didn't take his actions lightly.

"Hollingsworth doesn't fly with you?" he asked suddenly. While his gaze was homed in on his efforts, she couldn't help but believe that he'd noted her stiffening.

With a shake of her head, she averted her gaze to the fire while searching the bottom of the tub for the lump of soap she'd deposited there earlier. "No, he prefers devoting his time—" She stopped abruptly. The last thing she wanted was him recalling the night she'd been part of a wager.

"To cards," he finished for her.

"Yes, they are his passion."

"I'd have thought it was you."

She wasn't certain if he'd meant the words as an insult or a form of flattery. What was his passion? "A valuable mistress knows her place in her man's life and accepts it. And I am known for being valuable."

She hated that with him she felt a need to point that out. Every other gent in London recognized the fact, but if he did he wouldn't have changed his damned cards. Hollie had too much pride not to ensure that his peers were jealous of anything he possessed: fancy yacht, large country estate, fawning mistress.

If Langdon noted her tone was very much a reflection of someone educating the ignorant, he disregarded it, didn't comment.

After locating the soap, she applied it to a cloth before bringing her arms out from beneath the blanket. Shielding herself from his gaze was really rather pointless when he'd had an eyeful of her while removing her clothing, but his offer to stand in the doorway in order to preserve her modesty had made her feel uncharacteristically shy, almost virginal, in fact. She'd grown accustomed to Hollie's desire to keep her visible and flaunt her, to being on display. Langdon's attempt to provide her with privacy had taken her aback.

She'd expected he might attempt to take advantage of the situation to view as much of her as possible as often as possible. She didn't know quite what to make of his courtesies toward her, although perhaps they simply confirmed his lack of interest in her.

Sliding the linen along one of her arms, she was acutely aware of his gaze following her movements, his actions serving to make her a little more sure of herself. She'd always found distracting a man worked well when attempting to change the subject. They were such simple creatures, really. A little exhibition of skin caused their wits to abandon them completely.

She was at a bit of a disadvantage with her lumps, scrapes, and bruises, but displaying what had for a time been hidden worked in her favor. The brush ceased its movements, so she knew he was enthralled. But it wasn't as long as she'd anticipated before he was again applying his efforts to tame her wild hair. Really, she should just have him rid her of it. It might grant her the opportunity to truly be free.

"Why live in this crumbling structure away from polite society?" she asked, continuing to give her arm the washing of its life.

"I don't exactly live within these walls. I just come here when I need a bit of solitude. Why go off in a hot-air balloon?"

She couldn't stop herself from giving him a winsome smile. "Same reason, really. When I crave being alone, alone but surrounded by peace. Very few people inhabit the sky. And the birds seldom bother me."

"How did you even learn how to manage a balloon?"

"My father." The blanket tented as she drew up her knees and rested her cheek gently against them. "He was often away, tending to business"—or so he'd claimed—"but when he was at home, he'd take me up to touch the clouds. Or at least that was how he referred to it."

"What do clouds actually feel like?"

As substantial, as wonderful, as you. The response that ran through her mind was automatic because it was the sort of thing she would say to a man to make him feel more masculine, more appreciated, more . . . desired. She always knew precisely what to say in order to wrap a gent around her little finger, but she didn't want to play those games with this man. When she was in her hot-air balloon, she didn't have to play games. She could be herself. She was left with the impression that for the few days while she was here, she wouldn't have to play games either.

Wincing as he tugged on a particularly nasty knot, she slipped her arms back beneath the blanket. She didn't want to use her learned wiles to seduce him. "I don't know that I ever actually touched one. I suspect, however, that it would be very much like running your hands through smoke. Have you ever been in a balloon?"

"I went up in one at Cremorne Gardens. It remained tethered to the ground. It didn't travel with the wind."

"Then you haven't really been in a balloon. I'd give you a ride in mine, but it is no doubt at the bottom of the sea, causing a stir among the fish as they attempt to determine what sort of creature it might be. I don't suppose you saw any remnants of my conveyance on the shore where you found me."

"I was scouring around for survivors, not wreckage. Mostly, however, I was focused on you, and ensuring you continued to breathe."

He glided the brush through her hair, and she wondered when he had managed to rid her of so many tangles. "You're remarkably at ease around a man you don't know."

She was extremely comfortable around all men. "But I do know you, Langdon, and I'm well aware I appeal to you not in the least."

His brow furrowed and his hands stilled. "How did you arrive at that conclusion?"

"That night when Hollie made his ghastly offer—before he did—I saw your cards."

"I suspected as much. Upon your return, your hand going beneath the table was a signal to him, wasn't it?"

What was the harm in revealing the truth? "Yes, I was letting him know he couldn't beat you."

"Yet, he was still willing to wager . . . *you.*"

The last word was delivered so sharply that it could have cut glass. "I've never understood why you accepted his terms. You were so uninterested in me that you deliberately took action to lose."

He skimmed his finger along her chin, and she felt the touch clear down to her toes. "Do you truly believe any man in London is uninterested in you? Especially when you go to such bother to ensure they are?"

She didn't hear any censure in his tone—and yet, he'd tossed away his aces. "You proved you're not."

"Is that the reason you take no shame in baring your legs to me?"

With a scoff, she rolled her eyes. "Why must women's legs always be hidden?"

"Because they are the path that leads a man to paradise."

Good Lord, she was accustomed to seducing, not being seduced. She was fairly certain she'd grown so warm her body was reheating the water.

They were staring at each other, his silver eyes going dark. Was he interested? His previous actions indicated not, but at that precise moment he looked as though he might be contemplating kissing her. She was considering pressing her lips to his, but he didn't strike her as the sort who would stop with only a kiss. She already knew she would be unable to resist him, so if she did as she yearned to do, they might end up in this tub together. Most certainly they'd end up in that large, enticing bed.

While he might have once rejected her, he wasn't spoiled for choice here. Perhaps that was the reason she very deliberately and quite slowly moved her head back so her chin was no longer able to enjoy his gentle strokes.

A corner of his mouth hitched up. "Wise woman. With that cut on your lip still healing, it would have been painful to kiss me."

Her screech was tiny but shrill. "You arrogant man. I wasn't considering kissing you."

"Weren't you?"

"No." She didn't know why she was intent on lying. She knew only that in a relationship it did her no favors to be shown yearning for anything. It could turn the most innocent thing —a frock, a broach, an outing, a dog—into a weapon. Always, always, she had to show that nothing mattered. Only then would she matter.

Although truth be told, she wasn't in a relationship with this man. Wasn't even contemplating one. She was of the opinion that if he had been moving toward her and she'd said no that he would have stopped. He wouldn't take what she wasn't willingly offering. Perhaps that was the reason that she kept testing him. Or perhaps it was simply her nature now not to care what men saw of her. A foot, an ankle, a calf, a knee, a thigh. What did it matter?

The pathway to paradise.

She thought she might be blushing when she hadn't blushed since the evening Hollie had made his proposal that she become his mistress. All she had to do was lie with him and all her troubles would go away. She'd been nineteen and so naive. She hadn't realized other troubles would take their place.

"Where did you go just then?"

She snapped her mind back to the present. She'd locked away the past. Why was it suddenly here? She shook her head. "Nowhere of import."

How had he even noticed that she'd drifted away? Hollie certainly never noticed. Although he never noticed anything beyond the physical. He could never detect if she was morose or joyful or happy or sad. Their relationship was based on pleasure, all sorts of pleasure. They kept to themselves anything that would distract from it.

"I'll leave you to finish your bath." He unfolded his body, placed the brush near his razor, started to walk from the room, and stopped. "*I* was considering kissing you."

"I know. You have no skill at hiding your thoughts."

"Trust me, Marlowe, I am a master at hiding my thoughts when the situation warrants."

Chapter 7

At that particular moment, the situation warranted hiding his thoughts in a deep, dark cavern, away from even himself. The woman was injured, weak from her ordeal, cold . . . and still he wanted to initiate her in the pleasures to be found with him beneath the sheets. What the devil was wrong with him to even contemplate kissing her, to desperately want to tenderly skim his fingers over her face, to gently press his lips to every bruise and scrape as though that action alone had the power to heal her?

And once he'd done all those things, once he'd comforted and brought solace to all the places that ached, he'd carry her to the heavens, separate her soul from her body. If she wanted to fly, he'd gift her with wings of pleasure such as she'd never known.

He was left with the impression that it would be unlike anything he'd ever experienced as well. He'd harbored those very thoughts the night they'd sat at the same card table. He'd accepted Hollingsworth's terms simply to get the earl to shut the hell up. And because he'd hoped to give himself a graceful exit from the game.

Not want her? He'd wanted her from the moment he'd first seen her that long-ago night when he'd begun his search for a mistress. And every moment after, whenever he'd caught glimpses of her from afar. While she might appeal to him, the circumstances under which he'd have spent time with her at the Dragons if he'd held on to his cards did not. Just as the current situation was not conducive to their enjoying a joining. Forced proximity was hardly an acceptable *excuse* for pursuing pleasure. It should come about naturally, with two people of a like mind, yearning for what could transpire between them. With the fire of desire requiring only a bit of kindling to set it aflame.

In the kitchen, after removing his shirt and splashing cold water on his face, neck, and chest, he scrubbed vigorously at his flesh in an attempt to quieten it. He felt like his body was ablaze— because of a woman. A woman he shouldn't, couldn't, have. She was hurt, under his care. He'd failed others, wasn't going to fail her.

The frigid water doused his ardor, if not completely, at least enough that he could once again think rationally. When the rain ceased, he'd get her off the island. He had a boat moored in a small cove.

Strange how that thought brought him no sense of relief. He didn't want to be rid of her. Odd, that. He came here to be alone. He'd always been alone here. And yet from the moment he'd spied her on the beach, he'd had the sense that she belonged.

Not necessarily with him. It was ridiculous to even think that. But she belonged near, near enough that they could converse. Her balloon was to her what this fortification was to him: a place of refuge. Why had she craved solitude to such a degree that she'd risked being caught in a storm? Would she find the solace she needed here?

He'd been so distracted with his thoughts that he'd nearly scrubbed his skin raw. After drying off, he shrugged into his shirt and strode to the main room where he poured himself a glass of scotch before dropping down onto the sofa in front of the fire that he'd set to blazing earlier.

She was probably out of the tub by now, dry, and again covered with one of his shirts. He wondered if she was in his bed, beneath the blankets, or if she'd settled onto the settee near the fire. He should probably go upstairs to see to emptying the tub and removing it so she could get nearer to the fire.

Instead, he took a sip of his scotch and stared at the wildly cavorting flames. There had been flames another night when he'd rescued whom he could. At least he'd been spared those horrendous cries tonight.

Because of all the rushing about and activity that occurred during the London Season, Langdon always found it calming to travel by railway. As he looked out the window of the first-class carriage—the passing scenery only occasionally illuminated when the storm wanted more than raindrops to alert the travelers to its presence—he couldn't help but feel a measure of peace come over him. He loved the rain but loved even more traveling by rail. It was modern and quick.

While he journeyed alone, he wasn't lonely. As a matter of fact, he generally preferred observing the other passengers. They were all stories. That he didn't know their tales was unimportant. He often created lives for them.

The young woman with her head buried in a book because she was by nature shy and more comfortable with fictitious people.

The snoring gent who worked hard to provide for his family.

The dark-haired lady who was also asleep but only because she had six children waiting for her at home and this journey offered the only time she could truly rest.

The young boy with his nose pressed to the window because even though it was too dark to see much of anything, he'd never ridden on a train before and every aspect of it fascinated him—just as it had fascinated Langdon all those years ago when his father had first taken him somewhere via railway.

The animated gent telling his friend about the girl he'd been courting and was going to visit. Perhaps this time he'd find the courage to ask for her hand.

So many people, so many stories.

Langdon, himself, was headed down to the family estate in Cornwall to meet with the overseer regarding the income being produced. His father had endorsed Langdon's ideas regarding ways to increase the revenue, and so it was time to put them into practice and prove he would be a good custodian when the stint came. Not that he expected—or wanted—it to arrive anytime soon. His father was as fit as a fiddle and in the best of health.

But at six and twenty, Langdon was growing weary of the gaming, the drinking, and the whoring. He needed a purpose that was more substantial, more—

He came to on wet grass, the clash of steel, the grinding of metal, and the bursting of wood still ringing in his ears, still heavy on the air. With a groan and the clenching of his teeth to fend off the pain of his body protesting the tiniest of movements, he shoved himself to his feet and staggered to the heap of splintered wood that had once been a railway car. His head hurt so badly he could barely decipher his surroundings. A fire was blazing brightly where it appeared two locomotives, coming from opposite directions, had collided.

Like him, some people were standing about in a daze. High-pitched screams and wails of despair echoed around him. Several people were scurrying about, yelling for help.

He'd fallen into a nightmare.

Then he realized there were those who'd fallen more deeply. He started running toward the wreckage, toward the more horrendous cries. He hit a wall of shimmering heat but kept barreling forward—

Suddenly something—someone—rammed into him and he found himself on his back, landing on the cold soaked grass. Then someone else was on top of him, pinning him down. He tried to buck them off. "Let me go!"

"You can't help them, mate. They're already dead."

"No! No! Release me! I've got to get to them. I've got to save them. I've got—"

"Shh, shh. It's all right. Shh."

He jerked awake to find himself being held again, but not by the two bruisers he'd eventually bucked off, but by someone so remarkably soft that he felt as if he were in the clouds. Straddling his hips, she'd pressed his face to her linen-covered bosom and was holding him there. A blanket draped around her shoulders offered a shield from the biting drafts. His breaths were coming harsh and heavy, his chest nearly aching with the effort to draw in air.

He must have drifted off to sleep. And his horrifying memories had worked their way to the surface, as they so often did when slumber claimed him. But usually no one was about to hear his cries.

"Where were you?" she asked tenderly in the voice of an angel. He had the ridiculous thought that, having fallen from the heavens, maybe she'd been sent down to save him.

He barely shook his head. His arms were wound tightly around her. He had to be crushing her ribs, needed to release her. But the images were still there, so real he could almost touch them. He certainly felt them, deep inside him, wreaking their havoc. He'd managed to pull a few people from the railway car closest to the blaze, the one in which he'd been riding—or what was left of it. He'd dragged out the young woman who'd been reading. She would read more stories, but he suspected the wounds she'd endured that would eventually scar would make her even more shy. He'd held the animated gent as he whispered, *Tell Winnie I love her.* When his last breath came, it carried her name.

Eventually beneath rubble, he'd found the lad

who'd had his nose pressed to the window, his body completely broken. Something inside Langdon had broken then as well.

He'd not been with a woman since because he feared the lethargy after making love might cause him to fall asleep, where he was no longer in complete command of his faculties. Sometimes when he was locked in the throes of that horrendous night, he'd weep. And only the weak among men shed tears.

He was relatively certain Marlowe had gotten to him before that embarrassing happenstance. Still, she'd no doubt heard his keening, witnessed his mortifying display of losing control. This courageous woman who went up in a balloon when a storm was on the horizon. Madness.

Mad, the both of them.

"I was reminiscing about all the harsh challenges I dealt with before Hollie came into my life," she said softly. "Earlier, when you'd asked where I'd gone. This place, a world unto itself, so far from the maddening crowd, allows memories to slip in, especially those we fight to hold at bay. I wonder if they might die here and forever leave us in peace."

As he was escaping the remnants of the nightmare and was becoming more aware of his surroundings, he realized the blanket wasn't enough to prevent him from noticing that once again she wore *only* his shirt. He became acutely cognizant that it was her bare legs hugging his trouser-clad thighs. And the paradise he'd mentioned earlier was pressed intimately against his cloth-covered cock. And that particular appendage had not been in a stupor but was reacting to her nearness. She had to be aware of his body's response; however, she seemed unconcerned by it. But then she wasn't a virginal miss who had no idea what transpired between couples.

Loosening his hold on her, he eased back slightly, grateful no wet splotches marred the shirt she wore. Through the linen, he could see the dark circles of her nipples. Unfortunate that. Yet she'd come to him and offered comfort. She deserved better than his replacing the remnants of his nightmare with images of running his tongue over the taut peaks and taking the whole of the shadow into his mouth. He lifted his gaze to hers.

Before, in the past and tonight, the light surrounding them had always been dim, and he hadn't really noticed the exact shade of her eyes. A light blue, like when the sun was on full display and the day was at its brightest, when one could look up and know that no rain clouds would dare intrude. "I'd welcome the peace, but I don't know that I want to lose the memories completely." It seemed unfair to those who inhabited them. They should be remembered, even if only by a stranger.

"Who was holding you? Had you been attacked or kidnapped—"

"No. Railway accident. I was thrown clear. I don't know how. I have no specific memory of it. Just snatches of what happened. Horrendous noise as though the entire world had exploded. Seeing part of the railway car crumpling and flying apart at the same time. My body being grabbed and

shaken by the hand of an invisible giant. Soaring."
He shook his head. "Two trains collided."

"When did it happen?"

"June. Last." Only a couple of weeks after he'd
walked away from the card table where he could
have *won* her.

"There are so many railway accidents that they
all seem to muddle together. I may have read about
it in the newspapers, although I strive not to dwell
on the particulars of unpleasant occurrences."

She'd moved her hands up and was kneading his
shoulders. He wondered if she was even aware of
what she was doing. While he'd loosened his hold
and had intended to stop touching her completely,
he realized that his hands had gotten only as far
as her waist. They'd settled there, bracketing either
side of her.

Even with all the damage done to her face, he
couldn't take his eyes off her. At that moment, he
didn't know if he'd ever seen anyone more beautiful. It was the true concern, the caring—the way
she looked willing to slay his dragons, or at least
serve at his side to assist him in doing it.

He imagined the courage it must have taken for
her to appear in public with Hollingsworth and to
risk censure. Most mistresses were kept in secret,
to spare them Society's condemnation or to prevent
the revelation regarding the man's unfaithfulness.
However, Hollingsworth had no wife and, therefore, no qualms about parading his mistress about
town. He suspected the lord was overly proud of
landing such a beauty.

One of their outings to the theater had earned

a mention in the gossip section of the *Illustrated London News*. Had included an etching of her. The reporter had commented on her "legendary beauty," and Langdon had always suspected the man had been a bit smitten. Not that he blamed the journalist. She *was* striking, but it was her poise and confidence that enhanced nature's artwork. He wasn't certain most men took the time to analyze her appeal. He'd only ever heard them wax on about her features, as though she was little more than a sculpture, with no soul or heart.

But in the short time she'd been in his company, he was coming to the realization that she was far more complicated, and what rested below the surface was of much greater interest. Not that she was his to explore. He'd do well to remember that and to ensure they kept their distance from each other as much as possible within these small confines.

"Careful, Marlowe. Wearing so little, you risk getting more than you bargained for."

"I haven't bargained for anything. Besides you've already seen everything. After that, what's the point in hiding it all away or acting demure? You'd only lust for what is concealed. It's the way of men." She gave him an impish tilt of her head. "Women, too, if I'm honest. We want most that which we cannot have . . . and if we ever do acquire it, we're often disappointed."

"Based on your words, you lust for what I have concealed. Trust me, Marlowe, you wouldn't be disappointed."

Her lips twitched. "I assume you've moved beyond the remnants of your nightmare." Expertly,

sinuously, she slid off him, managing to provocatively wrap the blanket around her so he saw
nothing intimate. She curled into the corner of
the sofa, her torso and every limb hidden from his
sight. "Do you have them often?"

The memories never completely left him, but he
was usually better at controlling them. Tonight's
storm, however, had been playing havoc with him
since its arrival. He shrugged. "Are you hungry?"

Her eyes widened in surprise. "Actually . . . now
that you mention it, the bread you brought earlier
staved off the hunger for a while, but my stomach
is beginning to protest."

"I'll prepare something for us to eat."

"A lord who knows how to cook?"

"You'd be surprised by what I know." And by
how desperately he wanted to educate her and be
educated by her, for surely she had a few tricks
hidden up his shirtsleeves.

Chapter 8

*M*arlowe had wanted to traipse after him to the kitchen and watch him, but with a commanding voice, he'd told her to wait where she was, as though he couldn't stand the notion of having her near. She'd nearly disobeyed as she didn't like being ordered about but she was still weary from her ordeal and not up to a battle. Although she rather fancied the notion of engaging him in one, because she thought it could be challenging as well as enjoyable and entertaining.

With her bent legs pressed to her chest and her feet tucked in close, she studied the room. It was good-sized but not much thought had been given to furnishing and decorating it. No draperies adorned the large windows, which left the lightning visible whenever it appeared. She imagined on a clear night, the moon and stars offered a reflective bit of artwork. The fireplace, like the one in the bedchamber, was huge, a fire blazing. She smiled at the books scattered about. Perhaps that was Langdon's notion of *decorating*. She couldn't deny that their presence was both pleasing to the eye and comforting to the soul.

Although it had been obvious earlier that he'd not found comfort within this chamber.

She'd only just finished plaiting her hair, after managing to rid herself of all the tangles, when she'd heard his cry, like a wounded creature caught in an excruciating trap. Hence, following the echoes of his distress, she'd hurriedly made her way here. Her heart had gone out to him when she'd seen him flailing his arms about. It had also frightened her to witness this large, strong, bold man lost in the throes of a nightmare. From the moment she'd first laid eyes on him, he'd struck her as the sort of fellow who could defeat anything that posed a risk to achieving his goals.

Even his own lustful desires.

As close as she'd been to him, she'd been cognizant of his growing awareness of her as a woman, as a mate. The quickening of his breath, no longer in fear, but in anticipation. The flushing of his skin, no longer in embarrassment but in expectation. The hardening of his cock. If he didn't desire her, would *that* have happened?

But if he desired her, would he have left her so easily?

It suddenly occurred to her that perhaps he'd been more intent on escaping his own lustful yearnings, rather than her.

The man was a host of contradictions she wanted to sort through and sort out. The reason for her sudden need to do so was beyond her reckoning. The storm would no doubt end in a few hours and on the morrow . . . somehow she'd make her way back to the mainland. She furrowed her brow. He wasn't a prisoner here, surely. He had to possess a means for leaving. A boat, no doubt, rather than a balloon.

Her thoughts were interrupted when he strode in carrying two plates and handed her one before setting the other on a low table in front of the sofa. "I can offer you scotch, rum, or water," he said as he walked over to a sideboard.

"Scotch." She studied the offerings on her plate. Buttered eggs, bread slathered with butter, cheese, apple slices. Nothing fancy. Still, her mouth watered.

After placing two tumblers on the table, he settled down beside her and reached for his plate. "When the rain stops, I'll go fishing, get you something a little more substantial."

Using the fork that had been resting on her plate, she stirred the eggs. "I'd hoped when the rain stopped, I might be able to leave."

"What sort of host would I be if I sent you on your way with an empty stomach?"

"A rather grateful one, to be done with me, I expect."

A corner of his mouth hitched up. A dangerous action that made her think perhaps he was enjoying her company. She certainly didn't want to find herself enthralled with him. She wished she could return the gesture but had discovered moving her lip too much or spreading it too widely did her no favors. It not only brought discomfort but caused the cut to start bleeding again.

"Still, I'll feed you first," he replied, without

looking at her, concentrating instead on the food quickly disappearing from his own plate.

"Did you bake the bread?"

He chuckled low. "No. My mother brought it a few days ago when she came over to check on me."

"Do you have a close relationship with her?"

Taking a sip of his scotch, he focused his attention on the fire for a few seconds before nodding. "Family is very important to her."

"You mentioned your sister. You also have a brother as I recall."

He slid his gaze over to her. "Keep up with the nobility, do you?"

"Of course. It's important I do so because I never know when I might be in want of a different . . . provider."

"How is it—" He shook his head and returned to devouring the eggs.

"How is it?" she prompted.

Another brusque shake of his head. "It's none of my business."

"Isn't that a determination I should make? Ask your question."

"You're certainly not shy, are you?"

"There is no advantage to my being so. I'm not a young debutante who must act the innocent to gain a husband. Ask your question."

He studied her, took another sip of scotch. She enjoyed watching the way his throat worked as he swallowed. Men really should do away with wearing neckcloths. She liked the casualness hinted at by that small V of skin. "How is it that Hollingsworth became your benefactor?"

She'd expected the question to be of that nature. Still, it bothered her that he might care about the answer. "I'll answer if you'll first tell me why you accepted his offer that night . . . and then swapped your cards so you'd lose. And don't worry about hurting my feelings, because no matter what you say, I can promise you that I've had worse said to my face. I've erected armor over the years."

The intensity with which he scrutinized her made her feel as though he were mining her soul for the answer, but not to the question he'd asked. To what might have slowly built up her fortification. She couldn't help but think it was as strong as this castle-like structure that thus far had withstood the storm. "I know Hollingsworth well enough to understand that once he gets a notion in his head, he's like a dog with a bone. It was the quickest way to get us past a situation that was making you uncomfortable."

And just how in God's name had he discerned her discomfiture? Her intention had been to send a message of being haughtily put out with the notion of being something with which Hollie could barter—like a piece of furniture. Or his signet ring, which on numerous occasions she had seen him toss onto a pile of coins to cover his wager. On the rare times when he'd lost it, he'd made arrangements to purchase it back. She supposed the lessons he'd learned with the ring were the reason he had added the stipulation that she came for a limited amount of time. "You could have accepted his offer without swapping out your cards."

"It was the most expedient and gracious way to

leave no hard feelings. As I said that night, I don't take unwilling women."

"And if I'd been willing?"

"But you weren't."

"But if I had been?"

"You're beautiful, Marlowe. You know that. I suspect you have a thousand mirrors in your residence to confirm it. You're confident, flirtatious. But your power comes from your loyalty to Hollingsworth. Without that, you lose your appeal."

Her power didn't come from Hollie, and she was of a mind to teach him a lesson on that aspect of herself. But the earl had taught her not to care what people thought—a strange lesson from a man who cared very much what people thought. "Hence you still would have swapped out your cards even if it had been obvious that time alone with you was what I wanted?"

His grin was dark and filled with mystery. "We'll never know."

Oh, she suspected he did know, the scapegrace. He just wasn't going to tell her, preferring to leave her in a quandary, wondering which way he might have gone. Still, she was bothered by all that had transpired that night, more his reaction than Hollie's. "I can't make sense of your actions. You must have wagered at least a hundred pounds on that one hand. And you deliberately lost."

"Years ago, my father was a partner in that gaming hell, when it was Dodger's Drawing Room. As he always told us, there is wealth to be found in vice. Since we were old enough to understand the purpose of money, he has been incredibly generous with our allowance because he never wanted us to be put in the position of being so hungry we'd risk prison for a bit of cheese, as he once was. What I lost that night was pittance compared to what I hold in my coffers." He bowed his head slightly. "Excuse my vulgarity in discussing my wealth."

"How was it that your father, a child of the nobility, came to be so hungry?"

"Are you not familiar with the legend of the Devil Earl?"

"Your father is the Devil Earl?" She'd heard the moniker but hadn't known with whom it was associated.

He gave a slow nod. "As for how he came to be so hungry . . . when he was a wee lad, his parents were murdered in a London alleyway. He was with them but managed to escape their fate. He spent a good many years on the street, part of a gang of child pickpockets, before he was returned to his rightful place among the aristocracy."

"I've heard he killed a man."

"He never speaks about that part of his story, but knowing my father, I suspect the action was justified."

Setting aside his empty plate, taking another swallow of his scotch, he leaned back, his gaze on her focused as intensely as it had been that night. She felt completely unclothed as though, with his eyes, he had the power to burn away the blanket and his shirt. "Now, by your terms, I think I've earned the right to have my question answered."

*L*angdon was surprised by how strongly he wanted to unravel the mystery of her. He should not be intrigued by her and yet he was. It was the boredom that had settled in with the rain. While this place offered peace, it offered few entertainments. And he was, regretfully, finding her entertaining.

She offered him an overly bright smile, winced, and touched her tongue to the cut. It was a losing battle not to think of all the things she could possibly do with that tongue.

With a sigh, she shook her head. "It's a long story. To do it justice, I should probably wait for another time. I'm terribly weary."

Coquettish words, he suspected, would have accompanied the smile she'd misjudged. She'd planned to tease him, to use his curiosity against him. Flirting and tormenting seemed to come naturally to her. But with the injury to her lip, her full arsenal was not available, and he suspected she depended on it to make the most of her story. Although it was possible she was truly tired. She'd been through an ordeal. After the railway accident, for a while, he'd often felt he was wading through a quagmire when he was doing little more than lying in bed or sitting in a chair. He'd seemed to have lost the ability to concentrate, to focus on any one thing for more than a few minutes.

She placed her empty plate on the table. "That was quite good, possibly the most delicious meal I've ever had."

"Evading death's clutches does tend to make one appreciate the smaller pleasures in life."

He couldn't imagine she wouldn't be a pleasure. Based on her blush, she was very good at reading innuendos. With her about, they seemed to roll off his tongue without thought.

"Have you a couple of additional blankets? I could make a nest here in which to sleep."

"Don't be ridiculous. I'm not taking the only bed while a lady is in residence."

"You are very much aware I'm not a lady."

"However, I am a gentleman, so you'll be perfectly safe from any untoward advances . . . and alone up there." He jerked his head toward the ceiling and the room above them.

"While you'll be safe and alone down here." She picked at a piece of lint or something he couldn't quite see as her gaze traveled the back of the sofa like she was measuring it. "The bed is large enough that we could both snuggle into it, and it would probably be like sleeping in separate countries."

No, it damned well would not. Not when she was wearing only his bloody shirt. Would she keep it on once she was beneath the covers or, like him, did she prefer to sleep without any clothing at all? "Since the railway accident, I don't sleep all that well or that much. I'll be perfectly fine here."

Cramped, if not fine. He could always stretch out on the floor if need be.

"If you're certain. I hate to inconvenience you."

"Then the next time you see a storm brewing, stay on land."

"Where's the fun in that, in never taking a risk?"

"It'll keep you out of trouble."

"Knowing what you know of me, my lord, do you honestly believe I shy away from trouble?"

She unfolded herself and stood. He caught a peek at her toes. Since he was no longer tending to her, he decided that if she wanted to flash portions of herself at him, it would be rude not to take note. Because he *was* a gentleman, he shoved himself to his feet. "I'll see you in the morning, then."

She closed her eyes, opened them. "This is no doubt a pointless question, but you wouldn't happen to have a sewing basket, would you?"

Alarm skittered through him. "Have you a gash that needs to be sewn up?"

He hadn't seen one and could detect no bleeding now.

"No, but I will need something to wear when you take me back to the mainland. Your trousers are far too loose. I thought I could use a blanket to sew a simple skirt. I'll send you a replacement when I've returned to London."

Had she tried on a pair of his trousers? He didn't know why he was tempted to ask her to put them back on so he could see exactly how they fit. For some reason, the thought of her in his trousers was more alluring than her in his shirt.

"I do have a sewing basket." He walked over to a chair beside the fire and picked up a small wicker basket with a lid. "Actually, it's my mother's. She comes over to visit sometimes and is firmly against idle hands. Although I think most of the thread is embroidery silk." His mother had left the basket behind because *one never knew when one might be in want of needle and thread.*

As if he was going to mend his clothing should

it become ripped or frayed. Or bother to reattach a button. Or begin embroidering samplers.

Still he'd graciously thanked her because he knew she was worried about him. She tended to worry over all her children, not in a smothering manner, but in a way that demonstrated her deep love for them. His mother knew of no other way in which to love than deeply.

Having grown up watching the example set by his mother and father, he'd been unwilling to settle for anything less than the sort of marriage they had. Unfortunately, he wondered if he might be left with nothing at all. What woman—when she learned the truth of him—would want him as he was now? At least as a husband. A woman of ill repute might not give a bloody damn concerning his shortcomings as long as he kept her ensconced in all the trappings that had led her down that sinful path to begin with.

With gratitude in her eyes, Marlowe took the basket from him. "Thank you." Then she tossed aside the blanket. "I'll leave that for you. You'll need it down here."

Christ. Arches. Heels, ankles, calves, knees, and a portion of her thighs. The hem of his shirt lounged only a quarter of the way down her leg. Was that a freckle on her right knee?

"Good night, my lord." She began walking toward the doorway.

"You don't have to be so formal, Marlowe. After all, you're wearing my shirt."

"An expensive one at that, based on the softness of the linen and the tidiness of the stitching. Perhaps

I'll visit your tailor to have a shirt made specifically for me."

He could well imagine the controversy that would cause. But, after all, the woman attracted controversy the way a magnet did metal shavings. Then she was sauntering out, and it took everything within him not to follow her like a besotted fool.

He dropped down onto the sofa, poured the remainder of her scotch into his glass, and took a healthy swallow. There was the slightest change in its flavor, and he wondered if it was her. Good Lord, what was wrong with him? He never entertained such fanciful musings. But something about Marlowe captured a man's imagination.

Young swells often used her as the epitome of what they searched for in a fallen woman—whether she was to warm a gent's bed for only a night or serve as his mistress for an unlimited number. He even knew lords who had tried to lure her away from Hollingsworth, but her loyalty was as steadfast as the Rock of Gibraltar. Oh, she might flirt, tease, and give a man hope, but somehow it all seemed innocent, playful. She never gave the impression she was seriously considering anyone else.

While she'd claimed weariness tonight, tomorrow he would insist she keep her promise and tell him how she'd come to be Hollingsworth's mistress. And if she was still too exhausted to tell the tale, then he'd be like Charon and the answer would serve as payment for transporting her back to the mainland. He almost laughed as he envisioned the pique with which she might react to that.

While it was truly none of his business, he was keen to know some of her past. The earl was only a few years older than Langdon. Unmarried. When he did take a wife, would he let Marlowe go? She didn't strike him as the sort who was willing to share.

His search for a mistress last May had been for naught. Jamie Swindler had accused him of being too particular. But if he was going to go to the bother and expense of keeping a mistress happy, he wanted to ensure he would be content to spend swaths of time with her. That she'd keep him interested. That he would do the same for her. He saw it as a commitment of a sort. Not just sex, but companionship. However, not someone with whom he'd become too invested because their relationship would end when he married. He wouldn't be disloyal to his viscountess, to the woman who honored him by becoming his wife.

If he married.

It wasn't only nightmares that battered him since the railway accident. He hoped Marlowe would never discover that other aspect of his ordeal, for surely she would think he was mad. But she'd be here only a couple of days. In that time, he would be safe.

He tossed back the remainder of the scotch, welcomed its burning on the way down. Reaching out, he snatched the blanket she'd left behind. It smelled of her. Even though she'd used his soap, he could detect a lingering subtle fragrance unique to her. How was it that in such a short time, he already knew the scent of her? He had the unsettling thought that these rooms would always smell of her.

Ridiculous. She'd be gone once the rain stopped. He'd open windows and doors so the breeze that blew across the sea would chase away every aspect of her and leave behind the smell of salt water, brine, and fish. Within a short period, it would be as if she'd never been here. He could return to his introspection and shore himself up to face the Season.

On occasion their paths might cross. He would deliver a polite greeting . . . and imagine her flouncing about in his damned shirt. Which, truth be told, was much more enticing when it adorned her rather than him.

Grabbing his glass, he shot to his feet, began marching toward the bottles of liquor—

Her cry, sending shivers down his spine, momentarily stopped him in his tracks. Then he spun around, tossed the glass onto the sofa as he rushed by it, and hastened up the stairs. Very little light was coming from his bedchamber. His heart racing, he slowed his pace and glanced inside. Only the fire—and the occasional zag of lightning—provided light. The lamps and candles had all been doused. He'd never bothered to hang draperies around the bed, because when sleep eluded him, he liked to look out on the night. Therefore, he easily saw the lump that represented her curled beneath the covers. She was still, so very still.

He should have taken comfort in the affirmation she was sleeping, not in distress.

A fissure of concern slid through him with the realization that with her injuries, perhaps he shouldn't have allowed her to sleep. She'd obviously taken at least one if not several blows about the head. She might also have some internal damage. He should have at least stayed with her in order to more closely monitor her and to perhaps help her to hold the nightmares at bay.

Stealthily he padded toward the bed, his cold bare feet grateful when they landed on the large rug. As he neared, he could hear her soft soughing as she breathed. Finally, she was visible. Her head on one of his pillows, one hand beneath her cheek, the other fisted near the dip where her collarbones met, just above where the first button on his shirt was secured. For some reason he was surprised, albeit perhaps a bit disappointed, not to find her in the nude.

He wondered if she slept in a nightdress within her own residence. It seemed too innocent a thing for her. If she did, he imagined something gossamer that revealed without exposing completely. That teased and taunted, the way her smile did. That lured a man in as her knowing gaze did.

He shook off those thoughts. She appeared sound. Not fitful or frightened. If she'd been locked in the throes of a nightmare, she'd found the key to escape. Not that he was surprised. He was beginning to recognize that this woman found nothing daunting. Not Society's condemnation. Not her lover exhibiting her in public or his using her to shore up his wager. Not a raging storm. Not a turbulent sea. Not a lord who was idiotically annoyed that she'd wandered into his sanctuary. Because demonstrating annoyance was less dangerous than revealing that he was grateful for her company and the opportunity it afforded him to decipher all the intriguing aspects of her.

Her eyes, slumberous and heavy lidded, opened and a jolt of awareness shot through him. It was the look of a well-sated woman.

She didn't seem bothered by the fact he was standing there, but he felt compelled to explain his presence. "I heard you cry out."

"I was back in the storm, but the frightening dream faded away." She studied him a moment before purring, "Come to bed."

Dear Lord, she'd mistaken him for her lover, even if they looked nothing alike. Hollingsworth was fair, his hair so blond as to be nearly white. "I'm not Hollingsworth."

"I know." The fingers near her throat unfurled and she patted a spot beside her on the mattress. "Join me. Keep the horrid memories from returning."

Her hand stilled, her eyes closed. Had she been cognizant of the invitation she'd been proposing? Although truly, what had she offered? A place to sleep. No more than that. She did have the right of it. His bed was so large that they need not even touch. He might not even feel the warmth radiating from her body.

He probably should stay near. In case she needed him or took a turn for the worse. He was no physician. He didn't truly know how badly she might be hurt.

Looking over his shoulder, he studied the settee. That would suffice. It was near. But it wouldn't easily accommodate his length. Ah, but the bed was so much more comfortable. There were blankets to keep him warm. A pillow for his head. And he'd received an invitation—possibly clouded by slumber. He had the wherewithal, the strength of will, to resist temptation. He'd keep on his trousers.

The decision made, he tugged his shirt over his head and tossed it at the foot of the bed. Then slowly, ever so slowly, in case she awoke and objected, he lifted the covers and slid beneath them.

And was greeted with heavenly warmth. She was inches away, hadn't moved, and yet her heat seeped into his skin as though she was part and parcel of him. He couldn't recall ever feeling so . . . touched. Even though they weren't joined in any way.

He wondered if she'd learned this technique at a school for mistresses. Was there such a thing? How did a woman learn all the various ways of pleasure? By having a multitude of lovers, he supposed. How many had she had? He'd only ever heard of her being with Hollingsworth. She wasn't that old. Early twenties if he had to guess. How much experience could she have? Although with the age of consent for marriage only recently being raised from twelve to thirteen, he supposed she could have had a good bit.

However, her manner of speaking, while she claimed not to be one, was that of a lady. He shouldn't be so curious about her, and yet he was.

She shifted nearer to him, her hand curling around his upper arm, her cheek coming to rest against his skin.

He held his breath, waiting for her to fully

awaken and order him from her bed. His bed. But she slept on.

The storm was acting as a lullaby, luring him toward slumber. He was looking forward to the morrow when she'd finally answer the question he'd asked earlier. And in the answering, she might provide him with a clearer picture of exactly who she was.

Chapter 9

$\mathscr{M}$arlowe decided she was beginning to enjoy opening her eyes. No bare buttocks this morning but facing her was an incredibly handsome visage in need of a shave. She'd like very much to run her fingers over the thick shadow of his beard, but he'd no doubt object.

She had a vague memory of him standing beside the bed, an invitation issued. Obviously accepted, although she didn't recall him joining her. But his presence surrounded her in heavenly warmth and a sense of being protected. No doubt because of the strong arm curled over her side and the long fingers splayed against her back serving as a shield, as secure as one made of iron. She was left with the impression no one would be able to get to her, to harm her, as long as that hand rested against her.

Dear Lord, he was gorgeous but even in slumber he didn't appear particularly innocent. Or perhaps it was the positioning of their bodies that belied the virtuousness because sometime during the night they'd sought each other.

The shirt she wore had risen up her thigh, barely covering her most intimate area. While one leg was straight, the other was bent at the knee and nestled between his legs. Thank goodness he was wearing trousers. If he wasn't, the heat of attraction coursing through her would have no doubt caused her to ignite.

The storm had yet to abate, but the grayness pouring in through the windows allowed her to see him clearly. He was such a lovely specimen of manhood, and she'd always had a propensity for appreciating lovely things.

When she'd first clapped eyes on him in London, he'd been clean-shaven. She rather liked the scruffiness he was currently sporting. She supposed since he lived alone here, he kept his grooming habits to a minimum. Not that she blamed him. She imagined the pleasure to be found in simply brushing her hair back and securing it in place with a ribbon—instead of sitting for an hour while strands were artfully arranged to ensure another's satisfaction.

His black hair, traveling over his ears, curled loosely at the ends. That, too, had been different before. It had been much shorter, evenly cut, and tamed into perfect order. Now it was wild, like some feral creature that had been caged and then set free. It would do as it would, following no man's orders.

His eyelashes were the longest she'd ever seen. Resting against the curved upper edge of his strong cheekbones, they were thick and heavy. She was half-tempted to stir one loose of its mooring so she could blow it away with a gentle breath and make a wish. His eyelashes were sure to grant wishes.

She almost smiled. She hadn't had such fanciful thoughts since she was a child.

Then he opened his eyes, and she was no longer thinking of eyelashes. She was no longer thinking at all. The pewter gray of his eyes held her captive. Before meeting him, she'd never seen eyes of that shade. They were mesmerizing, reminding her of gray stone peered at through fog. The eeriness of Stonehenge. The mystery of it. He was full of mystery. She was rather certain of it. Here on this isle alone when, unlike her, he'd be welcomed as an honored guest into any home in Britain.

However, if he hadn't been here, she didn't know how she would have survived. She might have never woken up from the spot where the sea had deposited her. She'd have probably eventually frozen there. Instead, she was all warm and snug, slightly entwined with him, grateful she could still hear the rain pattering on the window. It gave her an excuse to remain where she was.

"I don't think I've ever slept so well in this bed," he said, his voice raspy and rough, and although she knew it was because he'd only just awakened, she imagined it sounded much the same after he made love to a woman. Or at least it was the way she'd want it to sound if he ever bedded her. She wanted his throat raw from his groans and growls. Wanted him demonstrating with grunts, thrusts, and muscles bulging with tenseness precisely what he endured as she turned him inside out.

Just the thought of him rising above her had dew

gathering between her thighs, her breaths difficult to find, and her body igniting to such a degree that she'd have to toss aside the blankets before long. "Rescuing me no doubt exhausted you."

"I'm not sure that's it." Moving his hand from her back, he laid it over hers where it rested against his chest, folded his fingers around it, and brought it to his lips where he placed the gentlest of kisses against her knuckles, never taking his gaze from hers. "Your body will no doubt protest any movement, worse than yesterday. The aches will have settled in to inhabit your bones. So move about gingerly."

"Have you experience floundering about in the sea and battling storms?"

A faraway look and pain entered his eyes before he shuttered all emotion. "In a manner of speaking."

She remembered what she'd learned of the railway accident, and how it remained within him. Surviving the storm might do the same to her. How did one escape the scars of trauma?

He released his hold on her hand, and she was keenly aware of more than his fingers withdrawing. She had the odd sense he was stacking boulders between them. "I'll bring up some warm water for the basin, then leave you to your ablutions. When you're ready, come down to the main room. I'll have prepared something for us to eat."

As he rolled out of the bed, she immediately felt the chill. It was more than cold air sweeping in; it was also more than the absence of his warmth. It was the distance she recognized that he was putting between them. Even though she told herself it was all for the best, she drew the covers more tightly around herself and wondered how he might react if she admitted she wouldn't mind him becoming one of her sins.

In a series of fluid movements, he grabbed his shirt from where it rested at the foot of the bed, dragged it on, and marched over to the fireplace. He crouched and began sacrificing logs to increase the heat. His shirt wasn't tucked into his waistband, so she didn't have a clean view of his trousers pulling taut over his backside, but she was treated to the delicious sight of the material hugging his thighs.

She'd never been shy about appreciating what a man had to offer. The lessons she'd learned after arriving in London probably had something to do with her lax attitude when it came to what most people found offensive. The human form had served as inspiration for any number of artistic works. How could it thusly be something about which to be ashamed, to be hidden away beneath layers of confining clothing?

It was one of the reasons that she dressed so simply when she was going up in her balloon. Clothes she could easily remove without the assistance of a maid. Who was to see her? Besides, it reduced the weight. The less cumbersome attire gave her a sense of freedom. One she never truly experienced when she was on the ground. Because she was always at another's beck and call. Although of late, she was discovering she wanted to be only at her own.

After dusting off his hands, he shoved himself

upright. It was a peculiar thing to think of his movements as poetic, yet they spoke to her in an odd sort of way, filling her with calm in much the same manner as reading a poem did. It was the rhythm of his actions, the smooth cadence, every aspect of him attuned to the whole.

He sat in a thickly stuffed chair and began pulling on a pair of boots that had been resting near the fire. "You might want to stay snuggled beneath the blankets as long as possible. As you've no doubt observed, this is a drafty old place."

"But it has its charms." Him being one of them, she was discovering.

"And its privacy. Usually."

"Sorry to have intruded." She sounded mulish, ungrateful, which she wasn't particularly pleased about. Men were wont to exhibit their displeasure if her attitude wasn't pleasant. And Langdon had no reason to be happy that he'd had to rescue her from the sea. She was an intrusion . . . and to an extent that would make her unwelcome company to anyone.

Except Langdon merely quirked up one corner of his mouth. "I usually relish the solitude, but last night I found myself wishing for companionship . . . and the sea delivered."

Strange how his words caused warmth and a measure of joy to wash over her. "Even though there were no stars upon which to wish?"

"I don't have to see the stars to know that they are there, and I've studied them thoroughly enough to know where they are at any given moment."

"I suppose I should be a bit miffed if it was your

wish that brought an end to my journey in the sky, but I do think they *have* to be visible to be wished upon. Hence I very much doubt you are responsible for my calamity."

"I shall hope not." He stood. "I won't be long." With that, he departed.

She pulled up her legs, nearly to her chest, grateful the warmth from his body hadn't dissipated completely. She wondered how he might react if she confessed that she'd be content to remain in bed with him as long as the rain fell. Longer still. It had been ages since she'd found herself so drawn to a man. Especially one who gave the impression he couldn't wait to be rid of her.

Perhaps that was his appeal. Like a good many people, she wanted what she couldn't have and being denied made the object all the more alluring.

*A*dding some butter to the eggs he was stirring in the pot, Langdon's thoughts shifted to earlier and how badly he hadn't wanted to get out of the damned bed. Certainly, he'd been in more intimate positions with any number of ladies, but with Marlowe's leg nestled between his thighs, her hand on his chest, and the narrow space separating the rest of their bodies, he'd been unable to recall when he'd ever been more aroused. Fortunately, the distance between her hips and his was wide enough so that, with his trousers keeping his cock confined, she'd been unaware of how much he wanted her.

And it was *want*. Not animalistic, savage need for mating that had possessed man from the dawn of time. No, something more had been driving this need within him to possess her. Something more personal, more directly related to her—as if she would provide the completion of his soul.

He'd thought he might go mad, simply lying there, eyes closed, absorbing her nearness. He'd been acutely aware of her studying him, as though her hands—rather than her gaze—were roaming over him, alighting upon him. How could he be so cognizant of her? And yet something about her called to the most primitive aspect of him: to protect, to cherish, to nurture.

In spite of all the bruising, swelling, and cuts marring her face that had greeted him when he did finally open his eyes, the warm appreciation in her light blue ones nearly undid him, as though she was enamored of him, curious about him. As though she wanted him as well—in spite of all the aches and pains that had to be plaguing her.

He hated the notion that she was suffering. Because of a tumble from the sky. Christ, he could hardly believe that she'd flown in a hot-air balloon. She was an adventuress, and perhaps that, more than anything, had him anxious to determine what sort of sexual escapades the two of them could experience. Surely a woman prone to not keeping her feet on the ground could welcome and provide less-than-routine sensual delights.

That evening at the Dragons, if the time they would have had together had come about in a manner that was clearly her choice, that didn't diminish her and treat her as an object . . . would she have been content with only the few hours allotted them or might she have wanted more? And what then? Was he to have called Hollingsworth out at dawn or convinced him to let his mistress go?

Sometime later, with two plates in hand, he strode into the main chamber and disappointment slammed into him because she'd managed to turn one of the more faded blankets into a makeshift skirt that reached the middle of her calves. She still wore his shirt, and he wondered if it would forever smell of her.

She turned from where she was standing at the window. "I was hoping to see the end of it, some clear skies in the distance."

He set the plates on the table before the sofa, one at each end. "Could rain for days or hours. Coffee or tea?"

She began sauntering toward him, and he decided the sensual walk was done out of habit, not in any attempt to seduce him. "Tea would be lovely. I'm in need of some comfort."

By the time he returned, she was sitting in one corner of the sofa, her legs stretched out, her feet flexing before the fire. The plate was on her lap, but she'd not touched anything.

"I have no milk." The storm had prevented him from returning to the family estate for weekly provisions. He lifted the cups just a bit. "One has no sugar, one has an abundance. Which do you prefer?"

"Surprise me. I'm not particular."

He wondered if the same could be said of the men in her life. He handed her a cup before settling onto the other end of the sofa, plate in hand. He set his cup on the table. "I'm sadly lacking in furniture, I'm afraid."

"And culinary skills. The offerings very much resemble those from last night."

"Eggs and fish are about the only things I've mastered when it comes to cooking."

"If I had the correct ingredients, I could make you a right proper meal."

"You don't strike me as someone who cooks."

"Like tea, I find baking comforting." Her tone carried the tiniest bit of defensiveness.

He'd meant no insult, but he supposed neither could forget exactly what she was, and that the path she'd chosen was always an undercurrent in conversations or actions, no matter how innocent.

They ate in silence for several long minutes, his gaze wandering to their feet seeking the warmth of the fire, hers so small compared to his. Such tiny toes. He wondered if a single physical aspect of her wasn't perfect.

Taking a sip of his sugarless tea, he mulled over how pleasant it was to be sitting here not alone, with the rain still falling, the thunder occasionally booming, the lightning flashing, and the dark clouds preventing the sunlight from getting all the way through. When he was younger, he and his brother would camp out on the island. Even if they stayed in the dwelling, at the time, it was hardly inhabitable. They explored, had adventures. He had the unsettling notion that the hours she was here would overshadow the memories from his youth. No matter how short her stay. He set his empty plate on the table. "I haven't forgotten that you owe me an answer."

Her voice was soft, warm. "I didn't think you

had, but it's such a lovely day and the answer isn't all that pleasant for me to reveal."

He'd begun to suspect as much and wished he'd never asked, wished he hadn't brought it up now when there was a coziness he'd never before experienced in this room. "Lovely day? There's a blasted storm out."

She slid her gaze over to him. "I've always loved the rain."

"Is that the reason you went out in it? To be in the sky with it?"

She was still struggling to smile, her tongue touching the tiny cut. "I hadn't considered that. If it affected my decision, I wasn't aware of it. No, I like to be indoors when it rains. This is a wonderful chamber, with its massive fireplace, in which to wait out a storm. I've been giving some thought to your dwelling. It was a lookout, wasn't it? A place to spot the enemy coming in."

"Legend would have it so."

"Will you live here when you take a wife?"

Was that jealousy he heard in her voice? He very much doubted it. "What woman would want to live in such isolation? To miss out on balls, shopping, and tea with friends?"

"Have you selected your lady?"

He gave her an indulgent grin and just held her gaze, until she blushed and looked away.

"Not my business, I suppose," she muttered. "I've read nothing in the gossip sheets, so if you have, I wonder if she even knows. Probably not. You're considered quite the catch, so I suspect she would be anxious for the world to know."

With a shake of his head, he chuckled. "I think you might be able to tell if I'm bluffing at the card table."

She slid her gaze over to him, and he felt like she'd pinned him in place as one might a butterfly to a board—to study and examine until all its secrets were revealed.

"It's to my benefit to be able to decipher men, what they think, what they want, what they would die for."

"And a good many would die for you."

She laughed, grimaced, licked that corner of her mouth again. "For *me*? No. For a chance to bed me? Possibly." She shrugged. "Probably. Hollie took me to a symposium once. The subject was insects, of all things. Did you know the praying mantis bites off the head of her lover after they've copulated?"

He'd never heard any woman use a term related to sex, and yet he couldn't envision her not being direct. Although the way she drew out the syllables of *copulated*, she might as well have said *fucked*. "Perhaps he disappointed her."

She laughed again, a sweet sound that reverberated through his chest. "Still, a rather rash punishment. I couldn't stop thinking about it for days after we went. The poor creature gets to make love only once. Good Lord, but I do hope it's an incredible experience for him. He pays a ghastly price for it."

He'd never spoken so openly about sex with a woman—even if it was insect sex. That she would feel sorry for a bug and worry about his enjoyment . . . he couldn't imagine she wouldn't give the same care and attention to a man's pleasure. He didn't want to contemplate what she might do, how exquisite the intimacy might be. Yet all the images suddenly fluttering through his mind were of her in various positions, engaged in various actions. If he'd had her those few hours Hollingsworth had offered, he thought her walking away might very well feel like dying. Even if his head remained attached.

"My apologies," she said. "Not appropriate breakfast conversation."

"Most women I know would rather crush an insect beneath their shoe than worry over its . . . happiness."

Her smile was small, as though she'd learned how wide she could spread her lips before her wound protested. "You may have failed to notice I am not like most women."

"I haven't failed to notice." He hadn't failed to notice anything about her. And that was the problem. He liked too much what he saw and was coming to learn about her.

And that placed him on a short path to disaster.

Chapter 10

Now what did I do to upset him? Marlowe wondered.

As though suddenly angry with her—or himself—Langdon had abruptly snatched her empty plate, grabbed his from the table, shoved himself to his feet, and stormed from the room as if the hounds of hell were nipping at his heels. Or someone was after his head. Had her tale of the praying mantis offended him? He hadn't seemed bothered by it. He'd looked at her as though entranced by every word.

At the symposium, she had been fascinated by the strange mating habit of the creature. She knew a few mistresses who would no doubt not mind having the ability to bite off the heads of their lovers. The women often complained that their chaps were either selfish or unskilled when it came to pleasuring them. Marlowe had the sense that Langdon would never have a mistress who was a member of the Praying Mantis Club.

She glanced around. The chamber seemed cold

and barren without him in it. She wondered if he was planning on returning.

Gingerly easing off the sofa—every muscle, bone, and joint was announcing it had been a casualty of the storm—she wandered to one of the huge windows and gazed out. Its size made it perfect for storm watching. She'd been able to see little last night. It appeared the dwelling was on the edge of a rise. Of course, it would be to allow for the best visibility when searching for those who were coming this way with nefarious intentions. She wondered how many ships might have crashed here on moonless nights or during storms. She suspected hers was the only balloon to have done so.

The clouds were still heavy and dark, the wind howling, and the rain a torrential downpour. How much life could the storm have left in it?

Perhaps she could amuse herself with a little exploring. Before she moved to London, when she was much younger, she would spend hours investigating all the various nooks and crannies of an abandoned and dilapidated abbey near her home. Once she'd found a red stone, a garnet she thought. Perhaps a ruby. Surely in its history it had been embedded in a religious relic. She had attributed magical qualities to it and made wishes upon it. The problem with wishes, though, she soon discovered, was that if a person wasn't terribly specific in describing the request, it might be granted, but in the end wasn't exactly what one had in mind.

Case in point: Langdon had wished for a woman

and, in the end, had gotten her. And seemed none too pleased by the wish granter's choice.

With a sigh, she snatched up the blanket she'd left the night before and draped it around her shoulders before leaving the chamber.

She detected some noises echoing into the hallway leading to the kitchen. She crept up to the open doorway and peered in. Langdon was tidying up from their meal.

She considered offering to assist, but based on the abruptness of his leaving, she didn't think he'd welcome her presence. So instead, she skirted past and made her way to a smaller chamber. It contained a large trestle table and one chair. Was this to serve as the dining room?

Although it more closely resembled a workroom. Scrunched-up paper was littering the floor. A mound of crushed papers filled a bin to overflowing. In the huge fireplace, the flames of a low fire waltzed.

Slowly, she approached the table as if it were a dangerous beast that could devour her in one bite. Whatever he was doing in here, whatever had been the cause of so much discarded paper, was absolutely none of her business. And yet she was craving an understanding of him. Why was he here away from everyone? Why wasn't he attending country house parties? Why wasn't he out hunting grouse or stag or whatever poor creature was presently in season? Why was he in this stark, dark, and frigid dwelling?

While she'd never been to Newgate, fortunately, she couldn't help but believe the prison's cells offered more comforts.

Eventually she was near enough to study everything that seemed to be haphazardly arranged. Pen with a gold nib, inkwell, stack of blank paper. And a maths primer.

Why in the hell would he need a primer on numbers? Perhaps he'd come here to study when he was a wee lad, still in school. But if that was the case, she was looking at nearly two decades since any of this would have been used. Wouldn't it be covered in a thick layer of dust?

Instead, not a speck of grime was visible anywhere.

Reaching down, she picked up a wadded piece of paper and untwisted it. It had a few more squiggles than those pieces that remained on the table, but she still couldn't make out what he was trying to accomplish.

"What the hell do you think you're doing?"

At the curt and clearly upset tone, she spun around, guiltily hiding the paper behind her back as if he hadn't already seen her studying it. She was rather certain that her cheeks were burning bright red at her having been caught snooping about. Still, she wasn't one to cower. She tilted her head haughtily. "I was merely exploring." She waved a hand toward the floor. "What is all this?"

"None of your bloody concern. Now get the hell out."

She watched in amazement as he charged into the room, scooped a handful of the scrunched papers from the floor, and tossed them onto the fire.

"So I'm restricted to two rooms?"

More papers tossed. "And the outdoors. You can go stand in the rain if you like."

"What I would *like* is to know why you are so upset. It's not as though I'd discovered that you'd buried a body."

He swung around and glowered. "Everything within this room is private. Explore anywhere else, but not this chamber. Nothing here is meant for you."

She gave a little curtsy. "My apologies for over-stepping. My curiosity got the better of me, I'm afraid. I usually know a good deal more about a man before he visits my bed. Although I suppose in reality, it was your bed and I the visitor."

She'd hoped to at least coax a smile out of him. Instead, he glowered more fiercely. "How many have been in your bed?"

Aware of her jaw dropping, she glared at him. The unmitigated audacity. How dare he ask such a personal question after chastising her for look-ing at a piece of paper. However, she refused to respond with fire, because she'd discovered that coolness could often cut deeper. Regaining control of her emotions, she lifted a shoulder so high she could have easily kissed it. "I don't keep count of my conquests. Do you?"

He began scooping up more bits of paper. "Off with you. Do your exploring. Be wary of the dun-geon, though. The door to it sometimes locks on its own. I'd hate for you to get trapped down there."

She was confident he would free her if she was. However, his tone contained less ire, but more wea-riness. As if he was the one in the storm trying to make it safely to land, but not quite sure he was going to make it.

She very much doubted he was even aware of her leaving the room, so focused was he on his task of getting rid of what passed as evidence for something he was determined to keep secret.

With every bone, muscle, and sinew of his body, Langdon was aware of her leaving. The relief should have been monstrous. Instead, the victory felt very much like a defeat.

Where would have been the harm in telling her? But she might have told Hollingsworth, who might tell his closest friends, who would then tell theirs until all of London knew that Viscount Langdon no longer had a knack for numbers.

He'd first noticed his inability to work with numerals only a couple of weeks after the railway accident. The leather satchel in which he'd been carrying the proposal outlining his plans for improvements to increase the estate's income had either been buried in the rubble or some enterprising soul had used the ensuing chaos to make off with it. Not that the contents would have been of any value to a thief, but the fine leather that had housed them might have brought a fair price from fences.

He'd taken some time to recover from the ordeal—cracked ribs had needed to heal, as had all the bruises, scrapes, and cuts. The headaches he'd suffered in the beginning had often laid him low.

But the day had come when he'd been determined to re-create his proposal. And he'd been unable to recall how numbers worked. It might have helped if he'd been able to identify the numerals or at least

determine their value, how many items composed
each one. He knew they were used for counting but
he had lost the ability to count. Not knowing the
value of each number made it impossible to merge
any of them and come up with a total, much less
merge a page full of them. Without that capability,
how was he going to comprehend the estate ledgers? How was he going to ensure the solvency of
the properties that would be entrusted to his care
when he inherited the title?

And if he married, bloody hell, he wouldn't
even be able to count how many children his wife
gave him.

With the aid of the primer, he'd been trying to
relearn numbers using the word problems because
he still maintained a grasp on words. But when he
got to a number, he could trace it onto paper but
everything else about it remained a mystery. It was
the damnedest thing.

His physician had diagnosed him with railway
spine. Said his brain and spine had gotten badly
shaken up in the railway accident. They didn't yet
have a cure for it because every case was different.
All he could do was hope that his ability to decipher numbers would return. But in his opinion
hope was a poor plan.

Hence the primer. And all his failed attempts to
rid himself of the problem.

And now he had another problem: Marlowe.

She could prick his temper without even trying.
She unsettled him. She was too curious, too smart.
Most women he knew would have been bored silly

with talk of insects. Squeamish at least. While she'd been fascinated.

With her inquisitive mind, she might determine what was happening in this room. Hell, she might be able to figure out his affliction by merely having a conversation with him. What if they waded into a topic that involved numbers?

His best recourse was to simply ignore her.

Chapter 11

$\mathscr{M}$arlowe had returned to the main chamber to stare out the window. During her journey back to this safe little corner, she'd become melancholy. "The morbs" was how her friend Sophie referred to this sadness that could weigh down a body as easily as it did a spirit.

She hadn't meant to intrude on Langdon's peaceful exile, but neither could she help being curious. She knew people who by outward appearances seemed perfectly happy, but inside they struggled with all sorts of troubles and strife. She wondered what it would entail to convince him to share his plight with her.

She wondered why she was desperate for him to do so.

Because it would help to pay him back for his rescue of her? Because she might have died without him and hence she owed him? It was so easy to try to find a convincing excuse when the truth was more difficult to face. She wanted to spend additional time in his company, wanted him grateful to her. She didn't want them at odds. As implausible as it should be, she rather liked him. While he'd certainly had a few instances of expressing his annoyance that she was here, far more moments had been spent showing her kindnesses.

At the soft whisper of sound, she turned and watched as Langdon entered, strolled over to a stack of books, lifted the top one, and took the second. His movements were so mesmerizing. It wasn't fair that she should notice, that he could be so alluring without even trying.

As if not bothered by her presence, as if not truly aware of it, he didn't even look at her as he went to the sofa, dropped onto one corner, and simultaneously stretched out his ridiculously long legs while opening the book to some spot in the middle.

She should leave him to it. Just stand there and idly twiddle her thumbs. He probably expected little else from her than lying around all day eating bonbons. Most envisioned the mistress life as one of glamour. Certainly, it had its moments. But a good deal more of it involved tedious tasks, ensuring every aspect of her, not only the physical, appealed to her consort.

Yes, she should give Langdon no attention at all. Respond to him as he was responding to her.

"You ought to build a large-cushioned seat against this window, make a little reading nook. The view is astonishing." Apparently, her tongue was not listening to her mind.

Looking up, with his brow furrowed, he seemed either surprised or irritated to see her standing there, as if he'd forgotten she existed or didn't much like being disturbed. She decided on the latter because it was inconceivable that he could forget she was here. Although maybe he had expected her to retreat to his bedchamber. The truth was, she'd never much liked being ignored. She'd spent a good bit of her energy over the recent years ensuring she would *not* be ignored.

"The view from upstairs is much better. You can see farther into the distance," he said flatly, and she couldn't help but believe that in his tone he was conveying that was exactly where she should be: upstairs, as far away from him as the storm allowed.

She didn't like the awkwardness that had settled in between them. Waking up with him this morning, she'd mistakenly believed they were at least willing to tolerate each other. Although she wanted more than that. Unaccustomed to gentlemen finding fault with her, she wanted him to at least like her, even if it was only a little bit.

"I want to apologize for my earlier intrusion into your . . . office. I didn't mean to pry." Of course, she had meant to pry but was hoping he'd be gracious enough to accept her apology.

"My apologies if I seemed harsh or hurt your feelings. I'm working on a proposal for the estate manager. A way to increase our revenue. Until I've completed it, I prefer to keep it close to the vest."

"Like you do your cards?"

A corner of his mouth tipped up. "Like I do my cards."

"You allowed me to see them that night."

He gave one slow nod before returning his attention to his book.

Since he magnanimously accepted her lie, she decided to return the favor and accept his regarding what was occurring within that room. All those scribbles had been for something else. She looked back at the rain. She could barely see through the sheets of cascading water. The clouds were so heavy and black that if she wasn't aware of the hour, she'd believe it was twilight.

"How did you know?" she asked.

"I beg your pardon?"

She did wish she didn't enjoy the deepness of his voice so much, like he was inviting her into a secret world the two of them shared. Slowly she began walking toward him. "Earlier, you opened the book and immediately began reading." Or pretended to. "But no ribbon, slip of paper, or favor from a ladylove marked your place. The corner has not been bent. I can detect no means by which you could succeed at such a feat, so how did you know precisely where you left off?"

He studied her intently, the way one did someone they were measuring up in order to determine if they could be trusted. "I've read it before." He waved his hand in a gesture to encompass the entire room. "I've read them all before. I like to open them randomly and start reading."

She lowered herself to the sofa. "You've read all these books?"

"Yes."

"And the ones in your bedchamber?"

"Those as well."

"Hence, you've been here long enough to read each one?"

"No, I bring books I've already read."

"Why?"

He released a long, slow breath, and she could see that he was striving to determine how best to explain. "These books . . . I draw comfort from them. I enjoy spending time with characters I know or going on adventures I've already been on. I can open these books to any page and I'm immediately . . . transported to someplace I know will . . . bring me . . . contentment." He shook his head. "I fear I sound rather mad."

"No, I never thought of it that way. I read a book and, when I'm finished, I never go back to it. I'm too eager to read the next one. I want the new, not the familiar. But I find no fault with either approach. And it's such a perfect day for becoming lost in a story. I don't suppose you could recommend one for me." She was interested in reading one of his favorite novels because she thought doing so might reveal something about him. How could a story be a favorite and not in some way be a reflection of the man?

"I don't know you well enough to know what you might enjoy," he said.

Therefore, to know him she was going to have to let him know her better. She supposed she could just randomly select a book, but of a sudden, she wanted him to do the choosing. "I fancy stories that offer hope and by the end bring me joy. Or even better, make me sigh and hold it close. It's all right if it saddens me in the middle, but if I have any tears at the end, they have to be because I'm happy for the characters. I want someone to fall in love. I want to *see* them fall in love."

"Frankenstein fell in love with his monster. I have that book somewhere around here," he said drolly.

She smiled softly, even though she experienced a little discomfort doing so. She wanted to believe he was teasing and not being an utter arse. "I think the scientist was more in love with himself. The story made me rather sad. I felt sorry for the . . . creature. But he wasn't the real monster. Frankenstein was."

He arched a brow. "I'm surprised you read it when it doesn't meet your requirement for happy tears at the end."

"When people are mentioning books they've read, or plays they've attended, or operas, or avenues for new entertainments . . . I find it useful to be knowledgeable about those things so I don't stand there like a ninny with conversations going on around me—and not being able to contribute or offer insights. Being a gentleman's mistress isn't all bedding, you know."

He scrutinized her as though she'd said something significant. After what seemed eons and was at least three lightning flashes, he asked, "Have you read *Great Expectations*?"

She shook her head. "Dickens's stories are a little too realistic."

He set aside what he'd been reading, got up, walked over to a stack of books, and took a tome from the bottom. He returned to his place and set the novel between them. "The character Pip falls in love."

She ran her finger along the spine. "Are they together at the end?"

"You'll have to read it."

She picked up the book and folded back the cover. "Ah, Charles Dickens signed this one."

"Yes, my father knew him, quite well actually, as did I by association."

"What was he like?"

"I was quite a bit younger and too much in awe to really notice." He opened his book—to a different page, she noted—and turned his attention to it.

End of discussion, then. Only she wasn't quite ready for it to be finished. "I shared with you what I like to read. What do you favor?"

Very slowly he closed the book and turned his head toward her. His eyes had gone that dark pewter again, and she was beginning to suspect they did that whenever he was aroused. She didn't think she was doing anything particularly provocative. She merely wanted a little more conversation.

But his gaze was intense, serious, his breathing slow and steady. He was still, so very still. He reminded her of a scorpion that had been on display in a glass case at the insect symposium. They'd dropped a huge spider into the enclosure. Both creatures had circled around the inner edges until suddenly the scorpion had gone deathly still—

With no warning whatsoever its tail had struck out with such swiftness that the poor spider hadn't a chance.

She was left with the impression that Langdon was

deliberating when and exactly how to strike. What sort of books did he enjoy reading that he would need to contemplate what to share or prepare himself to do so?

"I favor . . . long, slow kisses that last for days, the weight of a plump breast against my palm, and the sultry heat of a woman's tight core enveloping me."

Feeling as though the sofa had magically moved too close to the fireplace, she wanted to toss aside the blanket she'd wrapped around herself earlier. He had to have known she was asking about books, but he had chosen to respond with something else entirely. Something titillating, something he believed appropriate to say to her, a courtesan. He'd certainly never say anything like that to one of the ladies he swept around a London ballroom. And most certainly not in that low, seductive voice that confirmed for a woman that rewards for her were to be found on the other end of all those things he favored. Her lips had begun to tingle, her damned nipples had puckered, and dew had gathered between her thighs.

"Are you attempting to shock me, my lord, with such blatant sexual imagery?" *Or seduce me?* She dared not ask the latter because if he was, she feared she'd be unable to resist. *Damn Hollie for even giving her leave to entertain the idea of a night spent in the company of this man.* "It can't be done. Although I do find myself wondering . . . if you swapped out your cards that night because you were being offered a warm, moist kiss that would last only hours rather than your preferred days. Nor were you guaranteed either a plump breast—although mine are, which you probably discovered last night—or a tight core, which I also may lay claim to possessing. Perhaps you feared you weren't up to the challenge of gaining those when they weren't handed to you."

She thought he'd been still before. She wasn't certain he was even breathing now, although his eyes had jumped from her lips to her breasts to her lap and back up. If he'd been hoping to intimidate her with such raw words that created tawdry images, he was going to discover that she gave as good as she got.

Then she very deliberately and slowly returned her attention to her book.

𝒟amnation. He had been hoping to shock her . . . or perhaps seduce her. She didn't blush. She wasn't easily flustered. She teased. And she was so damned sultry. Every movement and pose calculated to entice.

Well, it was as she'd said that night. She wasn't a whore. She didn't give a man a single hour or even a night. She expected a commitment. Deserved that consideration. She wouldn't come cheap. With his squiring her about, Hollingsworth had ensured she could be demanding and particular when it came to her next lover.

He watched as she slowly turned a page and kept her focus on the words written by another. He considered confessing the reason he'd swapped out his cards . . .

Instead he turned his attention back to his own reading. Or tried to, but even when they weren't engaged in sparring words, he couldn't seem to focus on the material before him.

A hushed intimacy settled in around them, disturbed only by the crackling fire, pattering raindrops, and occasional thunder. *She* made not a sound. No occasional sigh. No whisper of movement beneath the blanket that he suspected wasn't soft enough for her skin. No sniffle, sneeze, or cough—it appeared she was not going to fall ill from her dunking in the sea.

Most of the ladies he knew would have decided the horrifying experience warranted some pampering, and yet she seemed to be taking it in stride. He'd done the same thing following the railway accident, carrying on as though it had been perfectly routine. Until the night he'd awoken drenched and shivering, as if he was back in that storm, comforting the dying and pleading with the living not to give up. At least she wouldn't have to deal with that aspect, being alone as she'd been, but he suspected that brought with it its own trauma. As much as he wished otherwise, he assumed eventually it would hit her full on as a force to be reckoned with. And all the sinuous moves, flirtatious glances, and tart words wouldn't lessen its impact.

Would Hollingsworth hold her, comfort her? Would he even be there if the nightmares came? Did he stay the night or only long enough to see to his purpose in arriving there to begin with?

His jaw began to ache, and he realized the thoughts had made him clench his teeth to such a degree he was surprised they didn't crack. The last thing he wanted was to envision the earl with her. What he wanted was to read his bloody book.

Half an hour later, he decided it was a damned good thing he'd already read *The Man in the Iron Mask*, because he was having a hell of a time concentrating on the passage resting before his eyes. Probably because his gaze kept shifting over to Marlowe as he sought to gauge her reaction to what she was reading—to what he had chosen for her to read. Why the devil he should care two figs whether she was enjoying it was beyond his comprehension. What did it matter if he'd selected a book that would be to her liking? He should have just told her to wander around until she found something that looked appealing. Or read a few pages and if it didn't draw her in, move on to another.

He'd expected her to favor reading matter that was tawdry, naughty. But then he supposed she encountered enough of those elements in her daily—nightly—life. Last night he'd assumed by the way she was moving about freely before him while wearing his shirt, not at all self-conscious about revealing those shapely legs, that she'd been attempting to seduce him, but watching the manner in which she turned pages, he was beginning to suspect that moving sensually was second nature to her. Whether it had come from practice or a natural inclination was open to speculation.

"Does Hollingsworth gift you with books?"

Why the devil had he disturbed the quiet with such an inane question?

As though coming out of a trance, slowly she lifted her head and turned it toward him. "No."

"Don't you like books?" He couldn't imagine anyone not treasuring them.

"Of course, I do."

"But you prefer fancy baubles or trinkets."

He suspected if her nose wasn't bruised and still slightly swollen that she would have wrinkled it in disgust at his statement. "I prefer giving to receiving but I have no preference when it comes to what sort of gifts I should be given. Which is good because Hollie is atrocious at determining what I might favor. He once gave me some jewelry to clamp onto my nipples."

He didn't know whether to be stunned by the gift or her casual use of *nipples*, a word most ladies would cut out their tongues before uttering.

She gave a little laugh. "Based on the set of your features, I'd say you were scandalized. My face was no doubt similarly arranged when I learned what they were for. I was wearing them as earbobs at the time."

Her eyes held a wicked gleam, and he fought not to laugh. He was not going to be like every other man in London and fall victim to her charms. He imagined her proudly strutting about, showing off the gift that was designed to be shared with a private audience of one. "How long have you and Hollingsworth been together?"

"Three years come May. You'd think he'd know my tastes by now. But he favors unusual objects, takes joy in purchasing them. And giving them. So I always make a point of reassuring him the gift is unlike anything I've received and thanking him profusely."

"How can he learn your tastes if you're dishonest with him?"

She angled her head to the side. "Am I being dishonest?"

"You're pretending to like what you don't."

"The gift is unique. That's not a lie. And I thank him because he thought of me and went to the trouble of bringing me something that brought him joy to present to me. The actual gift is not important. It is the act of giving and the pleasure that results for both parties, hopefully, that matters. When I look at the atrocious gifts lying around my residence, well, they do warm me because they remind me of Hollie and the way he smiled when he gave them to me."

He'd assumed she'd demand particular gifts, gifts that, if need be, could be taken to a fence or sold. That she'd be difficult to please. She was spoiled for choice when it came to benefactors. "I suppose it pays to keep him happy."

Her eyes dulled. Her small smile withered. "Ah, yes, Langdon, that's exactly why I demonstrate kindness: for the benefits doing so brings to me."

It seemed he couldn't go long without tossing an insult her way.

Although she merely turned her attention back to the book, it felt like a hard slap across his face. The woman was too damned skilled at communicating with her actions and body. He had no doubt that if she was drawn to him in the least, the desire would be fairly sizzling like the lightning across a darkened sky. It couldn't be denied.

Instead, he was left with the impression that she

could hardly be bothered with him. Which was fine. Which was how it should be. He shouldn't be bothered with her. Taking a deep breath, he focused on his book. But it couldn't snag his attention. His entire being was attuned to every aspect of her: each breath, each turn of a page, each twitch of a toe. She looked relaxed, content.

While he was strung so tightly, he thought he might break. It was the book he was reading. Or trying to. It wasn't doing its job to distract him. He needed something different.

He shoved himself to his feet, set the book on a random stack, walked over to another, and grabbed a different novel. He stopped by the fire to add a few more logs. There was a definite chill in the air, and he suspected it was coming from her following his last comment. He didn't want to like her. Certainly, when he'd first seen her in the secretive rooms at his club, he'd been drawn by her beauty but lust was more easily ignored when a woman didn't appeal to him on an intellectual level. She was beginning to appeal and in his defense, he'd been an arse.

If he were smart, he'd find an excuse to go out in the rain and stomp around for a bit until he'd worked her out of his system. The problem was, he didn't know if she was the sort that could be worked out of his system—not until he'd had her at least. Naked. Flush against his body. In his bed.

Putting distance between them by retreating to his bedchamber wasn't a viable option because he wouldn't be able to look at the bed without seeing her sprawled over it. At the settee without envisioning her lying along its length. At the washbasin without recalling the feel of her in his arms.

After unfolding his body, he stormed from the room, went to the kitchen, snatched up a box, opened it, and returned to the main chamber. Like a recalcitrant child, he sat in his corner of the sofa and placed the box between them. "I have a fondness for chocolate," he announced. "You're welcome to however many pieces you'd like."

Out of the corner of his eye, he watched as she slid her attention to his offering.

"Is that an apology?"

"I don't know how long the rain will last. It will be more pleasant if we're not at odds."

"I didn't realize we were." She plucked a bit of chocolate-covered caramel from the box and studied it. "I have a weakness for sweets, but chocolate is my favorite." She slowly pushed it into her mouth, her lips puckered as though she was kissing it.

He had to look away. He'd put too many logs on the fire and his face was probably turning red from the heat. "You can't help it, can you?"

A smack echoed between them, followed by what sounded very much like a lick—and that had him turning back toward her.

She arched a brow. "Pardon?"

"You can't *not* be provocative."

She picked out another piece and popped it into her mouth. "I suppose it's ingrained in me to put on a show when I'm not inside my residence. I'll try to be more attuned to your sensitivities."

"I'm not bothered by it. I was merely making an observation."

Bringing her feet up, she tucked them beneath her and twisted around slightly, closing the book, leaving a finger inside to serve as her marker. "You're not comfortable with me. I suspect because you don't quite approve of my . . . life."

"I find no fault with it. I recognize that choices for women who choose not to marry are limited." It was something Poppy continually complained about.

"*Who choose*? Not all women are given a choice. I wasn't."

He furrowed his brow. "What? Did Hollingsworth kidnap you?"

"Nothing quite so dramatic. If you find no fault, then why are you irritated with me?"

To lie or reveal the truth? The truth, he decided, would shock her down to her toes. Shocked him actually. He wanted her so badly he could barely see straight.

"Listen," he said in a low voice instead. Her eyes widening, as though that would improve her hearing, she went still. "Do you hear it?"

"What?" she asked softly, and he wanted that sensual sound repeated with her mouth against his ear.

"The rain."

She jerked her head toward the window, and he decided he liked her profile, the way it revealed her neck sloping down to her shoulder. "It stopped."

After tossing the book aside, she hopped off the sofa and dashed to the window, and he imagined how welcoming it would feel to walk through a door and see her dashing toward him with such unbridled enthusiasm.

"The sun is peering through the clouds, just barely, but they aren't as dark as they were." She spun around. "Do you think the storm has passed?"

"Possibly."

"Do you have a way to get off the island?"

"I have a small boat."

"Therefore, we can leave?"

It bothered him that she was so anxious to be rid of him. He'd been a terrible host. Standoffish. Caring for her while trying not to show he cared. He set aside his book, pushed to his feet, strode over to the window, and looked out. The isle was so small that there was nowhere in this dwelling where one couldn't see the water. "It's too choppy. It would be a struggle to row us across. Perhaps it'll be calm enough tomorrow." The disappointment in her eyes hit him hard, so hard that he was tempted to at least try to get her to the other shore. "What I can do is offer you fish for dinner."

Chapter 12

With fishing poles in hand, he knew it was complete madness to find Marlowe—charging ahead of him across rocks and bits of green—alluring. Over his shirt and her makeshift skirt, she wore his greatcoat, its hem nearly reaching her ankles. Or where her ankles probably were. He couldn't see them because she'd stuffed bits of linen into a pair of his boots so they at least stayed on her feet. She reminded him of a little girl playing at dressing to look like an adult.

Although she was far from being a little girl.

Unfortunately, she'd assumed herself invited on his outing. Not that he could blame her for wanting to escape the confines of what had no doubt felt like a prison. It wasn't her place of solitude. No, hers was in the sky.

He possessed additional fishing poles because sometimes his younger brother would join him for a lazy day of casting out a line and waiting for a nibble. Hence, he was carrying a pole for her as well as himself. For some reason, he was under the impression she wouldn't want to simply sit and watch; she'd want to participate.

The more he was coming to know her, the less he understood her willingness to become some man's ornament.

And the more he wished he hadn't changed his blasted cards that night at the Dragons. He wouldn't have bedded her, not under those circumstances, but he might have kissed her, might have touched his fingers to a cheek that had yet to be bruised by a storm. Might have trailed those fingers over the long length of her neck, along her bared shoulders. Might have taken some liberties simply to teach Hollingsworth that he needed to demonstrate more diligent care when it came to the woman who warmed his bed. He'd obviously begun to take her for granted, as men often did with their mistresses.

And Langdon was beginning to believe she never should be taken for granted.

Suddenly she stopped, like she'd rammed into a brick wall. But there was no wall, nothing about. They were still on the high ground, walking near the edge of the cliff. Then she lowered herself to the clover.

Immediately, he dropped his fishing gear and began running toward her. "Marlowe!"

Had her injuries overcome her? Were they worse than he'd surmised? When he reached her, he slid to his knees. "Did you grow faint? Swoon? Are you feeling ill?"

She looked at him, smiled softly. "No, the rainbow."

"Rainbow?"

With a slender finger, she pointed and turned her attention away from him. "I wanted to take a moment to appreciate it. How is it that nature can be so ugly, throwing about its wrath, and then create something so beautiful?"

Irritated by his near panic that she might have been in need of assistance, he dropped to his backside and scooted away just a little. The woman was turning him inside out. But he had to admit the rainbow was awe-inspiring, one of the largest he'd ever seen, stretching across the sea with one end disappearing somewhere in Cornwall.

"What do you think is on the other side of that rainbow?" she asked.

"Water."

She laughed, a sweet, noncynical sound that caused a strange tightening in his gut. "You're not very imaginative, are you?"

Oh, he wouldn't say that. He could well imagine trailing his mouth from her throat to that sweet valley between her thighs and lingering there until he'd had his fill. Could take days.

"When a storm isn't raging, it's rather peaceful here," she said. "I don't suppose we could stay a few days, even after the sea is not so choppy and is safe to travel."

"Don't think you'll grow tired of eating eggs?"

"Thought we were going to have fish."

"The weather might have chased them away."

"I should think you'd be able to lure them back."

"Wouldn't want Hollingsworth frantically worrying over your absence."

"He's at his country estate for a few more days, but even if he were in London, I very much doubt he'd be worrying over me."

I would. He didn't speak the words aloud because they had no place on this islet and were not appropriate to direct toward this woman. She wasn't his to worry over or care about. And she most certainly was not his to reach out and tuck behind her ear the strands of hair that the breeze had freed from their plaited mooring.

"I knew my father as the Earl of Wishingham," she said quietly, and every thought within his head stilled as he shifted his backside slightly so he could inch a little closer to her. If she was going to at last reveal something about her history, he didn't want to miss a word. "He arrived via balloon, near the small village in Northumberland where my mother grew up. At the time, I doubt as many as fifty people lived there. None had ever seen a balloon."

Her laugh was quick, sharp. "Nor a lord for that matter. When he married my mother in the small village church and moved into her tiny cottage that had once belonged to her parents, no one questioned why he didn't take her to the earldom to live. He told my mother he'd never been happy there. It was haunted by sadness, unlike her residence where she'd been loved. Where I came to know that love after I was born."

She drew her legs up, wrapped her arms around them as he wanted to wrap his arms around her, and pressed her chin to her knees. He refrained from urging her to continue, to show his impatience for her to finish the tale. He didn't know Wishingham, which wasn't unusual. Langdon didn't yet sit in the House of Lords, and he hadn't met every peer who existed, although he would ask his father if he knew anything about the man. He did find it odd that an earl's daughter would become another lord's doxy. Had she run away from home and been in need of money?

While it certainly wasn't uncommon among the lower classes, he'd never heard of a lady among the nobility falling on such hard times. Surely someone among the peerage would have helped her out. Was that where Hollingsworth had come in?

"People revered him. A lord living among them. From the moment I was born, I was addressed as Lady Marlowe. Or so I've been told. I don't recall the beginning of course, but any memories I have of my time in that village include being addressed as m'lady. I was special. The villagers celebrated my birth. We never did without. Individuals gifted us with this or that. I don't imagine royalty had it any better."

She released a long, slow breath. "My father would take me up in his balloon and show me the world from on high. I loved those magical moments . . . and I loved him. He was my hero. Seven years ago, when I was all of fifteen, he said he had some business to tend to, the Queen's business he said, would be gone for a few days. As he prepared for the flight—because he only ever traveled by balloon—I begged to go with him, but he wouldn't hear of it. Mother and I watched his ascent. The wind carried him away. We never saw him again."

He hadn't expected that ending to her tale. "Did you ever learn what became of him?"

She shook her head. "We never received any word. Mother assumed he crashed somewhere. Although I like to think that he sailed over a rainbow and landed safely in a magical land of leprechauns, sprites, fairies, and maybe even a couple of witches. Once the rainbow faded away, no avenue for him to get back to us existed because there was no colorful arch to go over."

She looked at him. "You can laugh at my silliness. I won't be offended."

In all likelihood her father had met a frightening and ugly end. He'd once seen a balloon catch fire and there had been no escape from death for the passengers aboard. All they'd been able to do was choose the ending to their story—either by fire or fall.

He much preferred the fantastical conclusion she'd drawn. "Losing someone we love—or even just someone we know—is difficult. I favor . . . your assumption. Maybe there is more than water on the other side of that rainbow. Perhaps there is that magical land you envision. I'm sorry I didn't know your father. I never met the Earl of Wishingham."

"Oh!" She laughed but this time the sound was a bit caustic. "That's because there never was an Earl of *Wish*ingham. My father was an utter fraud and merely *wished* he was an earl."

*M*arlowe still had a time of it, dealing with the truth regarding her father. She'd had a multitude of moments when she'd been unable to reconcile the man she'd known with the man he was. Why would he pretend to be something he wasn't? Because the villagers gave him deference and were so honored by his patronage that they never insisted he make good on his debts? To impress her mother? But she would have fallen in love with him anyway. He was kind and funny and dependable—until he wasn't.

"Well, now you can see why I put off telling you. It doesn't place my father in a very good light. Or my mother, for that matter. That she would believe him so thoroughly. But then why would she expect him to lie? She'd grown up in a tiny village where people were honest."

"Based upon what you've told me thus far, his subterfuge went on for years. How could no one know?"

"As I said, it was a small village. The people lived a simple, contented life. Few strayed far from where they'd been born. I'd wager not a single one had ever been to London. Even you didn't doubt. You just assumed you'd never heard of him."

"However, I'd have eventually asked my father about him or looked in *Burke's Peerage*."

"Until we came to London, we didn't even know a book that provided the lineage associated with each title existed."

"We?"

"My mother and I." She wished she hadn't started down this path. It was only that she couldn't see a rainbow and not think of her father. *One day we'll fly over a rainbow to a land of enchantment*, he'd often told her when she was small. And, oh, how she'd believed him. On a unicorn, she'd gallop over flower-adorned fields.

For some unfathomable reason, she'd needed to give voice to all the emotions swirling through her. Perhaps because she'd been convinced that she was going to die last night in that storm. Life seemed so precious and precarious at the same time. And while Langdon had not hidden his desire that she not be about, he had still managed to make her feel protected. "She waited two years for my father to return. Perhaps he had crashed, been hurt, needed to heal. Maybe he'd gone down in an isolated portion of England and had to trek over hill and dale to find civilization. At first, we discussed endlessly all the various scenarios that could be delaying his return. Over time, the discussions became less frequent. Neither of us ever voiced our worst fears. We loved him, you see. Neither of us wanted him gone."

Langdon held still and quiet, waiting, waiting for her to gather her thoughts and continue. How she knew this, she couldn't fathom. She experienced moments when she felt she knew him better and more intimately than she knew herself. Taking a deep breath to strengthen her resolve, she kept her gaze on the rainbow. "When I was seventeen, she decided that it was time we find his family, let them know what had happened. They would see to us, surely. See me educated in the ways of a lady. My mother was determined that I should have my coming out. After all, I was the daughter of an earl, and like her, I should marry a lord. Only properly, with all the pomp and circumstance the situation warranted. No small church and forgettable vicar for me. It was to be Westminster and the Archbishop of Canterbury. A white coach and white horses delivering me to the church. Bells ringing throughout the city. She wanted me to have what she hadn't. As an earl's daughter, it was what I deserved.

"The cottage sat on a small farm. We had a few animals: cows, pigs, chickens. Occasionally we'd sell one. So she had a little money set aside. But when the villagers discovered we were going to make a trek to London to claim our place among the nobility . . . well, goodness gracious. Some were dipping into their own coffers, a few giving us their last shilling. We were part of them, and they were part of us. We wouldn't forget them, surely. Once we were embraced by the earl's family, perhaps we could settle our debts.

"One of the villagers offered to ferry us in his wagon to a village where we could find a coach to take us to London. Then there was London. We found lodgings, the sort where we shared a room, a bed, with strangers. No one cared that she was Lady Wishingham and I was Lady Marlowe. We hardly knew where to begin to search for my father's relations. Mum decided Buckingham Palace. After all, Father had told her he danced with the Queen. You can well imagine that they thought we were mad. They'd never heard of him. After several tries to be seen by someone of authority or even the Queen herself, we were finally told by a fellow dressed in livery that we needed to make enquiries at the College of Arms. Things only worsened from there."

Watching the seagulls circling down below, she envied them their ability to fly while she was presently restricted to keeping her feet on the ground. Then something red caught her eye. Waving briefly, a quick hello, before scarpering off and disappearing. She shot to her feet. "Oh, it's my balloon!"

"*S*low down!" Langdon yelled.

The daft woman was going to break her lovely neck the way she was scrambling over the rough terrain in an effort to get to the small cove where he'd found her last night. Following in her wake, he'd already yelled at her several times to hold on, but she failed to heed his words, the stubborn wench. She was as independent a woman as he'd ever known.

Intriguing and secretive, no doubt grateful the bit of cloth that had made its quick appearance had given her an excuse not to finish her tale. He wanted to know exactly how she had gone from knocking on the door at Buckingham Palace to warming Hollingsworth's bed. He was striving not to be jealous but had the sense he was failing miserably. He didn't want to return her to London, didn't want to envision Hollingsworth there waiting for her to escort him to her bedchamber.

It was more than lust, more than physical attraction driving his thoughts. He was beginning to enjoy her company, especially when she opened up and shared parts of herself with him. He'd always envisioned that a woman who used her body for currency would be more callous and pragmatic, for surely a hard life had influenced her decisions. Yet in spite of her father being unworthy of siring her, she hoped he'd flown over a rainbow into a kinder existence.

Whereas Langdon wanted to beat the man bloody for his deception.

He also understood how a man falsely claiming to be a lord could be believed and revered by those of a small village far from London. He'd certainly never bothered to memorize every title. And a man with no coins in his coffers—there were merchants and shopkeepers so enamored of having the nobility as customers that they would never stoop so low as to actually *ask* their idol to pay up. Although he did have to wonder if her father had failed to return because his ruse had been discovered or his debts were in danger of seeing him in debtor's prison.

For her sake, as much as he didn't like the thought, he did rather hope the man had met an accidental end so she would at least be spared ever learning that her father was far worse than she imagined.

He skidded the last few feet to the beach and dashed around the outcropping behind which her balloon—and she—had disappeared. He found her on her knees, running her hands over long strips of cloth, each a different color—a brilliant red, blue, or purple—and he fought not to imagine her running her hands over him in the same manner. Her motions were almost loving, tender, as though she were examining wounds and expected the recipient of them to yell out in pain at any moment. Nearby, still attached to the balloon portion, was the basket, lying against a mound of rocks. Shattered and broken.

As she might have been.

Cold dread shivered through him, and he had a strong urge to pull her away from the blasted thing and order her to never again take such risks. He crouched beside her. "It doesn't look salvageable."

"The basket, no," she said in a mournful tone, "but the cloth I can repair."

"The cloth alone isn't going to get you off the island."

She looked at him. "Of course not. I'll need your boat for that. You did say you'd take me to the mainland when the water was calmer. I'm not in a hurry, however. It's rather nice to be away from the madness of it all. Is that the reason you come here? For the peace and the quiet and the isolation?"

Possibly at first, but now it was more so no one could hear his cries when the nightmares came. "Here, mamas can't toss their daughters my way, expecting me to catch them."

"How horrible indeed, to be so spoiled for choice."

"You are. You could have any man in London you wanted."

"Not at first. Oddly, it was Hollie who taught me how to ensure I had options when it came to my benefactor. Do you have a knife?"

The sudden change in topic took him aback, especially as he'd been considering how he might convince her Hollingsworth didn't deserve her loyalty. He'd obviously taken advantage . . . although Langdon had always known the earl to be a decent chap. "I do."

"Help me detach the basket."

He almost told her the price would be a kiss, but he wasn't fool enough to do that. He imagined one of the things Hollingsworth had taught her was how to pretend enjoyment. No, he wanted her begging for it.

While he sawed through the ropes that held the balloon fast to the basket, Marlowe wrung out small portions of the silk that made up the balloon. So many little rips and tears. A few large ones. Occasionally looking over at the basket where Langdon worked caused her stomach to knot up. She was damned fortunate she hadn't arrived on shore as crushed as the wicker. It was a sad, pitiful heap of broken dreams.

She wasn't altogether certain that dreams could be mended. Perhaps it was best to search for another. All the dreams she'd held as a young girl had shattered when she'd discovered her father's deception. In spite of him being weak and flawed, she didn't doubt his love for her. Still the truth had robbed her of her dreams. No noble husband for her. No love, no children, no family. *What is it you want of your life?* Hollie had asked her when they'd met. She'd once thought she'd wanted to be known.

Now all she wanted was to be forgotten.

She dragged more of the balloon from the sea and wrenched the salty water from it, ignoring the sting of protest from the few small cuts and scrapes on her hands. It was probably silly to go to such bother but what else did she have to do until the swells calmed and Langdon could deliver her to the opposite shore?

While she'd been enjoying the book she'd been reading, she cared more about her balloon. Besides, the cloth had saved her from carrying on with her tale. She'd told Langdon enough. He didn't need to know all of it. It was the unknown that made her such a mystery, that resulted in her being somewhat famous. *Never tell anyone everything,* Hollie had advised.

"What now?"

She looked up at the tall man looming over her, hands on his narrow hips. She wondered what it might feel like having those hands on her hips, pulling her close as he lowered his head . . .

She didn't want to admit that he had the most beautiful pair of luscious lips she'd ever seen. It was the reason she'd wanted to kiss them so badly that night at the Dragons. She could well imagine that they were quite skilled at delivering pleasure, for, surely, they'd been designed with that purpose in mind.

"Once I've gotten the rest of the envelope—"

"Envelope?"

"Yes, that's what this portion is called because it holds the air. Anyway, once it's out of the water, we can haul it up to your residence. Spread it out over the floor in that front room so it can dry. I could even begin repairing it."

"Wouldn't it be easier to simply purchase one anew?"

"Simpler isn't always the best way." She'd learned that through a series of trials and errors. "Besides, this one has memories associated with it."

"Right." He grabbed a handful of cloth and

heaved a massive amount of the material from the water with a single action. Corded muscles were extremely handy. She imagined running her hands over them as he tugged and pulled. Why was it that she couldn't seem to stop thinking about touching this man? Based on her reputation, he'd no doubt be surprised to learn that she didn't normally think about touching men. Few really appealed to her. She had exacting tastes, Hollie had once explained, just as he did.

The things that man knew about sex, desire, want, and need. It had frightened her at first, until he'd made it all seem so natural. It was one of the reasons she loved him.

Chapter 13

Waiting for a contrary fish to finally take a snap at the bait, Langdon sat on a boulder, shoulders hunched, elbows resting on his thighs, and the pole clasped between his hands. His mind not on the task, he was barely aware of the occasional nibble.

It had taken the two of them, him and Marlowe, working as a team, working together, each carrying a bunched-up end of the humongous amount of cloth, to get her balloon to the main chamber of his sanctuary, where she'd spread it out over the floor to dry. His having so little furniture was to her advantage, although she did relocate his books, so they were along the wall and no longer in her way. He'd built up the fire for her so the heat would eclipse the cold to such a degree that the material would dry more quickly.

Her attachment to the boldly colored cloth had made it seem like a rescue, no matter that the balloon was now useless. She had been caring for it as if it was ailing, rearranging areas of it as though to make it more comfortable—even though it was obvious she was simply moving the wetter sections nearer to the fire.

With a sigh, he craned his neck, rubbed the back of it. Usually, he enjoyed sitting on a rock and waiting. He liked having the moments to think while the waves lapped at the shore, creating a gentle lullaby.

But since her arrival, nothing was as it had been. He was anxious for the fish to bite, so he could make his way back to her. He knew she was perfectly safe without him nearby, and yet he found himself longing for her tart tongue and ability to put him in his place. He was intrigued by her when he bloody well shouldn't be.

Dusk was beginning to coat the land by the time he finally had enough fish in hand—enough for him alone, although he would share them with her. He didn't particularly like the way his feet sped up, urging him to hurry, or the manner in which his heart pounded rapidly. He *wasn't* eager to be with her again. It was late and he was chilled. More than ready to be surrounded by warmth and his books.

When he entered his residence, it felt different, not quite so . . . sparse or lonely. While he could hear no movements, he knew where he'd find her. He strode into the main chamber and came to an abrupt halt, holding his breath as she looked up.

Her smile was tentative, almost shy. He wanted to again see the joy that had quickly wreathed her face when she'd spotted the balloon. No, it was more than that. He wanted to be the reason for that joy.

Even as he acknowledged he'd given her no cause to experience a thrill at the sight of him.

"You're back." Sitting on the floor near the fire, some of the balloon gathered in her lap, the sewing basket beside her, it appeared she'd taken to mending up a tear. "I was beginning to worry. You were gone so long."

"The storm seems to have made the fish shy." He held up the basket in which he'd stored his catch. "Took longer than I'd expected."

She was once again wearing only his shirt and nothing else. Her skirt had become soaked when she'd waded into the water to rescue her precious silk, and she must have changed clothes while he was away. He had given the buttons on his shirts their freedom too many times to count—not that he possessed the ability to count—and yet at that moment he desperately wanted to ease the buttons of the shirt she wore through their holes—slowly and provocatively. He wanted to watch the material parting, little by little, revealing an ever-widening expanse of her cleavage, the inside swells of her breasts, the flat of her stomach—

Dropping his gaze before his trousers tented, he cleared his throat. "I'll prepare our dinner now."

She pushed herself to her feet, her lower legs encased in his socks. She was certainly making herself at home, and he was glad of it, wanted her to be at ease.

"I'll help," she announced enthusiastically.

He jerked up his head. The last thing he needed was her swishing around in his kitchen. "Not necessary."

Giving him a hard stare, she placed her hands on her hips. "Langdon, you don't have to wait on me. You spent the majority of your afternoon fetching us something to eat. The least I can do is help you prepare it."

"You always struck me as someone accustomed to being waited upon."

"You struck me as someone accustomed to getting his way . . . but you won't in this. I either help you or I cook the entire thing. Otherwise, I shan't eat. I insist upon doing my share."

Why couldn't she be as he expected? She was becoming harder and harder to resist.

*I*t was full-on dark by the time they finally sat down to devour the fish he'd caught. He had no actual dining room, no chairs in the kitchen that could be set against the large table where he prepared food. Therefore, they had taken their meal on the sofa in the main room. He thought he'd never be able to eat in there again without thinking of her.

When they were finished, she helped him clear up the mess. She washed the dishes and pans while he dried them and put them away. It seemed a domestic chore, one that people of his station certainly never experienced. Marlowe had probably expected to never experience it as a wife—tidying up with the noble husband her father had convinced her she would marry. While it seemed preposterous that the man could successfully live a lie for so long, Langdon knew it was possible. His friend, the Duke of Avendale, had married a woman who had spent years convincing people she was a widow who would soon be receiving a huge inheritance. With the promise of a future payment, shopkeepers had given her anything she desired, and she had lived in luxury. Her swindling days had eventually come to an end. Perhaps Marlowe's father's had as well, and that was the reason he hadn't returned. Langdon was tempted to go in search of the blighter.

When everything in the kitchen was as it should be, they returned to the main room, where she claimed her earlier spot on the floor and began working on repairing a tear.

As he sat on the sofa, book in his lap, he watched her efforts. The light from the flames danced over her hair, turning it from moonlight into wheat into pale yellow. What the devil was wrong with Hollingsworth to have her cover up something so mystifying? Why would he prefer black when he could have all the various shades of gold?

As he'd predicted, her cheek and the area around her nose looked worse. It would be another day or so before there was even a hint of the bruises going away, the scrapes healing, and yet she'd appeal to him no more then than she did now, because at the moment nothing on earth held more beauty.

She was so intent on her task, and he imagined she gave as much, if not more, attention to the man warming her bed. Just as she'd been fixated on the rainbow that afternoon. Whatever she focused on earned her undivided attention.

For a while, as she'd been telling her tale, her focus had been on him.

And his on her.

Now, when he should be falling into the words of the story, he seemed capable of only desperately searching for those rare moments when he could fall into the blue of her eyes.

When her gaze would dart over to him, he tried not to be caught staring at her, but suspected he was failing miserably. He'd come here to be alone, always came to be alone, but was having a difficult time imagining the place without her in it. He wondered how much time would pass before he'd no longer see the shadow of her presence wherever he looked. Somehow, he knew she was leaving an indelible mark in her wake. Just as she had that night at the Dragons. He couldn't visit his favorite club without being reminded of her.

From his position slouched on the sofa, he could detect myriad tears in the fabric. It would take her weeks, months, years to set it all to rights. To him, it truly appeared to be an impossible task and yet there she sat, one hand constantly in motion, poking needle and pulling thread through cloth. He had to admire her determination when he'd expected to never admire anything about her.

Quite suddenly the distance between them seemed far too wide. That he wanted to be nearer to her was unsettling. On the morrow he would deliver her to the opposite shore, no matter how unfriendly the water, because he was coming to like her, to desire her company and no good would come of his spending additional time with her. But at that precise moment—

Silently grounding out a curse at his own weakness and inability to resist her, he set aside his

book and came to his feet. To avoid stepping on
her precious find, he skirted the edge of the room
until he could feel the increased warmth of the fire
and detect her faint unique fragrance. It reminded
him of honeysuckle. He wondered if she normally
bathed in the perfume and its scent had become
immersed in her skin.

When he dropped down beside her, she didn't
seem at all surprised, reacted not at all, as though
she could hardly be bothered by his presence.
Strange how it made him want her more than if
she'd been fawning over him. The sewing basket
served as an ineffectual barrier between them.
He scrounged around in it until he located a
needle and thread. He cut off a length of thread
and tried to poke one end through the eye of the
needle. His fingers were too damned big and
clumsy, making him appear to be an oaf as he
kept missing his target.

"Here, let me," she said, taking both from him,
her fingers grazing over his knuckles, causing his
breathing to seize up. What the devil was wrong
with him? "Do you even know how to sew?"

She closed her mouth around the end of the
thread he'd been striving to slip through the needle
eye, and he was hit with images of her closing her
mouth around portions of his body: his finger, his
earlobe . . . his cock. Christ.

He cleared his throat, and yet still the words
came out raspy. "How hard can it be? You jam the
needle into the cloth and yank the thread through."

Her smile spoke of indulgence, and damned if
he didn't want to kiss those lips. Then she pulled

the thread from her mouth and slipped the end of it through the center of the needle eye—in one go. What sorcery was this?

She extended the seamstress's tool toward him. "You need to make the stitches small and taut so as little air as possible can escape."

He placed his thumb and forefinger above hers on the needle. They held still. Their gazes locked. His hand drifted around to cradle hers. Warm and silky smooth. He watched as the muscles at her throat worked while she swallowed. Even though no cleavage was visible because she wore his shirt, he could make out the slow rise and fall of her chest. It was uncanny how attuned to her he was. Nor could he believe how intimate the moment seemed. He'd bedded women and not felt as engaged.

The woman was sex personified. He wondered if she'd even had a choice at becoming a gentleman's plaything or if her destiny had been written on her bones the moment she'd been born.

Breaking eye contact, ducking her head, she finally released her hold. His hand itched to go after hers, but he held his desires in check, turned his attention to a small rip, and began weaving the needle and thread through the torn material. Blue. Hers purple. It was like having a rainbow spread out over his floor. He very much suspected that it was the various colors that had drawn her to this particular balloon. He couldn't envision her being content with a solid color carrying her into the sky.

He found himself taking extreme care with his stitches because he didn't want to be responsible for her crashing back to earth. His stomach tightened a bit at the thought of her—reckless and wild—daring to go back up in another storm. Yet he couldn't seem not to admire her courageousness, even if it was foolhardy. The woman was a series of contradictions and he wanted to explore each one.

"Based on the image you project in London, I wouldn't have thought you'd be content with something ruined." Something like him, broken and yet unable to fully heal. Not fixable with needle and thread.

"What do you perceive as being ruined, my lord?"

He snapped his gaze over to her quickly, before he'd finished with his latest stitch, and immediately felt the prick of pain. "Damnation!"

Hastily she moved the sewing basket aside, scooted nearer to him, and took his hand. He could see the blood pooling on the tip of his finger. Before he could tell her that it would be fine, she'd closed her mouth around it. His gut couldn't have tightened more if he'd taken a punch to it. He'd grown painfully hard. He could barely breathe. He certainly couldn't fashion a coherent thought. He seemed capable only of feeling her tongue traveling over his skin.

Then she lifted her gaze—heated and erotic—to his, and he feared he might burst right there on the spot. The most expensive woman he'd ever been with hadn't mastered that look of hunger, of need. He couldn't recall any other woman studying him as if she could devour him in a single bite but was contemplating the enjoyment to be found in nibbling him slowly, luxuriously, leisurely.

Marlowe might possess the power to drive him truly and completely mad.

Just as she had with the thread, she kept her mouth closed as she drew his finger from between her lips. "My mother would do that whenever I had a scrape. She claimed the wetness from a mouth had the power to stop the bleeding. It seems to have worked . . . in this case anyway."

She took away her hands, but his stayed where it was, hovering a few inches in the air, as if it had lost the ability to move without her assistance.

"You didn't answer my question," she said softly.

What bloody hell question was that? The one reflected in her eyes as she'd licked his finger: Do you desire me?

With every breath, every blink, every thought.

"About the ruination?" she added.

Who had ruined her? Hollingsworth? Or had it been someone before him?

She turned her focus to the balloon and looked at it lovingly. "I don't see something that's been torn asunder. Each of these rips, when repaired, will be like a scar. Scars fascinate me. They are a symbol that life came hard and fast and perhaps without mercy and the scar bearer told it to bugger off. Every scar is a story. Of survival, or pain, or, for some, perhaps the very worst day of their lives. Sometimes looking at them makes the unpleasantness difficult to forget. They're a reminder. However not only of what happened, but that we defeated it, that in the end we were stronger. We survived."

She turned her attention back to him. "But not all scars are visible, are they, my lord?"

He felt as if she was staring straight into his

soul, poring over it, encountering the scars, examining them. Yet he was powerless to see hers. Oh, certainly, he could view the injuries the storm had inflicted. Perhaps some might leave a shallow scar—but what others might she already harbor? For surely, she must have a few in order to speak so passionately about what they could represent.

She'd spoken with such honesty, such forthrightness, such conviction.

She'd held him mesmerized. So much about her did. She deserved his honesty. His truth.

"I determined not having you at all was better than having you for only a few hours. I switched my cards that night because never in my life had I ever wanted to kiss a woman more."

Chapter 14

*M*arlowe's breath caught, held, until finally like the air in a balloon, it slowly leaked out. The way he'd looked at her that night—no other man had ever regarded her with so much heat in his eyes, like a fire slowly simmering until it was smoldering.

Oh, certainly, she'd seen want, lust, and yearning. She'd reveled in her ability to bring it to the fore, to be able to create such desire. But it had been different with him. Terrifyingly so.

When Hollie had offered her up, she'd objected because her body had been reacting as his eyes had, until every inch of her was so heated, hot, that she'd been certain if he touched her, she'd combust. Perhaps they both would. Much as she'd once witnessed a hot-air balloon going up in flames. It had happened so quickly, so unexpectedly, there had been no time to react. She'd been able to only watch in horror.

Yet it hadn't deterred her from taking the same risk each time she ascended into the air. Sitting here now, she knew the same was true when it came to Langdon.

From the moment she'd awakened in his presence, she'd been tamping down her unbridled longing. How could she want a man who didn't fancy her? Only, he did. Quite powerfully, according to his words and the manner in which he now looked at her.

She'd misread him before, thought he'd been disgusted by her.

It was so much easier to be in his presence when she believed that to be the case. But the truth, dear God, the truth made it so much harder to resist the temptation that was Viscount Langdon.

Was he disgusted with himself, with his yearning for the woman she was, a woman kept? He hadn't treated her as if he had no respect for her, but then as a gentleman he was unlikely to show unkindness or be rude or give her a cut direct.

Reaching out, she grabbed the area of cloth she'd been working on and dragged it onto her lap. Quickly she plucked up the needle, hoping he would do the same with his. It would be easier to say what she wanted to say if he wasn't watching her so intensely. Everything about the man was extremely passionate whether he was reading, eating, or sewing. She suspected his kiss left a woman in a pool of fevered sensuality.

Finally, finally, he looked at the tip of his finger that she'd licked and, she assumed, after confirming it was no longer bleeding, returned to stitching up the cloth, creating a scar that would forever remind her of him when she was aloft. She'd already memorized the exact spot. Besides, it would be easy enough to find because his needlework was not as refined as hers. And yet in a way she thought it more beautiful.

"At the College of Arms, as I'm sure you're aware because you're no doubt included, is a document known as the Roll of the Peerage in which every title and the name of its holder is listed. A Registrar of Arms showed it to us and explained no Earl of Wishingham had ever existed. The gentleman, bless him, spent hours searching for my father's name, on the off chance we had the title wrong." She shook her head. "But he was nowhere to be found. My mother wasn't a countess, I wasn't a lady, and my father wasn't a lord." She was acutely aware of him going still, but she continued to pull needle and thread through the cloth, quickly, hurriedly, her fingers keeping pace with the memories dashing through her mind. "My mother decided we would return home—because we certainly hadn't the means to stay in London—but we wouldn't tell anyone what we'd discovered. She was mortified and didn't want her friends or associates to know what a fool she'd been."

"She wasn't alone. The entire village had been duped."

"Oh, but she'd married him, kept him there. They'd given him goods and services without requiring payment. She feared they might demand payment of her, if the truth ever came out. Of course, we had no idea who his family truly was. Where they lived. How to find them. If they were in a position to help. They could have been as poor as church mice. She didn't want to be a burden to them." She hugged the cloth briefly. "She never wanted to be a burden to anyone."

"How did you manage?"

She glanced over at him. One leg was bent, an arm draped across his raised knee. Did he always have to look so bloody masculine? "The cloth isn't going to mend itself."

A corner of his mouth hitched up. "Regretting that you ever started the tale?"

Slowly she shook her head. "Where I am, Langdon, is not where I ever expected to be. And yet, eventually, it seemed an inevitable course."

He skimmed his thumb along her jaw, stopping when he reached her chin, his forefinger joining the effort to stop her from turning away. "I'm not sitting in judgment, Marlowe."

"I thought you were that night. I believed that was the reason you cheated."

He tilted his head slightly. "Is it cheating if I lose?"

"Did you lose?"

"Much more than I'd wagered. It's only during the past couple of days that I've come to realize exactly how much." She was left with the impression that whatever he'd lost had something to do with her. Although perhaps that was just wishful thinking on her part. "I know a thing or two about painful memories. You don't have to tell me how you came to be with Hollingsworth if it's too agonizing."

But she wanted him to know. It seemed important that he know. It also seemed important she learn the specifics regarding his painful memories, only she wasn't going to beg for them. Although she suspected the railway accident was at the heart of it all. She felt like she was wandering through a forest of brambles, not quite sure of her footing, hitting snags along the way. Every time she was convinced she had him figured out, she discovered she didn't.

"We returned home, unexpectedly welcomed with cheers and excitement. Mum dashed a few hopes when she explained that we'd been unable to locate his family but were continuing the search. The falsehood didn't sit well with me. We were simply continuing the farce. I tried to persuade her to tell them the truth, but she just became more withdrawn, melancholy. I worried so. And then one day . . . she confessed everything to her dearest friend. As it turned out, she wasn't a friend at all. She announced it to the entire village. Just as my mother feared, the shopkeepers, tradesmen, and pub owners wanted what was owed. And we had no way to pay them. I tried to find employment in the village, but no one would hire me. They no longer trusted me. And that hurt, Langdon, so badly. I didn't know it was possible to be in so much pain without a visible wound."

"Hold there," he said before getting up, walking to the table that housed his spirits, and pouring scotch into a glass. When he returned, he handed it to her.

Grateful, she took a large, unladylike swallow before offering it to him and watching as he took a small sip.

"I'm sorry you experienced all that," he said.

"I didn't blame the villagers. All those years of debt." Just as she had then, she felt an urge to punch something. "My father made some payments over the years but when they each presented the balance of what was owed . . . it would take a lifetime to pay it back. Some were muttering about debtor's prison. I determined I would need to return to London. To be honest, I saw that as no hardship as I'd fallen in love with the city while we were there. It was so alive. An abundance of people moving about so quickly, chasing after life rather than just waiting for it to pass by. I was convinced I could find employment and a better wage. My mother was a true villager. She wasn't comfortable with leaving, so she stayed."

It was a relief in a way because not having her mother there gave her more freedom and allowed her to be not quite so honest regarding what she was actually doing to secure money. She appreciated that Langdon was patiently waiting for her to continue.

"I had very few coins when I arrived in London. I took lodgings in a less affluent area of town." A nice way of saying she'd moved to the rookeries. She hadn't even known people lived in such squalor. Her small village was lovely cottages with thatched roofs and colorful gardens. Oh, certainly, a house or two was in need of repair but neighbors helped neighbors. No one dressed in rags, went hungry, or slept in a bed with strangers. Fortunately, the boardinghouse in which she'd resided was clean and she had a tiny room with a small bed she shared with one girl. A girl who snored. "I found a position as a seamstress with a modiste."

She couldn't help herself. She held up the section she'd been sewing. "As you can see, I'm quite skilled with a needle. I was paid per piece, as long as the stitching was perfect. In theory, the faster I was, the more I would earn. The hours were long, but it was the only skill in which I had any confidence. I was there for two years. Then one afternoon, after I'd just finished a lovely sea-green ball gown, the shop owner was looking it over and decided the stitching wasn't up to snuff. Mind you, she didn't think it was untidy to the point it needed to be ripped out and redone. She simply wasn't going to pay me for it. Which as you can well imagine didn't sit well with me. We were in a back room arguing and I was threatening to quit if she didn't give me the money I was owed for my labor. Suddenly a gentleman walked in. I'd seen him on a few occasions, sitting in a chair in the front of the shop while a young lady was being fitted in the back. I assumed she was his wife. Turns out she was his sister. He asked if it was his sister's gown causing all the fuss. Madame said that it was, and he ordered her to pay me or he'd take his business elsewhere."

"Hollingsworth, I presume."

She nodded and took another swallow of the scotch. "Resentfully she did pay me. As soon as I had the coins in hand, I gave my notice. He invited me to join him for a cup of tea in a shop down the street. He filled me up on tea, cakes, and the promise of a life far better than the one I presently had. He'd caught glimpses of me at the dress shop on other occasions and was quite taken with me. I didn't accept his offer right away. I did try to find other employment. But nothing paid well when it came to earnings. At a couple of places where I interviewed—one was a mercantile shop and the other a grocer's—it was made clear that I would be expected to . . . lift my skirt on occasion. If I was going to do that, I might as well accept Hollie's offer. Leave the squalor behind. Receive an allowance that would allow me to pay off my father's debt more quickly. Bring my mother some peace of mind. And he gave me time for us to become friends first." She said the last because she didn't want him to think she'd felt that she'd been coerced or forced into the arrangement. "Who did I know in London who was going to care what I did? To be honest, I found it exciting, adventurous. He introduced me to a world that was very different from the one in which I'd grown up. My father had always told me someday I would have a lord. And now I did."

"Still, it couldn't have been easy, not at first. People being as judgmental as they are." True compassion floated through his deep voice. She was beginning to like him a little too much.

"It was easier than living in Vexham and seeing the condemnation in the eyes of those I'd known all my life. Because of my father's actions, not my own. In London, I'd met so few people, what did I care about the opinion of those I barely knew or didn't know at all? Nor did I understand why the manner in which I lived my life was truly any of their concern. I was doing nothing to harm them. Although I decided I would find a way to win them all over. I haven't achieved that end, but the gossip isn't quite as unkind as it was. So there's the answer to your question and now you know everything about me."

"I very much doubt that."

"Well, more than most." Even Hollie didn't know about her father's deceit or the massive debt she was striving to pay off. He'd never asked about her past and she'd never felt compelled to reveal the mortifying truth of it. She wasn't quite certain why she'd told Langdon so much.

"If your father were alive, I'd beat him to a bloody pulp."

"He couldn't foresee what our future would hold."

"He deceived your mother. He deceived you. He had to know no good would eventually come of it."

She sighed, felt the tears sting her eyes, and blinked them to purgatory as she always did when faced with the truth of the man who had sired her. "I know you speak true. I can't reconcile the man I knew with the man he actually was."

"And your mother left you to clean up his mess."

She heard the disgust in his voice and was disappointed in herself for taking comfort in it. She always felt guilty for wishing her mother had been stronger. But she also recognized that life's disappointments had battered her. While they'd done the same to Marlowe, she didn't feel they'd been quite as brutal. She hadn't *fallen in love* with a man who was more fiction than fact. Although it had made her wary of giving away her heart. How could she ever be sure she knew the absolute truth of someone? Perhaps that was part of the reason she felt so comfortable in her relationship with Hollie. He didn't ask for love. "It wasn't by choice, Langdon. Not everyone has the fortitude to withstand the onslaught of one more challenge. Instead of bending, some people break."

He studied her for the longest time, and she had the sense he was considering all she'd told him and was striving to arrange it into the nooks and crannies of what he knew about her. A softness finally touched his eyes. "I can't imagine you breaking."

"You don't view my accepting Hollie's offer as a possible crack? My becoming a kept woman?"

*H*e wanted to believe she'd had alternatives. There were always options. But he recognized that others had placed her on this path. She could have made far worse choices. One man paying for the privilege of being with her was better than many doing the same. And she'd taken the opportunity to put herself in a position where no one could ever take advantage of her again.

She'd recognized her value and capitalized on it. Business decisions. Yes, she was infamous. Yes, she would never be welcomed into an aristocrat's parlor. But she'd made a place for herself where she held power. Not an easy thing to do when the law still failed to recognize a woman as a man's equal.

His sister lived a life of privilege and yet lamented all she would lose if she married.

"I think you made the best of a horrendous situation." A situation Marlowe's father had led her into, despite her love for the blackguard. How any man could expect lies not to cause harm was beyond his reckoning.

Her head dipped slightly and her eyelashes

came to rest on her cheeks as she closed her eyes, perhaps not wanting him to see her relief that he hadn't chastised her for taking the route she had.

"Knowing the truth of me, do you still want to kiss me?" she asked quietly, lifting her lashes, capturing his gaze.

More than I did that night.

"You belong to another."

"Who isn't here. Besides, he gave us permission that night."

Only Langdon wanted passion, fire. He wanted to delve into her mouth, possess it, and make it his own. He wanted her thinking of him anytime she kissed Hollingsworth. He realized with a sudden jolt that it was terribly selfish of him, to make her yearn for him in place of the earl. Perhaps it was because he feared if he kissed her, he'd never be able to kiss another without thinking of her, that she had the power to brand herself on his soul.

With something as simple as a kiss. But even without her mouth pressed to his, he knew it wouldn't be simple. It would be complex, vastly so. He wanted to know her taste, her sounds—sighs or moans—her heat.

If a kiss could be so much, what the devil would fucking her do to him?

Could he be content with only kissing her, content with a part when he desired the whole?

He didn't recall her moving. Perhaps it had been him. But suddenly their breaths were mingling, and he could see the black outline that circled the blue of her eyes.

"You're battling what you should do against what you want to do." Her voice was low, throaty, intimate. "I have the means to make you surrender if you don't want to take the responsibility for kissing me."

He wasn't half-tempted to demand she make him surrender. He'd never much enjoyed losing but suspected she would make it reverberate as a victory.

"You can say it was all my doing," she added.

"When I want something badly, I'm not gentle when it comes to taking it. After that cut on your lip heals enough that you can smile fully without grimacing, I'll give you a kiss that will drop you to your knees."

She touched the tip of her tongue to the corner of her mouth, perhaps testing it, and he was torn between hoping to see a wide smile and dreading how kissing her might destroy him. He was going to put her in the boat tomorrow morning, row her to the far shore, and get her to a railway—no, not the railway. He wouldn't risk taking her from the world. A coach, then. He would ensure he never crossed paths with her again, never saw that bright smile, never had to honor the vow he'd just recklessly made.

"I look forward to it," she said, easing away from him, and returning to her stitching.

The breath he hadn't realized he'd been holding came out on a rush. It was then that he realized he had indeed been hoping to see a wide smile. He wanted to kiss her that desperately, so desperately at that precise moment that he would willingly accept the possibility that she would ruin him for any other woman. He hoped to hell he would ruin her for any other man, that with his kiss she would experience a tempest of desire such as she'd never known.

Chapter 15

She'd never done such shoddy stitching before, but her fingers were shaking. She had been tempted to force that bright smile, but she didn't want to have any discomfort mar her memory of his kiss. When he said he wouldn't be gentle, she didn't think he would be rough or brutish but instead would pour all his passion into it. It wouldn't be like sailing through the clouds in her balloon. It would be like striving to survive the storm. Frightening. Exhilarating. Unforgettable.

She shouldn't have been trying to tempt him. He was dangerous. He made her long for things she'd never had. He made her long for things she would never have. A man who loved her, a man who would marry her.

She had known when she accepted Hollie's offer what she was giving up. But at the time it hadn't seemed at all like a sacrifice. Her father had taught her that even marriage wasn't safe. That the only safety was in being able to stand on her own.

And she had taken that knowledge with her and used it to make herself invincible.

But Langdon made her feel vulnerable. He made her feel like he possessed the power to break through the walls she'd erected to protect her heart. A heart that had broken when she'd learned the truth about her father, a heart that had never completely healed. A heart that didn't trust love.

One of the reasons she went up in her balloon was to remember how special he'd made her feel. Perhaps, too, a part of her was searching for him, wanting an explanation. Or a confrontation.

He'd taught her men could be disappointing. Her relationship with Hollie was on her terms. While it might not look like it outwardly, she held all the power. With Langdon, she feared the power would go to him and much like the kiss he'd promised, he wouldn't be gentle with it. He could turn her inside out. He could make her *want* as she never had before. Even now, her tongue kept testing her lip to see if it could withstand a broad smile, endure his kiss.

Tomorrow perhaps. And if it didn't happen before she left the island, she'd collect when she was in London, for surely their paths would cross at some point. Hollie certainly hadn't been bothered by the notion of her spending time alone with Langdon. Why should she feel guilty over a kiss?

Even if she wanted it now, later would have to do.

She knotted off the thread, snipped it free, and tucked the needle back into the sewing basket. "I misjudged my healing after last night's calamity. I'm going to retire."

He studied her as one might a jewel he was assessing for flaws. "Are you ill?"

"Merely weary. Surviving takes a toll, I suppose. Will you be—" She stalled, wondering why she was suddenly shy about what she wanted to ask. It seemed, however, that knowing he wanted to kiss her made anything that hinted at flirtation a more serious endeavor, not to be taken lightly. She cleared her throat. "—joining me?"

"You're far too enticing, Marlowe. I'd best not."

"I possess the will to resist you."

He leaned toward her. "Would you like to put that will to the test? Not with a kiss, but with a good many other things that are just as pleasant?"

"For some reason, I don't see your kiss as being *pleasant*." Pleasant wouldn't drop her to her knees.

Grinning, he settled back. "It's good you know what to expect."

She couldn't stop the retort from rolling off the tip of her tongue. "I wonder if you do, my lord, if you know what *I* will deliver."

With that, she pushed to her feet and walked from the chamber. When she reached the stairs, she dashed up the steps. Every other man had been in awe of her beauty, and she'd been able to easily wrap each around her little finger. Langdon was different, not easily wrapped.

If she experienced Langdon, would she want to give him up? Perhaps he was merely an itch and if she scratched it, this obsession with him would go away. Although in her experience, a scratched itch usually became more intense, wanting to be scratched, scratched, scratched again.

It might be best to never give him that smile, never receive that kiss.

She strode into the bedchamber and rubbed her hands up and down her arms. It was chillier, the fire reduced to embers since they'd not been in here to keep it blazing. She knelt before the fireplace and lifted a log from the stack beside it.

A large hand swooped in and took the wood from her. "I'll see to it."

Jerking her head up, she stared at Langdon. "I can manage."

"Don't need you getting a splinter. It occurred to me after you left that the fire had probably gone out." He jerked his head to the side. "Go on. Into bed with you."

Since he had no steps, getting into his massive bed required a little running start and a hop. She managed it without revealing too much, settled on her side, and brought the covers in snugly around her. She watched as he added logs, stirred the embers, and brought the fire back to life, much as he'd brought her last night, with care and attention to details.

"I wish you'd sleep in here. I feel badly about kicking you out of your lovely bed."

"Before I brought any furniture here, I was sleeping on the floor. The sofa is a luxury compared to that." He gave the appearance of speaking to the fire, not her. If he looked her way, would he be tempted to join her?

"We slept splendidly together last night."

"I know you better today."

"And that's made a difference?"

"You're more complicated than I expected." Resting on the balls of his feet, he twisted around. "That makes you more intriguing. I have a weakness for things that intrigue me."

"I told you all about me. It seems only fair that you share the truth of you."

He unfolded that magnificent body of his, leaned a shoulder against the mantelpiece and crossed his arms over his chest. "My father is an earl—not a pretend one. My mother is the daughter of a duke. They came to know each other when she sought out his help."

"What sort of help would the daughter of a duke need?"

"She wanted him to kill someone."

She was well aware that her eyes had rounded, big like saucers. "That's your parents' story. Not yours. I want yours."

He looked at his stockinged feet and back up at her. "You're proof that our parents' stories shape us. He had an unsavory reputation, my father. My parents have worked hard to see it forgotten. I'm very much aware that as their legacy, I must be above reproach." He shrugged. "I went to Eton, then Cambridge."

"At which did you learn to cheat?"

He grinned. "My father taught me that. Further proof that our parents shape us. Until last summer, until the railway accident, I don't know that I'd ever faced a true challenge. Now I face it every day."

She sat up. "What do you mean by that?"

He shook his head.

"The nightmares?"

"Among other things." He shoved himself away from the wall. "Sleep well, Marlowe."

He left the room as quietly as he'd entered. She almost slipped out of bed, rushed after him, and demanded he tell her of the other things. But she certainly didn't want to beg. She wanted him to confide in her of his own accord. However, she couldn't help but wonder if the challenge to which he'd referred had anything to do with the discarded papers she'd found in the room that was forbidden to her.

Reaching out, she extinguished the flame in the lamp on the table beside the bed. With the storm's passing, the sky was clearer and moonlight filtered in through the windows. The flames from the fire caused shadows to dance over the walls and ceiling.

She snuggled down beneath the blankets and drifted off to sleep.

The lightning flashed and the thunder bellowed. The stinging rain pelted her. She was up too high, in the midst of it, the core of the storm. The wicker gondola rocked wildly. She clung to the ropes but even as she did so, she knew they wouldn't save her—

The fire had gone out. No hot air was filling the balloon. The cold air surrounding her was causing it to deflate rapidly and she was falling . . . falling . . . falling—

Jerking free of the nightmare, Marlowe was flailing about, her hands constantly hitting something hard, but warm. Nothing at all like the frigid air in which she'd been. She was vaguely aware of being wrapped up in something. Had the ropes that attached the gondola to the balloon wound themselves about her? Had she gotten tangled up in them?

"Shh, shh. You're safe," a deep voice rumbled near her ear. "You're safe now."

She was taking in great gasps of air, shivering—but she wasn't cold, because a massive amount of warmth was pressed against her, holding her close. Large hands were stroking her back.

And that voice that had once made her feel unwanted was doing the opposite now.

"Nothing is going to hurt you."

He wouldn't let it. Somehow she knew he would protect her.

"I was back in the storm. Terrified. I thought I was going to die. No, I didn't think it. I knew it. The craft has no steering mechanism. I go where the wind takes me. By the time I realized I needed to land, it was too late. It had swept me out over the sea. Then I was hurtling to the earth—" She was clutching his shirt with both hands, just as she'd clutched the basket of her balloon. But he was sturdier, not tossing her about. One of her hands was up against his chest, and through the linen of his shirt, she could feel the hard, steady pounding of his heart.

"You made it to shore," he said briskly, as if she needed reminding. "You never have to go up in the air again."

Oh, but she did because if she didn't, the storm would have won.

"I don't want to think about it, the storm thrashing me, the sea dragging me under. But I don't know how to stop the images from bombarding me. I don't know why tonight I feel like I'm back in the tempest."

Maybe having found her balloon and seeing the wreckage of it had brought home how she'd barely escaped death's clutches. It forced to the forefront the memories she'd been able to ignore as she'd focused more on surviving her time with Langdon. But something had shifted between them, and he was no longer the threat she'd originally perceived.

He was holding her close, stretched out beside her, his body partially covering hers, his face mere inches away.

"I just want to forget the terror." And she knew just how to make that happen, at least temporarily, at least for now. She closed the distance between their mouths.

He immediately deepened the kiss with an urgency, a hunger, his tongue delving—

She released the tiniest of whimpers, and he quickly pulled away, resting his cheek against hers. "I'm sorry. I wasn't thinking."

Had he wanted her as badly as she'd wanted him?

"It's all right. It wasn't unbearable. And I . . . I started it."

He shifted slightly, and with his tongue, outlined the shell of her ear. Warmth spiraled through her. "I could kiss another pair of lips." His voice was low, throaty.

Then he was holding her gaze, and within the moonbeams filtering through the windows, she could see the heat of desire burning in his eyes.

Lowering his head, he kissed her cheek, her chin, her throat. "Say yes," he growled.

She knew what he wanted. And she knew she absolutely should say no because it could lead to other things, more intimate things. "Yes" came out on a breath.

He rolled over until he was covering her completely. Another kiss pressed to her throat. One to the skin at the V where the first button of the shirt she wore was secured. He closed his mouth over her breast, and she felt the heated dew seeping through the linen, her nipple going taut in response. A kiss midway down.

Then his torso was nestled between her legs. He slowly, so slowly and provocatively, eased the shirt up past her hips to reveal the haven he sought. He lifted his smoldering gaze and captured hers, as her breaths, not quite steady, sawed in and out.

She considered ordering him to remove the shirt he still wore but there was something intoxicating about a man in shirtsleeves looking at her as he did, from such an intimate spot. It made what was about to occur seem even more forbidden while at the same time more sensual, more necessary.

His eyes never left hers as he took a slow, deliciously wicked lick. Her whimper this time was filled with pleasure, not pain. His lips closed around the tiny bud. He stroked and suckled. She scraped her fingers along his scalp, entangled them in his hair, could have sworn satisfaction touched his eyes before he went to his task in earnest, with all the ungentleness he'd promised her earlier.

Her entire body reacted as though she was soaring through a storm and the lightning had actually struck her, causing every nerve ending to shiver with delight in response. "Oh, dear Lord."

Sensations of pleasure swept through her. She'd never experienced anything like it.

Langdon was an expert at knowing exactly where to lick, when to suck, how much pressure to apply. A slow roll of his tongue in a figure eight. A long swipe that parted those lips and took him nearer to her core.

Marlowe thought it was her screams while lost in the throes of a nightmare that had brought him to her. She wondered if her screams while lost in the throes of pleasure would have him staying with her tonight. Last night there had been no nightmare. Perhaps she'd been too exhausted or maybe it was simply because this man's presence in the bed with her was strong enough to hold dreadful dreams at bay.

She was reluctant to admit it to herself, much less to him, but his refusal to warm the bed earlier had been a disappointment. The sound of his breathing, the heat of his body, the scent of his skin were all a calming aphrodisiac.

Oh, but the sight of his broad shoulders spreading her thighs, his head moving as he taunted and teased, and his hands inching up beneath her shirt were the opposite of calming. They made her mad with desire, with want, with need.

Perhaps it all made him mad with desire as well because his low groans seemed to signal his own satisfaction. He was pleased with her reactions and for some reason, that was suddenly important. She

wanted him to know that he had the power to drive
her to distraction. She released all the little sighs,
moans, and squeals building within her.

His large hands finally reached her breasts,
cupped them, and kneaded. His thumbs flicked over
her nipples as his mouth flicked over sensitive flesh.

She threw her arms back, over her head, bent
her hands at the wrists, and pressed her palms
to the sturdy headboard. She began gyrating
her hips, moving against his mouth, his lips, his
tongue. Laying her knees on the bed like the
spreading of butterfly wings, she pressed her feet
against his buttocks. She did wish he wasn't wearing trousers, but she didn't want him to cease his
ministrations in order to remove them.

Then her body began tensing, the pleasure
building to a crescendo—

"Let go, Marlowe," he ordered even as he continued feasting with urgency. "I'll catch you."

Suddenly profound pleasure shot through her
and she was crying out, soaring among the stars,
her back arching off the bed. His name was reverberating on the air around her.

Still he licked, but more slowly, leisurely. And
with each swipe of his tongue, her body gave a
little jolt. Until it had no more to give, and she lay
there completely sated and replete.

Slowly, languorously, he prowled up her torso
and wrapped his arms around her before flopping
onto his back and drawing her up against his side.
"I should think that would keep the nightmares
away for a while."

She released a low chuckle while settling more

comfortably into the curve of his shoulder and fiddling with a button on his shirt. "Will you stay?"

"If you like."

"You could remove your shirt if it would make you more comfortable."

"It would. I don't mean to shock you, but I'm accustomed to sleeping in nothing at all."

"You forget what I am if you think such a confession would shock me. Besides, I sleep in the nude as well."

"Christ." His arm briefly tightened around her. "By all means feel free to remove my shirt that you're wearing."

She didn't know why she'd felt a need to try to unsettle him. Especially when he'd been kind enough to chase off her demons. "For propriety's sake, my shirt will stay in place, and I think you should keep your trousers on."

In tandem, as though they'd done it a thousand times, she eased away, he sat up, drew his shirt over this head, tossed it aside, dropped back against the pillow, and she settled in against his side as his arm came around her.

It was both reassuring and a bit unsettling to discover they were so in tune with each other.

"I wonder if my nightmares will last as many months as yours," she said quietly.

"I shall hope not."

It was strange how she was aware of him pondering something, knew a question was on the tip of his tongue. Finally it came.

"If you can't steer the balloon, then how do you land where you need to?"

"I don't have a destination, which is one of the things I like. The randomness of it. But I pay a young man to follow me in a wagon. He returns me and my balloon to London."

"It doesn't seem a very efficient means of travel."

"I'll have to take you up sometime." But even as she said it, she doubted she ever would. Once she left here, it would be best to avoid him as much as possible. She was coming to like him far too much. Besides the sexual attraction between them was frightening.

"I'd enjoy that." But there was a distance in his voice. He, too, understood what their reality would entail.

Chapter 16

$\mathscr{L}$angdon awoke to a summer blue sky. Not outside. But here in his bed. Resting on her side, one hand beneath her cheek, a contented look on her face, Marlowe was watching him. His hand was curled over her hip, the shirt providing a barrier between their skin. He supposed even in sleep, he recognized that she wasn't his to take liberties with.

"Did you sleep all right?" he asked.

Her smile was soft, not one broad enough to give him permission to kiss her as he wanted. "Mmm. I woke up well rested."

Her slender fingers feathered along his throat, slipped beneath the chain around his neck, and skittered down until she was holding the silver medallion his chest had warmed. "Why do you wear this?"

"My mother gave it to me. The image etched on it is of St. Christopher. Patron saint of travelers. She thought it would protect me during my journeys." He wore it because he loved her and to make her feel better, not because he attributed any special powers to it.

"Are you Catholic?"

"No, but saints are for everyone." Her hand was resting against his skin. He wrapped his fingers around it and brought it to his lips. "Even with your bruises, you're still beautiful. How is your lip?"

"Tender but healing."

"And your other lips?"

"Hoping I have a nightmare tonight."

He laughed. "You are—"

"Ollie!"

He released a low groan and a solid curse as he heard the feet stomping up the stairs.

"Ollie?" she repeated.

"Oliver." He threw back the covers and scrambled out of bed. "Wait here."

"Who is it?"

"My brother."

He'd just snatched up his shirt from where he'd tossed it the night before when the scoundrel dashed in, his gaze going directly to the bed, and he staggered to an abrupt stop like he'd slammed into a stone wall. His jaw dropped and his eyes widened. Of the three children his mother had delivered, Stuart was the one who most resembled her, with his blond hair and fairer features. But his eyes were the Claybourne eyes, pewter gray.

"Mother sent me to check on you now that the waters have calmed. She was worried about you being in the storm, but it appears you survived exceptionally well."

"Get out."

"Not going to introduce me to your lady fair?"

"No. This is hardly the appropriate setting for introductions. We're not properly attired for God's sake." As soon as the words were out, he wished he'd stilled his tongue before they were uttered.

His brother bowed, his gaze focused on Marlowe. "I'm Stuart. Unfortunate younger brother of Ollie here. I daresay it's a pleasure to make your acquaintance."

"Get. The. Hell. Out."

Stuart had the audacity to wink at her before spinning on his heel and heading from the room.

Langdon turned to look at her. She was sitting up, her back against the headboard, her gaze aimed at her hands folded primly in her lap. Her cheeks were pink, and he couldn't recall if he'd ever seen her blush. "I apologize for bringing attention to our disheveled state."

She gave her head a slight shake before glancing up. The sadness in those blue eyes was like a punch to the gut. "It's all right. I'm accustomed to not being introduced."

He took a step toward her and noticed the tiniest of flinches. His back being flayed wouldn't have hurt more. "I was striving to protect you, your reputation."

She arched a brow. "You think he doesn't know who I am? And what reputation? It's not sterling, I'm not a lady with any hope of dragging a lord to the altar."

He sat on the edge of the bed, cupped her chin, grateful she didn't jerk away. "I handled the entire matter poorly and for that I apologize. I'm not ashamed of being seen with you—even if I've no right to be *with* you. There are better ways to have conveyed that to my brother. And I'm a bit put out with him for disturbing what was a lovely beginning to the morning. Still, I need to make sure he understands that no one is to learn that you were here." Leaning forward, he pressed a kiss to her brow. "I won't be long."

As he descended the stairs, he dragged his shirt over his head. The stone was cold. He should have taken the time to pull on his boots, but he wanted Stuart gone as quickly as possible. He found his brother in the front chamber staring at the multicolored cloth spread out over the floor, his hands on his hips. Some instinct must have alerted him to Langdon's silent arrival because he abruptly turned, a bit of censure marring his otherwise handsome face. "You *do* know who she is."

"Of course I do."

"How did Marlowe end up here? Did you steal her from Hollingsworth? Does he know? When you return to London, are you going to be facing a pistol at dawn?"

"No pistol at dawn because you're not to tell anyone she was here."

"But you're cuckolding him."

"I believe that term applies only to a husband." He released a deep sigh. "But no, it's not what you think. The storm delivered her to my shore. I have only the one bed. Nothing untoward happened within it." Nothing *very* untoward at least.

With a curt laugh, Stuart shook his head. "You

have London's most beautiful and infamous courtesan in your bed, and you *don't* fuck her?"

Langdon saw so much red that he thought he might drown in it. He was also very close to punching his brother. "Don't use that word when speaking about her."

"Which one? Beautiful? Courtes—"

"Fuck. And no, I did not."

His brother stared at him. "Christ, I believe you. Don't think I could have said the same."

"You're not to touch her."

"I wasn't planning to. After all, we've not been formerly introduced." He didn't attempt to hide his sarcasm, and Langdon realized he'd insulted his brother as well as Marlowe by not introducing them, but then he'd have never introduced any woman found in his bed. It simply wasn't done.

Turning slightly, Stuart waved his arm in the general direction of the cloth. "What is all this?"

"An envelope."

"Have a lengthy letter to post, have you?"

His brother tried so hard to be humorous when all he was succeeding at was being irritating. "Apparently that's the official name of that portion of a hot-air balloon. It's how Marlowe ended up on my shore. She flew the bloody thing. Unfortunately, it crashed in the sea. Only that was salvageable."

His eyes widened in awe. "She's an aeronaut?"

"Yes."

"She might get more respect if people knew that."

His hands closing into fists, he took a menacing step forward. "Who doesn't respect her?"

The irony of the question struck him once he heard the words spoken aloud. He'd once viewed her as a ruined woman and given her less respect than she deserved.

Stuart opened his mouth to speak, closed it. Grinned broadly. "Hello, Marlowe. Ollie was just telling me you're an aeronaut. Well done."

Langdon swung around to see her standing in the doorway, wearing his shirt and the blanket skirt, her hair plaited. Christ, how much had she heard? He prayed nothing.

"In London, I've never heard anyone refer to him as Ollie."

How often had she heard anyone refer to him at all?

"Oh, he hates it. That's why I do it. Younger brothers are supposed to be a nuisance and I take my role in his life very seriously."

Her smile was small, no doubt because of her injured lip, but it was obvious by the twinkling in her eyes that she was charmed. Stuart had that devil-may-care sense about him that gave the impression he was jolly good fun. Who was Langdon kidding? Stuart was always up for a good time. He had no responsibilities weighing him down. As the spare he was free to do as he pleased.

"Ollie was explaining the unfortunate circumstances that brought you to his shore. I would be more than delighted to take you back across to the mainland."

"That won't be necessary," Langdon said so sharply that both Marlowe and Stuart snapped their heads around to stare at him in surprise, like maybe they'd forgotten he was even there. He feared they could see the green-eyed monster presently sitting squarely on his shoulder. He was swamped with possessiveness and jealousy when he had no right to either emotion because she wasn't bloody well his. "I'll be taking her across this afternoon."

It was ridiculous for him to go to the bother of doing so when Stuart would already be taking the same route. He was certainly capable of getting her to the village and ensuring she boarded a coach that would get her to London. But Langdon wanted to be responsible for her, care for her, and, in essence, be her hero. Could he be any more of a fool?

He expected both to object or to argue the ridiculousness of his plan.

"Would you mind if I stayed a bit longer?" Marlowe asked. "Just until I've finished mending the balloon. You have so much more room here, and your lack of furnishings allows me to spread it out. My town house has no chamber as large as all this and it's not nearly as sparsely decorated."

Langdon was very much aware of his brother's rapt attention. Still, he nodded. "Very well. It won't be a bother for you to stay." Could he sound any more disaffected, especially as he was grateful to have her to himself for a few more days? He turned to his brother. "I'll walk you down to your boat."

Stuart's sardonic grin conveyed that he knew Langdon was striving to get rid of him. Once more, he bowed toward his guest. "It was a pleasure to meet you, Marlowe."

"You as well, my lord," she said sweetly.

Where was her tart tongue when it came to his

brother? On the other hand, he rather liked that she reserved it for him.

It wasn't until they were outside, walking down the path, that Stuart said, "I think you've stolen her from Hollingsworth without even realizing it."

"Don't be ridiculous."

"So you do realize it."

He growled. "I've not stolen her. She's as loyal to Hollingsworth as I've seen any woman be loyal."

"But she asked to stay."

"Because she cares about her bloody balloon."

"What do you care about?"

Nothing he was interested in discussing. "Assure Mother that I'm fine. I'll visit in a few days so she can see for herself. Do *not* tell her about Marlowe. Mother will want to come over to check on matters, and I'd rather she not." Selfishly, he wanted whatever time was left to him and Marlowe to be theirs and theirs alone. "I'll introduce Marlowe when we arrive."

They walked along in silence for several minutes. Langdon preferred his brother quiet.

"I heard you once had an opportunity during a card game to win her from Hollingsworth. I'm surprised you didn't take matters in hand to ensure you won."

"It would have been only for a few hours."

"I would have cheated to have her alone for a few *minutes*."

Langdon was hardly aware of quickly twisting around and grabbing his brother by his shirtfront. "If you cross paths with her in the future, you will show her the utmost respect. You won't be leering at her the way you did in there." He jerked his head toward the tiny stone castle. "And if you wish to retain all your teeth and continue to receive an allowance after Father passes, you will absolutely do nothing in order to *have her* at all." He gave Stuart a little shake. "Have I made myself perfectly clear?"

"Good God, you've fallen for her."

Releasing his hold, he shoved his brother away. "Don't be daft."

He'd come to like her. Certainly. But fallen for her? He was too practical to make that sort of tragic error in judgment.

"You seem terribly protective."

"I've read that in some cultures if you save a person's life, you become responsible for them."

"Not in ours."

"Still, I saw the woman near death—and I've seen others succumb to its call—so yes, I suppose a part of me doesn't want to see any harm come to her and feels a need to defend her from those who might use her callously."

"I wouldn't, but"—he held up his hand before Langdon could issue a retort—"I'll honor your request to steer clear of her."

"Very good."

Stuart began walking, and Langdon fell into step beside him. He loved his brother and didn't usually go about issuing threats but the thought of anyone seeing Marlowe as a source of momentary amusement made his blood boil. She was worthy of a man who appreciated every aspect of her. Hollingsworth might not be her husband, but she seemed to care for him and he for her . . . except

for the one night when he'd offered her up. That
continued to vex and made no sense.

"At dinner the other night, Mother speculated
this might be the Season you settle on a wife,"
Stuart said quietly.

Langdon sighed. "Why are mothers always so
anxious to marry off their children?"

"I think it makes them feel their children become
someone else's responsibility."

"I'm twenty-eight. She's no longer responsible
for me."

"She feels differently. Why else have me come
check on you?"

"She'd probably feel responsible for us if we'd
seen a hundred years. Perhaps it's just the way
of mothers." He wasn't quite certain Marlowe's
mother had done right by her. He tried not to sit in
judgment, but he wondered how different her life
would be if her mother had stepped up and taken
care of matters instead of relying on her daughter
to do so. He also understood how hard it was to let
others see you bruised and broken. His family all
believed him scarred but mended. However, some
wounds simply wouldn't heal.

They reached the shoreline where Stuart had
moored his boat. Two men Langdon recognized as
serving as footmen up at the estate were sitting on
a large boulder staring out at the sea of blue. "You
didn't come alone."

"No. Water might look calm, but I don't quite
trust it." He grinned. "If you'd known I wouldn't
be alone with her, would you have let me take her
across?"

"We'll never know."

"Oh, I think we very much know. How does it work when a mistress wants to be mistress to some other gent? It's not as if she has to divorce the first. Does she just leave? Would you have to duel for her honor?"

"She's not going to leave him."

"Conferred with her about it already?"

He sighed deeply and with frustration. "No. And I'm not going to discuss it with you. Get in the damned boat."

With a deep laugh, Stuart swept his arm through the air. "All right, gents, we're headed back to Heatherwood." It was the name of the family estate.

After everyone was situated in the boat, oars at the ready, Langdon pushed on the skiff, wading into the water until he could properly shove it and its occupants off.

"Don't do anything I wouldn't do!" Stuart yelled.

Shaking his head, Langdon waved. Then he stood there, the water swirling and eddying around his calves, and wondered how a mistress *did* go about breaking things off with her lover. He knew men who had let their mistresses go, usually by purchasing them expensive gifts, but he'd never wondered how a woman might instigate the proceedings. And would Marlowe have any interest in securing him as her protector?

On the other hand, did he want to be associated with a woman of such notoriety?

Chapter 17

*W*hen he returned to the residence, he found her in the main room, sitting on the floor beside the fireplace, and already working to mend the fabric. There was a homey feel that had never been part of this dwelling. It was a bit disconcerting, making him think that at long last he could find the peace that he'd come here seeking.

She glanced up. "Your brother is a bit of a scamp."

"He is that."

"And you're wet."

He looked down at his sodden trousers. He'd left his boots just inside the doorway. "I shoved him"—at her eyes widening, he decided an amendment was in order—"his boat into the water. I won't be long."

After dashing up the stairs, he was surprised to find the bed set to rights. He seldom bothered to make the bed, because he'd only unmake it later.

Nothing about the room seemed the same. The sunlight appeared brighter, coming through the windows. He couldn't look around without seeing her within these walls or hearing her cries of fear soon followed by shouts of pleasure.

He shrugged out of his coat, stripped off his trousers. He set them in front of the fire to dry before drawing on another pair. He followed that with a dry set of boots. His stomach rumbled. Stuart's arrival had delayed breakfast.

He made his way down the stairs and into the kitchen. He smiled at the large wicker basket resting on the table, not needing to look inside to know what he'd find. He added a few things before popping back upstairs and grabbing a quilt from the cupboard.

He didn't know why he suddenly felt lighter, like he could float on air. Did she feel this way when she was in her balloon? It had been so very long since he hadn't felt weighted down. Perhaps that night of the railway accident was finally leaving him.

With wicker basket in hand, the quilt draped over his arm, he returned to the front room, crossed over to where she sat, and held out his hand to her. "Come on."

She studied the items he was holding. "What's that?"

"My mother sent food. We're going on a picnic."

*T*hey didn't go far from the dwelling, just to the edge of the cliff, where he'd spread out the quilt and she'd lowered herself to it. She'd stuffed her feet back into his boots that she'd borrowed the day before. His coat was draped over her shoulders. Wearing only his trousers, shirtsleeves, and boots, he didn't seem at all bothered by the chill in the air as he spread out the fare: Scotch eggs, ham, scones. His mother had even included clotted cream and jam. The last thing he pulled out was a crock and two earthenware mugs. "My contribution," he announced and poured her some tea.

Still a trifle hurt by the entire introduction fiasco—even though it had been obvious his brother knew who she was—she refused to be charmed, even when he stretched out on his side, rose up on an elbow, and snatched up a piece of ham with his fingers.

"We're to eat like barbarians?" she asked.

He grinned. "I suspect most of my ancestors who lived here did. Besides, I find it refreshing from time to time not to have to follow all of Society's strictures." He waved the hand holding the ham over the food. "Help yourself."

She took a sip of tea instead. He must have put half the sugar in England in it. She didn't know if she'd ever had anything quite so delicious. Setting the mug aside, she went for a scone.

"You like sweet things," he murmured.

"I do. Although I'm sweet enough without them."

"You've no idea." He looked out over the narrow strip of water separating his island from the mainland, leaving her with the impression he was referring to *her* taste.

If she stayed any longer, she might discover the taste of him. She wasn't quite certain that would be a wise thing to do. "While you were seeing your brother off, I took an inventory of the tears. I estimate I'll be able to finish my task in only a few hours." He was staring out over the water, but she was left with the impression that he was bracing himself for an onslaught of words he didn't want to hear. "We should go back to the mainland today."

Without looking at her, he nodded. "I agree."

She didn't know why his answer disappointed her. It was the correct answer. It assured they didn't quarrel. "I think you should know, in case you should ever cross paths with Hollie, that I'm not going to tell him about my little adventure."

He did look at her then, his face set in a somber mask. "That's probably for the best."

"He wouldn't be jealous. But he would be upset by my dunderheadedness."

He rolled a little more onto his side so he was more squarely facing her. "And which dunderheadedness would that be?"

"Placing myself in a position to fall from the sky." *To fall for you.* "I never tell him when I've gone up because he worries so."

His brow furrowed. "But it's a part of you. Not to share it with him . . . how can he fully appreciate you?"

"That's the way of mistresses. You don't give your benefactor the whole of you. You have to keep a portion just for yourself, something to which you can remain true." She shook her head. "Or perhaps it's necessary for survival for everyone, not just mistresses. Like you, with your room of crumpled paper. Other than you, who knows about the reasons behind it?"

He chuckled darkly. "It's not an aspect of me that I want or intend to keep. But if I was going to share it with anyone, I might share the reason behind it with you." He grinned. "But I'm not."

Chapter 18

*T*he last time Marlowe had felt any sadness at all at leaving someplace was the day she left Vexham without her mother and began her solitary journey to London.

For some strange, preposterous reason, she was experiencing some of the same sadness now as Langdon rowed them toward the mainland. His small stone keep was not home, and yet she didn't know if she'd ever felt safer anywhere else. She'd been rescued, warmed, and pleasured.

In a way, she was sorry to be headed back to London, although she knew she needed to go. Hollie would be calling on her as soon as he returned, and they had some things between them to settle.

She didn't want to admit that part of her melancholy was a result of leaving Langdon. Which was utterly ridiculous. They didn't mean anything to each other really. The only reason she couldn't take her eyes off him at the moment was because he was wearing only shirtsleeves, trousers, and boots, and his lack of jacket or coat made it easier to see the strain of his muscles as he rowed. His actions were so smooth, so damned masculine.

He'd rolled his sleeves up past his elbows and she could see his muscles bunching, his veins bulging, and she imagined them doing the same as he levered himself above her.

Hollie was slender, his pallor that of a man who seldom frequented the outdoors. She found no fault with his build, but it didn't make her mouth water. As a matter of fact, no gentleman's ever had until she met Langdon.

And then he became all she could think about.

She brought his greatcoat more tightly around her to ward off the chill of the wind that wasn't strong enough to blow them off course, but offered a bit of a challenge when it came to reaching the other shore. It had taken them a while to bundle up her balloon and secure it with rope so it wouldn't unfurl and become ungainly. It also made it easier for Langdon to haul to the boat. She'd offered to carry it with him, but he'd insisted on doing it alone, as though he needed to show off his masculinity. Much to her chagrin, she'd quite enjoyed his efforts and the way in which they'd made his muscles bulge. He hadn't even breathed heavily, had simply carted the monstrously large item that was composed of yards and yards of cloth as though it was no bother at all. Although once he'd settled it in the boat, he'd rubbed his lower back before reaching over to assist her in climbing aboard.

"Were you part of the rowing team while you were at Cambridge?" she asked.

He nodded. "I was. It is easier when there are more hands at the task."

"I offered to row. You said you only had the one set of oars."

"I wasn't complaining. Merely making conversation."

"You like your outdoor activities."

"I do." He grinned devilishly. "Indoor ones as well."

"Those that involve ladies, I suppose."

"Depends on the lady."

She shouldn't ask. It was absolutely none of her business, and yet—

"Do you have a mistress?"

"Don't now, never have."

She was beginning to wish she hadn't started down this path, and yet she was curious. "I suppose there's no shortage of women willing to warm your bed."

"Are you one of them?"

She definitely shouldn't have started down this path. "I've never been unfaithful to Hollie." She felt her cheeks go pink. "Although I suppose last night might count."

"Only partially. I wouldn't feel guilty about it. Whatever happens on that bit of rock stays there." He glanced over his shoulder. "We're almost where we need to be."

She wasn't certain she knew where she needed to be any longer. Although thoughts along those lines had been plaguing her for a while. It was part of the reason she'd recklessly gone up that evening in spite of dark clouds brewing in the distance.

Twisting around, she looked back at the small castle-like structure and wondered why she wished she was still there. It certainly wasn't the fanciest of dwellings or even the most welcoming, and yet she'd had an odd sense of belonging there.

A sudden lurch had her gasping and struggling to catch her balance. They'd hit shore.

With one smooth, easy movement, Langdon leapt out into the shallow water, took hold of the bow, and dragged the boat onto the sand before securing it with a rope to a post beside another boat. She supposed this was a favorite mooring spot for his family.

Returning to her, he helped her stand. "Place your hands on my shoulders," he ordered.

When she did so, he circled his strong hands around her waist, lifted her out, and carried her beyond reach of the waves before returning for the balloon.

"This way," he indicated with a nod, and she began to follow him up a series of wooden steps.

At the top, she stopped to admire the front of the massive manor house. A large drive circled in front of it. A time would come when Langdon, his wife, and children would live there. When his heir would row across to the small island and wander the halls in the fortification as she had. She'd once thought that eventually she'd live in a house such as the one she now studied, whether it was her father's or her husband's. She'd loved her father, and yet he'd irrevocably hurt her. And the path she'd chosen to travel put marriage beyond reach.

Turning, Langdon continued walking, only backward. "You coming?"

She hurried to catch up and he swung back around to face the manor. "It's quite impressive," she said.

"To the right of it, at the bottom of the cliff, is another cove. Within the residence is a secret passage that leads down to it. Stuart and I spent many an hour playing within it, pretending we were pirates."

They reached the pebbled drive, and he turned toward the house.

She staggered to a stop. "Wait. Where are you going?"

He walked back to her and dropped the parcel he'd been carrying. "To change out of my wet trousers and boots. And to have a carriage readied in which to transport you to London."

"I can walk to the nearest village and hire transportation there. I assume it's at the end of this path."

"Taking my coat and boots with you? And what of your balloon? Are you going to haul that?"

"Perhaps you could provide a footman to assist me. As well as a letter of reference stating I will pay what is owed once I reach London, so hopefully I'll have less bother obtaining a ticket. I'll just wait here."

He shook his head. "Come on. You'll like my mother."

When he reached down to pick up the balloon, she grabbed his arm to stop him. "You know what I am. You can't introduce me to her and you most certainly can't take me into her parlor."

"With all your confidence, I've always had the

impression you thought you were worthy of dining with the Queen."

"I might give that impression, but I *do* know my place, and it most certainly—"

"Oliver!" An older woman, with pale blond hair, was dashing down the front steps. A dark-haired gentleman was following at a more sedate pace, although his long legs allowed him to nearly keep pace with her.

"Too late now." Langdon's tone was one of victory and satisfaction.

"Bugger it," she muttered beneath her breath.

"Careful or you'll find yourself in a cursing match with my sister." Turning, he opened his arms wide and embraced the woman as she rushed into the circle of his arms. They hugged each other tightly. Marlowe didn't know if she'd ever seen such an enthusiastic greeting among the aristocracy. The gentleman who'd been accompanying her reached them and looked on with affection. She didn't need anyone to tell her that he was the Earl of Claybourne, because his son so favored him— except for the nose. The earl's appeared to have been broken a time or two.

The woman leaned back, patting her hands against Langdon's cheeks, his shoulders, his chest. "I've been so worried about you. That storm was awful."

"Stuart should have told you I was fine."

"He did, but I like to see for myself."

He stepped back. "Mother, Father, allow me to introduce Marlowe. The storm saw fit to deliver her to my shore in her hot-air balloon."

The countess smiled. "The aeronaut Stuart told us about. It's a pleasure to make your acquaintance, Miss Marlowe."

Before curtsying, she caught sight of Langdon's jaw tensing, no doubt because Stuart was not to have revealed her presence within his dwelling. Without a chaperone, it would have been scandalous. On the other hand, being a mistress probably overrode that. "It's just Marlowe, my lady."

"Still, it's a pleasure. Do come inside and rest before dinner."

"We're not staying," Langdon finally said—thank God. "I need to change and have my carriage readied so I can return Marlowe to London."

"But if you leave now, you won't get far before you'll be traveling at night."

"We'll stop at an inn—"

"Your mother would like you to stay," Claybourne said, in a tone that would brook no argument. "Besides, after that storm, the roads are likely to be muddy and treacherous. You risk getting stuck. Best to wait until the morning to leave."

"I'm not properly attired to join you for dinner," Marlowe said.

The Countess of Claybourne patted her shoulder gently. "Poppy will have something you can wear. You're about the same size. Come up to the residence and we'll get you settled."

She slipped her arm around her husband's, and they began walking away. Marlowe looked at Langdon and he gave her a sympathetic yet small smile. "It won't be that bad. We might as well surrender."

"Do you think they have any idea who I am?"

He nodded. "My father has long made it his business to know who everyone in London is. My mother and sister scour the gossip sheets, although they probably won't know about Hollingsworth. I don't think he's ever referred to by name when you're mentioned. But they won't be judgmental, Marlowe. They're not without sin. But if at any minute, you tell me you don't want to stay, we'll leave immediately."

She gazed past him to the residence. "Do you know I've never been to Hollie's estates?"

"I would think a woman who ascends into the heavens would have nothing to fear."

Especially, she thought, with him at her side.

$\mathcal{A}$s they walked into the main entryway, she fought not to be awestruck, but the impressive surroundings took her breath. The high vaulted fresco ceiling, the wide staircase with its red runner, the walls bearing portraits of his ancestors. The furniture with its intricate carvings, polished to a shine. The statuettes, the vases, the adornments. She couldn't help but believe that her mother had expected, at some point in her life, to have been living in a mansion such as this. To have servants at her beck and call, similar to the footman relieving Langdon of her balloon and carrying it away, after he'd been ordered to see it well cared for.

As though it were a person. A treasure as fine as any that surrounded her now.

His mother was standing at the foot of the stairs. "Come. I'll show you to your chamber, and we'll see about finding something of Poppy's for you to wear. She and Stuart are out riding, so you'll meet her later. Would you care for a bath?"

"I'd love a bath, if it's not too much of a bother."

"No bother at all."

Marlowe was acutely aware of Langdon following behind her as his mother escorted her up the stairs. She was also very much aware of the elegance of his mother. Marlowe had practiced for hours to portray the same sophistication, and yet she couldn't help but feel that her movements were shadowed by a bit of coarseness, a bit of striving too hard to be what she was not—a true lady.

After they reached the landing, everything passed in such a rush. A couple of lady's maids—obviously the countess's and then her daughter's—were already waiting, as if the countess had known all along her son and his guest would be staying the night. Langdon disappeared, no doubt to get out of his wet trousers and perhaps enjoy his own bath.

In a mauve room of white furniture, a gown was located as well as all the sundry undergarments necessary. In a blue bedchamber at the end of the hallway, a bath was being prepared, a fire was dancing on the hearth, and Marlowe found herself being assisted in undressing. She had her own servant to help her dress and undress, to fix her hair, and to tend to anything else she required, so she was quite comfortable being waited upon.

"I'll leave you in the care of these two," the countess said, her hand on the doorknob. "If you require anything at all, let Jenny here know." Jenny bobbed a quick curtsy. "She's served me for many years now. Feel free to rest and relax before coming down to dinner."

"Thank you, my lady."

When the door closed behind the countess, Marlowe wondered if perhaps she should sneak out and make her way to the village on foot. If she couldn't carry the balloon all the way herself, she could leave a note for Langdon to deliver it to her when he returned to London.

"Lord Langdon has never brought a lady here before," the younger of the maids said a bit slyly.

"It's none of our business," Jenny scolded her.

"I got caught in the storm, and he's helping me get back to London," Marlowe assured them. "I certainly hadn't intended to impose on the earl and countess. My being here is more nature's doing than the viscount's."

When the last of the water was poured into the tub, Marlowe lowered herself into the heavenly warmth. "The road in front of the estate, does it lead to the village?"

"Aye," Jenny said. "When a body gets to the fork, they just go to the right, away from the water."

"Is the village far?"

"Not too far."

Perhaps she would head there after she washed up. She'd always believed herself good enough for a place like this but at the moment she was wishing they'd never left the island.

Chapter 19

In the library, scotch in hand, Langdon leaned against the window casing, staring out at the elaborate gardens. The sun was setting. Night would be upon them soon. He shouldn't have waited until it was so late in the day to bring Marlowe to the mainland. By doing so, he'd ensured they wouldn't be traveling to London this day, because he knew his mother well enough to know she'd worry about them traveling in the dark.

Although he'd planned to seek refuge in an inn along the way, he still wasn't certain whether he would have requested a room for himself and Marlowe to share or if he would have ensured she had her own room. However, he also recognized that he'd left their departure until he knew an invitation would be offered because he'd made a mistake that morning by not introducing Marlowe to his brother.

The disappointment on her face had nearly cleaved him in two.

Hence he had decided that he bloody well would

introduce her to his parents. They might disown him afterward—

A corner of his mouth hitched up because he knew they wouldn't. They didn't sit in judgment of good people, and in spite of the majority of London questioning her morals, Marlowe was a good person. Life had tossed her a series of unfair disadvantages, and she'd made the most of a society that valued women for their breeding potential and little else. Certainly laws were changing to make life more advantageous for women, but it was a slow process.

Besides, it was no secret that his parents had been married only a few months when he made his arrival in their lives, so they certainly weren't going to cast stones at a woman who lifted her skirts without the benefit of marriage. She lifted them for only one man. And maybe a little for Langdon. Although technically, she'd lifted his shirt.

"The estate manager says you haven't discussed with him those plans you showed me last summer for improvements that would increase the estate's income."

His father's voice held no censure, only curiosity and a bit of bafflement. Langdon had been incredibly anxious to get the improvements underway but the railway accident had derailed him—literally. He turned slightly to face his father, who was sitting in a nearby chair. "I need to map out the plans again, recalculate figures." *I need to bloody well remember what they all were.* "They didn't survive the crash."

"You had only the one copy that you were carrying with you?"

"I didn't think I needed more. They were in a satchel beside me. But I was unable to locate it in the wreckage."

His father nodded. "How are the headaches you were having?"

Debilitating. "Not as bad as they were."

"I used to have massive pains in my head, whenever my past—which I couldn't remember—tried to intrude on the present."

"Dr. Graves told me that headaches are common following a collision such as the one I endured. Something about being knocked about."

"He's one of the best physicians in all of England. You go see him again if those pains don't improve."

"I will."

"Your mother worries that you're spending too much time alone of late."

"She always worries. In this case, she worries for naught."

His father didn't move, merely studied him, and Langdon knew that when utter stillness overtook his father, the lord was at his most dangerous—uncovering secrets, divining the truth.

"I am fine," Langdon stated succinctly, pouring every bit of deception he could muster into the words.

"Your mother will be relieved to know that."

But he heard in his father's tone that he had failed to convince him fully. However, he wasn't yet ready to reveal his struggles. He was the first-born, the heir, and as such he needed to be stronger than most. He needed to deserve what would be handed down to him. Felt a yearning to prove he would be a good guardian of his heritage for future generations.

Feminine laughter wafted into the library only a few seconds before his mother, sister, and Marlowe strolled in. He'd forgotten how utterly elegant Marlowe appeared when wearing an evening gown, how gracefully she moved when not clomping about in his boots. When her hair, upswept and artfully arranged, brought attention to the graceful slope of her neck and her enticing shoulders.

Although he realized he'd only ever seen it arranged when it was black. The blond strands suited her so much better. Hollingsworth was a fool to want anything at all about her altered. Even with the healing injuries, no one matched her beauty.

Staring at her, he found it difficult to breathe, while his gut clenched.

She gave him a quick glance, her smile small, as if she was embarrassed to be caught wearing so much clothing. He imagined the joy to be found in divesting her of every layer, stitch, and bit of lace.

His father was handing each lady a small glass of port when Stuart ambled in and greeted their guest by taking her hand and pressing a kiss to her knuckles. Langdon was hit with an overwhelming urge to shout, *Mine!*

Only she wasn't his. She belonged to Hollingsworth.

Belonged. As though she were a piece of property. She was her own woman. She wouldn't be with Hollingsworth if she didn't want to be. He wondered what it might take for her to leave the earl.

He wandered over to be nearer to the group congregating around her, butterflies to a bright colorful petal. It amused him that she had the same impact here as she did at a soiree in London; people naturally migrated to her. When he'd seen it happening before, he'd assumed it was her beauty, but he was beginning to suspect she possessed a natural, welcoming mien. Seeing her encouraging his sister, who usually needed no encouragement, he realized she possessed a kindness that put people at ease. Thinking back on it, he recalled noticing shy gents who were prone to stammering around women speaking to her without issuing a single stutter.

He wanted to pull her aside, ask how she'd enjoyed her bath, being pampered, looked after. He wanted to ask her to cross back over to his island for the night and they'd leave in the morning. He wanted her to himself. He wanted to speak with her alone to ensure she was feeling comfortable, although he couldn't envision any member of his family saying anything that would make her feel uncomfortable.

The butler strode in, came to a stop. "Dinner is served."

Before Stuart could, Langdon offered Marlowe his arm. "May I escort you in?"

She seemed surprised by his action. Even though it was only family, still the ladies were escorted. His father was already leading his mother out of the room by the time Marlowe nodded.

"Looks like you're stuck with me," Stuart said, presenting his arm to his sister.

"I suppose in a few years, you'll be saying that to the woman you marry."

He chuckled darkly. "I'm never going to marry."

"The famous last words of many a bachelor," Poppy said, before slipping her arm through his and urging him to head for the door.

Langdon waited until they were no longer within hearing distance to begin escorting Marlowe. "Has everything gone to your satisfaction?" He kept his voice low, intimate.

"As kind as your family is, I very much wish we were on our way to London."

"Tomorrow we will be."

And once there, she'd be in another man's keeping. An unfortunate realization struck him: he wished she were in his.

Chapter 20

"How did you ever find the courage to go up in a balloon?" Poppy asked, from her place beside Marlowe at the dining table.

"My father was an aeronaut and, when I was a little girl, he would often take me with him on short tours around the countryside. Hence I was traveling through the sky before I was old enough to realize the dangers of leaving the ground. Once my balloon is repaired, I could take you up sometime if you like."

Poppy's eyes widened slightly, and Marlowe realized too late the inappropriateness of her words. They might be welcoming her tonight, but the earl and countess certainly weren't going to allow their impressionable daughter to spend time with a lord's mistress.

Stuart laughed. "Poppy can't even stand at the top of the stairs and look down without swooning."

His sister blushed. "'Tis true, I'm afraid. I get dizzy."

It was the girl's excuse not to spend time in

Marlowe's presence, and she should let her have it. But she didn't want Langdon's sister to never experience the wonder of flight if another opportunity came her way. "Look across, not down," she said kindly. "You'll trick yourself into believing you're only inches, not yards, from the ground."

"Truly?" Poppy asked. "Is that what you do?"

"I think if I looked straight down, I'd be in danger of growing lightheaded and tumbling right out of the gondola."

"Perhaps I will give it a go sometime."

"You won't regret it. Up there"—she looked toward the ceiling—"you're remarkably . . . free, unencumbered by any of Society's rules."

"I so hate Society's rules. Especially the one where I must have a chaperone."

Since she'd never had one, Marlowe had no desire to get into a conversation about chaperones. She'd always gone where she wanted when she wanted. She supposed once her mother learned the truth regarding her husband, she'd given up on any notion that her daughter might marry a respectable man who would want a respectable wife.

"Only because you'd like to visit Aiden Trewlove's club for ladies," Stuart said, teasingly.

"Or the Fair and Spare," Poppy added. "Have you ever gone to either of those, Marlowe?"

"No, I've not." She went to the sort of clubs in which a lady like Poppy would never set foot.

The conversation drifted to plays, operas, concerts, and books. She was included, what she might have seen or read, but no inquiries that were particularly personal. She was tempted to ask if they—especially the ladies—had read *My Secret Desires*, a scandalous memoir that had recently taken London by storm as it revealed the wicked exploits of one of their own, a certain Lord Knightly. She wondered if they considered it obscene and were in favor of it being banned. She hadn't and wasn't. But she'd had a heated discussion with Hollie concerning it, and she wasn't really in favor of ruining the pleasant mood that no doubt kept everyone's digestion on an even keel.

She liked when the focus wasn't on her and she was able to more closely observe the dynamics of the family. Especially Langdon. He was very much like his father, serious and reserved, his smiles rare.

She'd assumed he'd seldom given her a smile because of a dislike for her, but he was giving her more than he'd given his family thus far, and she was beginning to realize each he'd bestowed upon her was precious and to be treasured.

Rarely did his gaze stray from her, but when it did, it quickly returned as though he needed to be assured she was still there. She'd thought with others about he'd have an excuse not to give her any attention, and yet it was almost as if they were alone.

Dressed in dining finery, freshly shaved, his hair trimmed, he'd stolen her breath when she'd first walked into the library. Having grown accustomed to him in his shirtsleeves, she'd forgotten how gorgeous he was when outfitted for the evening. It was wholly unfair that without any effort at all, he could cause her heart to beat erratically, her body to warm, and the sensitive spot between her thighs to thrum.

Whenever he took a sip of wine and touched his tongue to his lips to ensure he enjoyed every last drop, she would recall him touching his tongue to her, and she would feel as if she were in danger of going up in flames.

And she wondered if she had any effect on him at all.

"I have a bit of news to share," Lady Poppy declared, a touch of giddiness in her voice. "If courtship is on your agenda for the upcoming Season, as Mother believes, I think you'll find what I have to say of particular interest, Oliver."

He looked at his sister, his patient smile telling Marlowe that he always indulged her. What must it be like to be so loved by him?

"Oh?" he asked.

"I received a letter today from my dear friend, Lady Euphemia. She's to marry Lord Hollingsworth."

*S*tanding at the edge of the cliff, Langdon stared out over the moon-glistening water. If Poppy knew that Marlowe served as a mistress, it was evident she didn't know whose mistress she was. Otherwise, she'd have never made that announcement during dinner, because she wasn't in the habit of making people uncomfortable.

But her revelation had rocked him to his core.

When he'd jerked his gaze to Marlowe, she'd averted her eyes but couldn't have appeared less bothered if Poppy had said, *Oh, look, a pea has fallen off my plate.*

She'd known about the betrothal.

When she'd given him a sultry glance, when she'd looked as though she might ignite if he touched her, she'd known.

Last night when he had pleasured her with his mouth, and she'd cried out, when he'd felt her pulsing against his tongue . . . she'd known.

She could have told him at any time and it might have changed things between them. Had she feared that it would . . . or that it wouldn't?

"Your entire family cheats at cards."

Unable to help himself, he smiled as Marlowe's soft voice reached his ears, but he didn't turn toward her, not even when she came to a stop beside him.

"The whole point of the game is not to give yourself away."

Following dinner, they'd all gone to the billiards room, which included a baize-covered table for cards, as well as several sitting areas where people could gather for smaller conversations.

"I think they were taking pity on me, as I won a few hands. Your mother seemed surprised to win as well."

"She never manipulates the cards, although I'm fairly certain Father taught her how."

"Is that the reason you didn't join us—because you're more skilled than all of them?"

He'd seen a spark of disappointment in her features when he'd declined and instead had opted to sit nearby and watch. Until he'd begun to regret that he couldn't join them. Because as Marlowe had noted, when it came to cards, his family had no qualms about cheating, regardless of whom they were playing. And he'd yet to reveal that since the railway accident, he'd lost his ability to cheat. He could no longer decipher the cards nor were his hands as quick as they'd once been.

He'd known that when his family noticed—and they'd have noticed—they would have demanded an explanation, and he wasn't yet ready to give one. He held out hope it was a temporary loss and yet of late, nothing felt temporary. "I simply wasn't in the mood for cards."

"What were you in the mood for?"

He looked at her then, captured her gaze, and held it, all the while daring her to acknowledge the answer. "I think you know."

Chapter 21

God help her, she did know. She wanted it, too. She tested her lip. A kiss wouldn't hurt too terribly badly, and she suspected the pleasure he'd deliver would far outweigh the pain she'd experience. The challenge would be producing the smile he required without grimacing.

"Much more than a kiss," he said darkly, before turning his attention away.

"But it starts with a kiss."

"It doesn't have to."

He hadn't needed to kiss her last night to send her soaring. She hated to admit that she wasn't looking forward to sleeping alone tonight. Strange how after only two nights, the notion of not having him with her in bed made her feel that something important was missing.

Stepping back, he faced her and traced a blunt-tipped finger lightly along her cheek, careful not to touch any of her injuries. "Poppy's announcement during dinner came as no surprise to you."

She'd hoped he'd let the entire matter go, ignore

it, give it no credence. She should have known he wouldn't. With barely a shake of her head followed by a nod to shore up her resolve, she forced out the words that she'd been striving to escape ever since she'd read them, words that in a way had delivered her to his island. "The day of the storm . . . the *Times* included an announcement regarding . . . Hollie's betrothal."

She was rather proud of the fact that her voice had come out neutral, giving away none of her riotous emotions concerning the matter. The shock of it. She hadn't anticipated they'd stay together until their hair turned silver, but neither had she expected a parting to come out of the blue. Rather like a storm that had arrived without warning. One minute the sun was shining, and, the next, black clouds obliterated it.

"Why didn't you mention it?"

"I've been striving to determine exactly how I feel about it." And it was convenient to have Hollie as a buffer between them, saved her from doing what she ought not with Langdon. But she'd done some of it anyway. And she suspected she was on the verge of doing a good deal more.

"Is that the reason you went up in your balloon in spite of the dangers?"

"To be honest, the dark clouds were so far in the distance, on the horizon, I was certain I'd descend before they became a problem. However, I became so lost in thought that I was being swept out over the sea before I even realized how far I'd actually traveled. Then I got into a spot of bother and . . . well, you know the rest."

"The rest, but not all of the before or how you feel about it now."

Normally she took a great deal of pride in her ability to capture someone's rapt attention, but she was rather wishing Langdon would turn his focus elsewhere. Instead, his gaze was thoroughly assessing her as though searching for rips in the fabric of her being, much as she'd searched for tears in the silk of her balloon. Did there have to be a full moon tonight that made her so easy to see? She cleared her throat. "The announcement came as a complete surprise because I was unaware he was even courting anyone. No hints appeared in the gossip columns, so it was a bit of a shock. Did you know he was wooing someone?"

"No."

"As Lady Euphemia Harrington is a dear friend of your sister's, I assume you know her. What can you tell me about her?" She hadn't meant to ask, wasn't interested in others' opinion of the lady. She'd thought she only cared what Hollie believed. Strange to realize she cared a great deal more for Langdon's assessment.

"Her father is the Earl of Wakefield."

She detected a measure of sympathy in his voice. She'd never been comfortable with sympathy, had always believed that receiving it indicated a weakness in herself, a lack of strength when it came to facing the world. And yet from him, it seemed more comforting than it should.

"I've always found her to be agreeable," he continued.

If it wouldn't have started her lip bleeding again,

she would have laughed uproariously. "That's very noncommittal."

"She's very much the opposite of you."

"Upstanding and without sin."

He shook his head. "She blends into the wallpaper, but even wallflowers are worthy of attention. I doubt her name will ever grace a gossip column. Do you love him?"

She was very skilled at reading the messages relayed in men's posture. She'd picked up the talent from Hollie. When they'd first begun their association, whenever they went to a club and wandered through it, he'd pointed to one man or another and asked her what he was conveying without words to his partner or someone else to whom he was speaking.

The language of the body, Marlowe, is always far more honest than the language of words, he'd told her.

And so it was that based on the tightening of Langdon's jaw and the subtle stiffening of his body, he was bracing for a blow. She wished she could climb into her balloon and go up into the sky where it was remarkably quiet and still, so she could decipher why he might react in such a manner. Reading a man's body didn't always allow her to read his mind.

"Quite possibly but not in the way to which you might be . . . alluding. Certainly, I hold a great deal of affection for him, but I'm not *in* love with him."

"Love is love."

"Poppycock. There are as many different facets to love as there are stars in the sky. You should see the stars from a balloon, up above the earth. They are like diamonds strewn across black velvet. They look close enough to pluck."

"You fly at night? You didn't get caught out after dark by accident?"

"Dusk is the best time to go. You can see the magnificence of the sunset from on high. In addition, at night, the wind currents are at their calmest. It's like being surrounded by peace."

"That's what you were looking for. Peace."

Perhaps he was as skilled as she at reading people. "I had always assumed when Hollie met the woman he intended to wed or began a courtship—whether or not it came to fruition—he would seek my opinion on the matter or at least extend the courtesy of letting me know his thoughts were occupied with someone else. I've not seen him in a little over a month, but that's not uncommon when the Season isn't fully underway and he's spending more time at his estate than in London. Still, I can't imagine that he hasn't been pursuing her for some time."

"His talk of another woman wouldn't have made you jealous?"

It should have, shouldn't it? However, she'd never considered him truly hers. He was simply . . . on loan. She liked him well enough, enjoyed his company, but she'd never invested her heart, because she'd known as an earl, he was obligated to marry. While he was perfectly comfortable flaunting her about London, he'd never flaunt her inside a church. She was someone with whom he could have a bit of fun. Not someone to whom he'd have a duty.

"Mistresses don't have the luxury of jealousy," she said, wishing she didn't sound so bitter about it. "So now you know why I made such a poor decision the night of the storm." And why she'd asked to put off her return to London. And then decided it all needed to be faced.

She felt the tears sting her eyes and furiously blinked them back. "Truth be told, I have been melancholy . . . and angry that Hollie hadn't the courage to tell me to my face but had left me to discover his future plans in the newspaper."

"For what it's worth, he should have told you before having the announcement printed."

"Is that what you would have done?"

"If I had a mistress and a similar situation arose."

"You say that now but when it comes to actually facing a woman's hurt or wrath—"

"I'm not a coward."

He said it with such conviction, she had no choice except to believe him. And she was much more interested in discovering things about him than continuing to discuss Hollie's upcoming nuptials. "You mentioned that things don't always have to start with a kiss."

"Did Hollingsworth teach you that they were required?"

"He has his own way of doing things, and he doesn't stray from them."

His fingers went into her hair, and she felt a little tug. In what would be darkness without the moonlight, she couldn't see what he held but it appeared he tossed it aside. And then a few tendrils of her hair fell down to her shoulders.

"Hence, with him, it's always the same," he said, his voice low, speculative as though he was striving to envision what her life in London might entail.

Another tug, more tresses falling.

"When he comes to me, and we stay in, we never stray into uncharted territory. You, my lord, are uncharted territory."

"Does that frighten you?"

Terrifies me. Excites me.

"I think it's important for you to know that while the law does not require that I remain faithful to Hollie—after all, we took no marriage vows, signed no church registry—I have never strayed. However, of late, there has been a discontentment in me"—she squeezed her eyes shut. A discontentment that had only grown since the night at the Twin Dragons— "that I think Hollie has recognized. It may be the reason he made that atrocious wager with you."

She felt his pull on the hairpin, was aware of him tossing it aside. More strands falling. Suddenly she was finding it difficult to breathe. Her body was growing warm.

"I wouldn't have bedded you that night. Although I may have indulged enough to kiss you silly. I like Hollingsworth. But I like you more." Another hairpin was tossed aside, and the rest of her hair tumbled down around her shoulders. Placing his hand between the wayward strands and her neck, he moved the tresses aside and lowered his head. "I wouldn't want to do anything to make you feel . . . tawdry."

Then his mouth, heated and open, was covering her skin, just below her jaw, near her ear. Her knees went weak, and she found herself clutching his upper arms as his hands clamped around her waist and drew her near. "I'm a mistress. I'm supposed to be tawdry."

He growled. "You smell so good. You feel so good. You taste so good. I want to taste more of you."

"I want to taste you."

"Christ." He pulled back and studied her. The moonlight captured the silver of his eyes and turned them molten. They were smoldering with desire.

Hollie had never looked at her that way. It created a burning low in her belly and between her thighs. She knew what Langdon could give her, desperately wanted it. "Although he and I have not yet officially parted ways, I don't see that Hollie could fault me for wanting this, for taking it."

"I would if you were mine." He looked toward the residence, where only a few windows revealed the glow of lamps.

"They were all retiring for the night. I came out here to let you know . . . and got distracted."

"Mother gave you a chamber in the family wing."

"Beside Poppy's room. We'd have to be very quiet."

"The other wing has bedchambers." He lifted her into his arms. "You have until we're nearer the residence to let me know if I turn to the left to deliver you to your bedchamber in the family wing, where you'll sleep alone. Or if I turn to the right, toward the guest wing, where you'll be mine until just before dawn."

As he began striding forward, she circled her tongue around the shell of his ear before whispering, "Turn right. For the love of God, turn right."

Chapter 22

$\mathcal{L}$angdon was not a thief. He'd never taken what belonged to another. If he hadn't learned about Hollingsworth's betrothal, his steps wouldn't be quickening, and he wouldn't now be on the verge of taking this woman as though she belonged to him.

They reached the door that led into the other wing. Without hesitation, she reached down, released the latch, and shoved open the door. He carried her into the entryway that wasn't quite as grand as the one leading into the main portion of the residence. If he continued down the hallway, he'd pass a number of small parlors, reading rooms, and libraries that were available so guests could make themselves at home and have a bit of privacy. He considered going into one and grabbing a bottle of spirits to take with them up the stairs but nothing he drank was going to be as intoxicating as Marlowe.

He crossed over to a table where a lit lamp threw their shadows onto the walls. "Grab that," he ordered her, surprised by the raspiness and fervor he heard in his voice.

She did as he bade. "Wouldn't it be easier if you set me down, so I could walk?"

"I've thought about carrying you like this since the night of the storm." He started up the stairs.

"You did carry me. How else would I have gotten to your bedchamber?"

"Not like this. I carried you as I would a sack of potatoes, over my shoulder. I could have kissed your bum, it was so near."

She released an indignant squeak, and he laughed, definitely glad he'd brought her to the other wing and not to his bedchamber. He had no desire whatsoever to keep her quiet. He wanted her squeals, sighs, and moans. He wanted her calling out his name. He wanted to be surrounded by all the sounds they could elicit together.

If this was to be their only night together, he wanted nothing held back. And if he could convince her to give him many more, he wanted tonight to be the start of it all, to begin as he intended for them to continue.

Having finally reached the landing, he turned into the first bedchamber, kicked the door closed, and set her on her feet. He took the lamp from her and placed it on the nearby dressing table. It revealed a room that was more shadow than light. She was limned by moonlight pouring in through the large window.

If she wasn't still healing, he'd take her in his arms and slash his mouth over hers.

"Would you care for a fire?"

She shook her head. "I have a feeling you're going to be warming me."

"I intend to set you alight."

He heard a rush of breath escape her. "I know I shouldn't be nervous."

He stepped forward until the toes of his boots touched the toes of her slippers. "You have held me enthralled since the first moment I saw you. You have fueled my fantasies."

As if in disbelief, she shook her head. "I'm likely to disappoint, then."

"I very much doubt it."

And he lowered his head.

*S*he didn't know how it had come about, but as he laid his mouth against the curve of her throat, it was hotter than when they'd been outside. Wetter. More intoxicating. Of its own accord, her head dropped back, giving him easier access, as her hands slipped inside his jacket and slid up his chest, over his waistcoat and shirt.

She rather wished they were back on his island, where neither of them would be wearing much in the way of clothing. His mouth trailed down and followed the outline of the path designated by the low cut of her borrowed gown. Her breasts seemed to swell, reaching for his attentions. Her nipples puckered and became far too sensitive, begging for release and not to be flattened against the irritating fabric.

While she suspected he was accustomed to being in control, she couldn't imagine that he wanted a docile coupling from her. He would want an equality between them. To give and to take similarly.

Therefore she didn't hesitate to skim her fingers

along his waistcoat buttons and begin giving them their freedom. She took satisfaction in his encouraging groan. His hands left her as he shrugged out of his coat and then his waistcoat. She unknotted his neckcloth and pulled it free. Then she went to work on the buttons of his shirt. She'd barely seen to three of them before he was tugging his shirt over his head and casting it aside.

He spun her so her back was to him and he draped her hair over one shoulder before he began loosening the lacings on the gown. His mouth took a journey over her nape before he shoved the shoulders of the gown down her arms, then down her body until she was able to step out of it.

Her petticoats and underthings came next until she was soon covered in only moonlight. He placed his hands on her shoulders and slowly turned her around.

In spite of the shadows surrounding them, partly layered over him, she could read the appreciation in his eyes. She thought of all his books. Her memories would be like them, stacked and scattered about, and she'd often return to those from this night, but she thought the way he was looking at her now would always be her favorite moment. She didn't know how anything could make her feel more . . . fancied. She dared not consider *loved* because a woman who had traveled along her path was certain to be denied such an incredible gift. But it didn't mean her own heart wouldn't fall. And she was beginning to fear that where he was concerned, it already had.

"My God, but you are lovely. Perfection."

"You really didn't look the night you found me in the storm?"

"I saw bits. There was no way to avoid it. But not the whole. And the whole is . . . remarkable."

He reached for her, and she jumped back. He stilled, his face suddenly somber. "You've changed your mind?"

"No. Now *I* want to see the whole." She arched a brow. "Although I did get a view of your lovely backside when I awoke on your settee that first night."

He laughed. Deeply, richly. "I had a sense I was being watched."

"But when you turned, the front was already covered so"—she waved a hand impatiently—"get on with it. Show me what I've yet to see."

He dropped into a nearby chair, tugged off his boots, and tossed them aside. He shoved himself to his feet. With arms outstretched, he approached. "You seem to enjoy loosening buttons. Have at mine."

She swallowed hard. *Let him give you what I, of late, have failed to deliver*, Hollie had told her. She'd been frightened then and angry. But hurt, so hurt when Langdon had tossed down his cards, and she'd realized what he'd done. To avoid being with her, she'd thought. Yet here he was, confessing the loveliest of accolades. As she slowly ran her hand up the fall of his trousers, she realized his body was offering its own accolades to her.

He'd wanted her then and he wanted her now. And perhaps in between. And he'd resisted until this moment. And now she was his. Completely. Absolutely. At least for tonight.

These hours she would hold close, the memories to be relived when doubts surfaced and the need to be loved overtook common sense.

Her mother had loved and it had ruined her life. Marlowe certainly wasn't going to make that mistake. She was mistress of her fate.

And for tonight she was Langdon's mistress.

She almost chuckled at the absurdity of her musings, but he was straining against his trousers where her hand had come to rest, his breaths easing in and out in shuddering pants. She didn't know if she'd ever possessed this much power. Oh, certainly, there were swells in London who fell at her feet, who promised her the world if she would leave Hollie to become their mistress.

No one promised what she wanted most: to be loved and respected, to escape her past, to embrace a life that the little girl inside her still innocently believed was possible to possess.

This man had come the closest. Removing her drenched clothing and not gawking sleazily at what was revealed, touching only with permission. Preparing her eggs, bringing her fish, sitting beside her and sewing her balloon. Talking with her about things that didn't involve sex. Looking at her as though he would devour her and make her glad he had.

Pressing her hand more firmly against him, she reached around and squeezed his backside. His eyes closed as he groaned low. "The buttons. You'll like squeezing it with no cloth in the way."

She did laugh then, taking care to open her mouth only a bit, just enough for the sound to escape. She didn't want to delay the cut's healing. Because she *would* get that kiss he'd promised, one way or another.

Her fingers were trembling when she released the first button from its mooring. The next and the next. As the material parted, he sprung free. It was her breath suddenly shuddering. She moved slightly so the lamp could cast its glow over him. She'd long had an appreciation for the male form. His didn't disappoint.

He rid himself of his trousers before drawing her up against his body, his mouth just a whisper over hers as it skimmed down to her breast, his tongue circling her nipple, eager yet gentle, then lapping at her skin before his mouth closed over the sensitive flesh. She wove her fingers through his hair and held his head, keeping him there until she'd had her fill of the sensations.

Languorously, his mouth open, leaving a trail of dew in its wake, he moved to the other breast and gave it the same intense attention. He was masterful, licking, nipping, sucking. All the little sounds she couldn't hold back seemed only to spur him on to lingering and continuing the assault. She cursed her mouth for the injury that would prevent her from teasing him in the same way.

With one hand still on his head, she slid her other one down his ribs, counting as she went, along his flat stomach before wrapping her fingers around heated velvet-covered steel. He groaned low and deep, the sound reverberating through her.

She would not compare him with Hollie, and yet already she knew she would be experiencing something she hadn't before. He was so much more passionate, so much more attuned to her needs.

And then it was as though he'd been dark clouds on the horizon, warning of what was to come, holding himself in check, giving her time to prepare—

Because suddenly it was as if the tempest was upon them, and they were caught in a storm of desire that would leave nothing as it had been.

He swept her into his arms, carried her to the bed, lowered her to the mattress, and followed her down.

"I don't think there is so much as an inch of you that isn't beautiful," he said on a rasp, his hands trailing the length of her, down to her toes and back up. "But you know that already."

"Still, a woman likes to hear it."

"But you are more than your beauty, Marlowe."

He straightened until he was able to hold her gaze with such intensity that it was almost frightening to behold, his palm cupping her jaw. No one had ever looked at her as if his soul was striving to meld with hers, as if where they touched was only wrapping, while the true gift inside was waiting to be revealed. "You intrigue me. Your strength, your daring. Your confidence. I can't imagine you doing much cowering when you realized you'd be overtaken by a storm. I suspect it was the storm cringing when it realized it had you within its grasp."

She laughed lightly but was also deeply touched, and no doubt blushing because of the sort of praise that had never before been heaped on her. She wasn't accustomed to men looking below the surface, and yet it seemed he was an expert at exploring more deeply than most. "I'm not that formidable, I'm afraid."

"You kept your wits about you, well enough to know your clothing was a liability. You did what had to be done, regardless of propriety. I know women who would have swooned at the first stirring of their hair by the wind. Men as well, to be honest."

And then he became the storm.

*L*angdon was accustomed to bedding gorgeous women. Like most men, he had an appreciation for beauty, and he couldn't deny that Marlowe reigned supreme when it came to physical perfection. He suspected most men, being what men were, looked no further than the blue of her eyes, the small nose, the rounded chin, the sharp cheekbones, and the long golden eyelashes. They might not recognize that what made the surface so remarkable was everything within her, like hot springs, where what was hidden bubbled up to make them valuable.

He couldn't be sure that even Hollingsworth realized what he had.

And she brought all her confidence and daring to the bed, matching the intensity of his passion and desire. No passivity with her, and yet he'd known there wouldn't be.

She was fire, molten and scalding, with the most wicked hands that knew where to touch, how to touch, in order to make him beg. "Yes, more, you're driving me mad."

He imagined that if her mouth was healed and

added to her arsenal that he might not have the strength to survive the onslaught of pleasure.

It mattered not where she stroked. Every part of him jumped as though struck by lightning. She left behind sizzling nerve endings. That she was aware of her power over him, relished it, served to enhance the prelude to their eventual joining.

Her skin was silk, gliding over his as positions changed. Rolling to their sides, his back, her straddling him, rubbing her sultry, lavalike core along the length of him, flagrantly teasing the tip of his cock with an introduction to what awaited him between those sweet lips he'd kissed the night before. He knotted his hands into the sheets with the pleasure that engulfed him with so shallow a touch.

He bucked his hips and she lifted hers with a raspy, "Not yet."

He doubted there was a torture device at the Tower of London that could cause more torment than he was presently experiencing. To want with every fiber of his being—to experience excruciating pleasure in the waiting to possess.

With her, even when everything was fast and frenzied, there was a slowness, a savoring . . . a knowing that ultimate indulgence hovered on the horizon. A thunderstorm that couldn't be quieted or tamed. That would have its way with them and make them grateful it had.

Marlowe cursed the split lip. She could take only small nibbles, tiny tastes. But when she touched the tip of her tongue to the head of his cock, he jumped with such force as to nearly throw them both off the bed.

"Have mercy," he ground out.

She lifted her gaze to his, smoldering with such intensity, she was surprised it didn't ignite the room. Never breaking eye contact, she nibbled her way down the length of him, taking so much satisfaction in his strained features that she almost experienced her own release.

Suddenly he grabbed her, tossed her on her back, and settled himself between her thighs. "Two can play at that game."

And then down he went.

With the first stroke of his tongue, a strained whimper escaped and she squeezed her eyes shut. Last night had been the first time she'd ever experienced this particular method of receiving pleasure. She'd never even imagined it, but she supposed her reaction had indicated that she thoroughly enjoyed it. Yet everything with him, even the things she'd experienced multiple times, seemed . . . novel. Perhaps it was the method of his delivery. It was as if he possessed her, owned her, controlled her.

Yet she felt that she did the same with him.

Each striving to ensure the other experienced the ultimate in ecstasy.

And together they ensured they would.

He took hold of her hips and raised them to his feasting mouth, and she very nearly came undone. So many sensations. So deep. So lasting. So incredible.

It was obvious he was enjoying it as well . . . or at least her reaction to it. His moans and groans served to amplify her enjoyment. She was close, so very close.

"Langdon."

Without ceasing his attentions, he captured her gaze.

"I want you inside me when I fall apart."

"Christ." It was more a feral groan than an exclamation.

He pressed a kiss to the inside of one thigh and then to the other before easing up, bracing his arms on either side of her, hovering over her. "Guide me home."

Oh, God. She might not have been able to smile with her mouth but the rest of her grinned with giddiness—like receiving on Christmas morning something she'd been lusting after all year. She wrapped her fingers around him, angled her hips, and brought him to the cusp—

With a tortured groan, he slid deeply into her and stilled, as though savoring the closeness achieved. She wrapped her legs around that incredible backside of his, squeezed.

And then they were moving in tandem. Him thrusting, her meeting those thrusts with equal fervor. The pleasure building, rapidly climbing to impossible heights—

Untethered, she soared, crying out, tightening her hold on him. His guttural groan echoed around her as his back arched with his final thrust.

Breathing heavily, he lowered himself to his

elbows, buried his face in the curve of her shoulder, and pressed a kiss to her damp, and still singing, flesh.

*H*e was resting on his back, Marlowe draped over him. She'd thought she was a woman of the world, and yet he was teaching her things, showing her things, making her feel things she'd never imagined possible. She'd never realized what she lacked in education.

"There's a hell of a lot about being with you, Marlowe, that I've not experienced with another woman. I'm trying to convince myself that it's an illusion because it's been months since I've been with anyone." She was very much aware of him going so still she wasn't certain he was even breathing. "But I don't think that's it."

He shifted them both until they were lying side by side, facing each other. He threaded his fingers through her hair, resting the heel of his hand against her jaw. His voice was low, sounding almost confused. "I do know I don't want to take you back to Hollingsworth."

She knew she didn't want him to take her back. But neither did she want him to ask her to be his mistress, and she suspected it was all he would offer. He was decent and proper; his family was decent and proper. And she was anything but.

"I don't suppose"—he closed his eyes, opened them, and held her gaze—"you'd consider becoming my mistress? I would give you twice whatever he gives you. A larger residence, more servants, a more generous allowance."

Why did it hurt so bloody much to have her suspicions confirmed? From the moment Hollie had taken her in, she'd worked to be flamboyant, eccentric, noticed. And she had succeeded beyond her wildest imaginings. Unfortunately, she'd also managed to create a trap for herself. She had taken what Hollie needed her to be, embraced it proudly, refusing to cower before those who looked at her with disdain, as though she had fecal matter spread over her face.

Only Langdon wasn't looking at her with disdain. He was looking at her with something akin to hope and woven within it were need and passion.

But being invited into his parents' residence had awoken something within her, something she'd forced into the farthest corners of her mind, where it could remain dormant. However, tonight it was lumbering through her thoughts like a brown bear disturbed from its hibernation. And it was hungry. For all the things she'd been told she'd have when she grew up: a lordly husband, children, love. But she wouldn't attain them with Langdon. She would be to him as she was to Hollie: something to be taken out on occasion and flaunted.

"I should probably make my way to my bedchamber now to avoid getting caught later."

She started to roll over, but he stayed her with a hand on her shoulder. Why did it have to be so hard, so large, so powerful?

"I take it the answer is no," he said somberly.

She gazed at him over her shoulder. "I don't know that I want to be another man's mistress."

"Even knowing how things would be between us?"

"Is that what this was? An audition?"

"No." He abruptly sat up, the sheets falling to his hips, his upper torso bared. How she wanted to run her fingers over every inch. Had she no pride? "No," he repeated. "But if you can have something wondrous with me . . ."

His voice trailed off, his expression a bit thunderstruck and confused, as though he suddenly found himself immerged in a quagmire, the mud pulling him under, and he had no idea how it was he found himself in such a dire predicament.

"Everything isn't always about sex," she said quietly. She shifted and scooted until she was sitting up with her back pressed to a bedpost at the foot of the bed. "Three years ago, when I was nineteen, the thought of being a courtesan sounded exotic, bold, and daring. But it came at a cost I'd not considered. I'm no longer content, and I don't yet know what will make me so. But I know I won't find it with you, as your mistress. And you can't have me any other way, can you?"

He looked away, shifted his position, like someone who'd been given a problem to decipher and was without the means to work it out. She knew the truth: if they'd been in London his family never would have welcomed her into their home. But this place, so far away from everything, was safe for doing what one ought not.

"I'm weary, Langdon. Is there a trick to getting to my bedchamber from here or do I just go out the way we came?"

"We can get there easily from here. I'll escort you. But at least let me hold you until dawn."

Chapter 23

The hours without monstrous rain were hardly sufficient for the roads to dry out completely. Hence the journey to London was a bit rough, with Langdon's carriage bouncing more than it would have on a dry path. Although it seemed not to affect in the least the gentleman sitting across from her. Langdon barely moved as the coach swayed. While in contrast, on several occasions, Marlowe found herself curling her hands over the edge of the bench seat upon which she sat, clutching it, holding on for dear life, just as she'd held on to her balloon in the storm, just as she'd held on to Langdon last night when ecstasy engulfed her. Just like she wanted to clutch him again.

The sun had just begun creeping over the horizon when they'd returned to their respective bedchambers with no one else the wiser.

Marlowe had considered slipping into bed for a couple hours of sleep since most of her night had involved short increments of dozing off woven between wild frenzies of lovemaking. Mistresses weren't made love to. Neither were whores.

However, she couldn't help but believe that was what had passed between them each time they came together. She didn't know if she could claim to love him—love was an emotion she'd been determined to never feel because it made her too vulnerable. Love had clouded her mother's judgment, because surely she should have insisted upon some proof her husband was who and what he'd claimed to be. On the other hand, why would she have ever suspected a lie?

Still, Marlowe hadn't returned to bed, because they'd both agreed they needed to begin the journey as early as possible.

She was now wearing one of his sister's traveling frocks, along with all the various accoutrements that went with it. She desperately missed wearing only his shirt, enjoying all the freedoms that came with it. At the moment, her breathing was restricted; she was wrapped in a cocoon. No, not *a* cocoon, but several. The undergarments, the outer garments, even the coach had her hemmed in, so she couldn't move about freely.

All she could do was watch him watching her, as if things needed to be said but were too dangerous to utter. Confessions that would make the parting all the more challenging.

Strangely, she'd found it difficult to say farewell to his family. They'd joined them for breakfast. How the legs of the sideboard didn't snap with the weight of all the food spread out over it was beyond her imagining. By the time they were finished eating, the coach had been readied and was waiting for them, the yards of cloth that made up the envelope secured to the roof of the coach. She imagined how brilliant, bright, and colorful they appeared traveling through the countryside.

If they had any hope at all of not being noticed when they reached her terrace home, they would need to arrive beneath the cover of night. Like thieves. Which was how she felt. As though she'd stolen something precious—time with Langdon— and needed to return it. However, that was an impossibility. All those minutes were now part of her memories, to be hoarded away.

Looking out the window, she noted the sky— with fluffy white clouds dotting it here and there—was a serene blue, completely opposite to the tempest of emotions roiling through her. So tempted to accept his offer of becoming his mistress. So aware that it would bring misery because at some point he would have to take a wife. Would he discuss the selections with her? Would she discover who it was because of a notice in the *Times*? Would they part ways? Or would he lead two very different lives? One with her? One with another? While she couldn't remain mistress to a married man, could she let him go?

"A ride in a balloon isn't nearly as choppy as your convenience," she said teasingly, striving to rid them of the somberness that seemed to be traveling with them within the confines of the coach. "Presently I feel as though I'm bobbing along on the crest of waves."

"I could ask the driver to slow but he worries

we'll get mired in the mud if he goes at too leisurely a pace. I imagine he is as much an expert at driving this conveyance as you are at handling yours."

At his acknowledgment of her skills, she cursed the corset for preventing her from inhaling deeply and thrusting out her chest with pride. "I wish I could take you up someday. I always feel as though I'm made . . . of air." She gave an awkward chuckle. "It's impossible to describe."

"I don't know if I'd like having you made of air. I like you solid. I like the way my hand curls around the side of your waist or the nape of your neck. I like the silkiness of your hair running through my fingers. I like the weight of your breast in my palm."

How differently would any of that feel, for her, for him, if they were among the clouds? Would she continue to experience the weightlessness she was accustomed to when caught in a stream of air? Or would he keep her anchored to the earth, even when she was above it?

Now he was the one looking out the window and she knew it was because he'd conjured up images of what had transpired between them last night. She'd halfway hoped that once they were beyond sight of anyone, he'd cross over and take her into his arms. That they would do on this bench what they'd done in his bed.

She didn't think the cut on her lip would split and bleed if she gave him a generous, come-hither smile, but she couldn't be sure. Yet a hundred times she'd thought about testing it. She didn't want to leave him without experiencing his kiss, and yet she had the uncomfortable sensation that his kiss, more than making love, would make it harder, nearly impossible, to leave him.

But the harsh reality was that she didn't want to be his mistress. She feared what she wanted was to be his wife. His viscountess, the mother of his children. His partner in all things.

It was full on night by the time they finally crossed into London. Marlowe could sense the miles they'd traveled increasing and the ones to be traveled decreasing. Like sand through an hourglass, their time together was drifting away.

During the days and nights since they'd begun the journey, occasionally they'd stopped at a tavern or inn for a meal and a change of horses. But they'd never taken rooms anywhere. Instead, they'd stayed on the road. Lighting lanterns to guide them through the darkness when it had arrived.

Perhaps Langdon had determined it was the only way to ignore the desire rampaging through them.

She wouldn't see him again after tonight. She *couldn't* see him again after tonight. It would be too difficult. She suspected he was mulling over similar thoughts, because a few times she'd noted him studying her lips to such an extent that she was relatively certain he could have perfectly sketched them. With the tip of her tongue, she pushed at the inside corner of her mouth, where the gash was healing. She grimaced and cursed at the discomfort. Was it ever not going to hurt when she applied pressure to it? Was she going to go the remainder of her life without fully knowing his kiss?

"Does it still hurt?" he asked quietly, and she

wondered if within the dim confines, he'd been able to see her testing it.

"I'm afraid so. I'm beginning to think it might have needed stitches."

"You've seen my handiwork. It would have no doubt left a horrendous scar."

"I'll pay a visit to my physician tomorrow."

"Scoot over."

She did as he bade, then watched his shadowy form cross over to sit beside her. She shifted slightly to more squarely face him, not at all surprised when his warm and slightly chafed palm cradled the side of her face that had escaped bruising. Without any thought at all, she found herself leaning into it, a puppy seeking a petting.

Or a woman who had traded passion for security.

Although the path she was currently on wasn't exactly what she'd wanted either.

It had taken a brush with death to teach her that lesson. When the hour of her demise had been upon her, snippets from her life had passed before her in a slow unwinding. Very few had brought her satisfaction or joy. They'd left her feeling miserable and alone, so very alone, and crying out to the heavens, *Not yet!*

Who would remember her when she was gone? Who would mourn? What evidence of her existence would remain when she was no longer about to serve as a reminder?

She placed her hand over his, where it rested against her cheek, turned her head into it, and pressed the gentlest of kisses against his palm. She didn't know exactly why she'd done it. Perhaps as a demonstration that a whisper of a kiss was better than no kiss at all.

He could hold himself in check. Their mouths could come together. They could go slowly, lightly, testing the waters, increasing their zeal—

"Be my mistress, and I'll pay off your father's debt," he said somberly, a mourner speaking at a wake. It felt like her heart stopped for a second or two before carrying on with pumping blood through her body. She'd gone as cold as ice but now the heat of embarrassment was flooding her. "All of your allowance will be yours to do with as you please."

She wondered if he'd been pondering this notion during the entire journey, if he'd been considering what his life would entail with her and what it would without her. The same sort of thoughts had been tumbling through her mind.

"But you won't be exclusively mine, will you?" she asked, nearly losing the battle to keep her voice steady, to give no hint to the turmoil swirling within her, a tempest with the strength to engulf ships and deliver them to the bottom of the sea. "You're a viscount who will one day become an earl. You have a duty to marry, to provide an heir. How many mornings will I awaken to find you in my bed, in my arms? How many nights will I wait in vain for you to come to me? How long will you stay in my company? How long before the only thing between us is fornication?"

"*I* won't marry for a few more years." He was taken aback by his tone threaded with desperation.

He didn't want to voice aloud that she could leave him then, find another protector, do as she pleased. He wasn't certain he'd ever be ready for her to be with someone else.

But the disgrace that would arise if he were to marry her . . .

His parents had survived scandal, but it had taken a toll on them, their children.

The coach was slowing. They were in London proper now. She would be with him only a little while longer.

She hadn't responded to his earlier statement, and he assumed it was because it didn't matter. A few years together wasn't worth the heartbreak that would follow. Arrogant of him to think she would find the parting as hellish as he would.

The glow from streetlamps eased in and out of the conveyance, casting her in a different light each time. So many facets to her. During the short time they'd been together, he'd been able to explore only a few of them, when he desperately wanted to explore them all, every single aspect of her. He might possibly need a lifetime to study them all.

"We're almost there," she said.

Looking past her, he could see the residences. No shops, no taverns, no pubs. Only dwellings lined up, side by side. He would soon be without her, the realization nearly unbearable.

As light as a whisper, he touched his lips to hers. The kiss was neither passionate nor fiery. He didn't urge her to open her mouth to him. Yet, he didn't know if any kiss had ever branded him more. With his thumb, he stroked her unmarred cheek, while his mouth lingered on hers.

He didn't want to consider all the kisses they'd never share. All the nights, all the days. All the smiles and laughter that would not be theirs.

Aware of the coach coming to a stop, he pulled back, his gaze holding hers. They were so near to a streetlamp that he could see her clearly. Her eyes shone with a brightness. Not tears, surely.

Releasing his hold on her, he slipped his fingers beneath his neckcloth, located the chain that held the St. Christopher medallion, and dragged it over his head. "For your future travels," he said as he draped it around her neck.

He heard a tiny mewl, almost painful. She closed a hand around the disk. "I'll treasure it."

"Should you ever need me—"

"I won't."

Crossing over in front of her, he shoved open the door, leapt out, and handed her down. His footman was already at the top of the short steps, handing off the balloon to her butler.

"Take care of yourself, Langdon," she said flatly.

He watched her until she disappeared into her residence.

Chapter 24

Although she never turned around, never so much as glanced back, she was keenly aware of his gaze following her movements. When she passed over the threshold, closed the door, and slumped against it, she could still sense him standing there, waiting.

She wondered if he was holding his breath as she was. Until her chest ached with the need for fresh air.

She was still standing there when her butler returned after taking her balloon someplace out of the way.

"Will there be anything else, madam?"

"No" came out on a croak, most likely because she wanted to utter a different response. Because there was something else she wanted, but it was futile to ask him for what he hadn't the power to give her.

Love.

Through the oak, she heard the distant slamming of a coach door, quickly followed by the clomping of horses' hooves and the whir of wheels. In all these years, she'd never been angry at her father. She'd been dumbfounded, confused by his actions. Most assuredly, she'd hated what her mother had been forced to endure.

But in her mind's eye, memories of him had never been tainted. He'd always remained the loving father, the one who lifted her onto his shoulders when she grew tired of walking or needed to see into the distance during the village's annual fete. He was the one who had shown her the world from on high.

I lay the world at your feet, he'd once told her just before he'd hugged her close and laughed.

She'd always believed his laughter to have come about because of joy and love. But she was having a difficult time at the moment not hearing his words as anything except a horrendous joke, his laughter a sinister foreshadowing of a life that stole away dreams rather than granting them.

Belatedly, she realized her butler still stood at attention, scrutinizing her, striving to determine how to be useful. For surely, it had to be apparent that something was amiss with her. She suspected he was trying to determine exactly how much he could pry before he'd be stepping over a line that separated servant from mistress of the household.

"Have the balloon spread out in my study." She wanted to ensure she hadn't missed any tears. Lie. She wanted to run her fingers over Langdon's needlework. "And please see to it that a bath is prepared."

With tasks in hand, he visibly relaxed, all the

air seeping out of him as it did the envelope when the balloon needed to return to earth. "Very good, madam."

She might have chuckled at the swiftness with which he departed, but she wasn't certain if she'd ever laugh again.

Trudging up the stairs in her gaslit residence, she found herself comparing the trek to one recently made on darkened stairs where she'd needed a lamp to guide her. How uneven the steps were, but how full of character they seemed. It was ridiculous to miss them, to regret that she'd never again climb them.

In her bedchamber, she stood before the cheval glass, hardly recognizing the woman reflected back at her. It wasn't the cuts, scrapes, or dark blue bruises. It was the light gray frock, with buttons done up to her throat. Within her wardrobe was no frock to match it in portraying innocence or virtue. Everything had been designed to reveal, while not slipping into the area of obscenity. It seemed odd to have so much of her covered and hidden away.

Her discomfiture served as further proof that she wasn't meant for Langdon's world.

She wandered over to the window. The draperies were drawn aside. Gazing out on her streetlamp-lit surroundings, she found herself wishing she was looking out on the blue water, turbulent or calm. That she could hear the wind whistling through ancient cracks. That she could reach down and pick up a book from an ungainly stack.

Why was it that after only a few days she could be missing so much? Langdon most of all.

God, not even an hour had passed, and already

she had so many things she wanted to discuss with him.

A knock sounded. Her bathwater. But before she could bid the servant to enter, Hollie was strolling into the chamber.

"Where have you— What the devil happened to your face?" Quickening his step, he reached her, gently took hold of her chin with his thumb and forefinger, and tilted her head this way and that, striving to take note of all the injuries. They looked worse than they had that first night. The lump on her head had flattened, but below her eye now was a dark bruise. Blood draining down, no doubt. "Did someone attack you?"

True depth of concern echoed through his voice.

"Mother Nature, I'm afraid. When did you return to London?"

"Yesterday. I tried to get here sooner but the rain slowed me down."

"Yet your announcement in the *Times* had no difficulty winging its way to an editor's desk."

With a grimace, he released his hold on her and stepped back. "I was hoping to get here before you saw that."

She lowered herself to the chair by the window and indicated the one opposite her. "Tell me about Lady Euphemia."

Ignoring the chair she'd indicated, he leaned against the wall, his shoulder digging into the edge of the window as though he was striving to punish himself, because while she had tried to speak flatly, she was aware the tiniest sliver of hurt had edged its way along her tone. And he'd noted it.

"Have you seen a surgeon?" he asked, ignoring her previous request.

"I'm not in need of a physician. I have only scrapes and bruises."

"I came by to see you yesterday. Your butler said you'd gone up in your balloon and had yet to return." He looked out the window. "I was afraid . . . afraid you might have suffered your father's fate."

"I don't know his fate."

His gaze came back to her. "Which is all the worse. I feared I might never know what happened to you, might never see you again."

He looked diminished and indeed fearful. She knew he cared about her, but she'd never felt any emotion containing much depth coming from him. They were cordial toward each other. Certainly from him, she'd never experienced the fire that raged within Langdon.

Hollie was a few inches shorter, his shoulders not as broad. And bless the man, he didn't have much of an arse. Three of his front teeth overlapped each other, which gave him a bit of a boyish look. His nose was too wide for his face, his lips too thin. But she'd never minded that he wasn't classically handsome. He'd always been kind and introduced her to new experiences.

His hair was nearly white, but she didn't think it was prematurely lacking in color. His sister's, from what Marlowe remembered of her visits to the modiste, was the same shade. He'd never introduced her to any family members, hadn't really introduced Marlowe to his sister. She'd never been to any of his residences, so had never seen portraits of any of his ancestors. In truth, they'd never shared much beyond the surface of their lives.

She'd told him about her interest in ballooning because of her father and how he'd never returned from one of his flights, but she'd certainly never confessed how he'd managed to convince an entire village that he was an earl. Why had she told Langdon?

It had seemed so natural to share so much of her past with him.

"I crashed into the sea, near an island that was inhabited. I was rescued."

His brow furrowed. "Which island?"

She shook her head. "I don't believe it had a name."

"The inhabitants must have called it something."

"Inhabitant. There was only one. Lord Langdon."

Blinking, he eased away from the window edge. "You were with Langdon?"

"He was a perfect gentleman." Perfect, at least. The gentleman part might be up for debate. "As you are well aware, since you offered me to him, he has no interest in me." A little lie because what had passed between them was for her and her alone to hold dear and reminisce about from time to time.

"I don't know why he switched out his cards that night—perhaps because he *is* a gentleman—but he was definitely interested," Hollie assured her.

"Did you offer me to him because you knew a betrothal was on your horizon?"

"The way you two looked at each other . . . I fairly came away from that table scorched. Hence, I decided where was the harm in letting you test the waters. Magnanimous of me, I thought. Perhaps when the time comes, he'll be your protector."

"I don't think we'd suit." To have him for only a little while when she wanted him forever. Had she known that becoming Hollie's mistress would have prevented her from having Langdon into eternity, she wouldn't have become a mistress. But had she never become a mistress, she'd have never met him. Oh, the ironies of life. "As for when the time comes, it's now, Hollie."

With a brisk nod, he finally lowered himself to the chair. "I really did want to get to you before the announcement appeared. Her family was quick to see it done. I suppose they wanted to ensure I didn't back out, or if I did, they could sue me. As for your inquiry"—he gave her a wry smile—"she's very timid, my Effie."

The depth of affection surrounding the name took Marlowe by surprise. She'd no idea that Hollie could feel so strongly about anything. "You love her."

He nodded. "I have for years. She is so lovely, Marlowe, and she comes with a substantial dowry. Not that I care about the dowry, but I knew it would mean competition for her hand. At first, I had to patiently wait for her coming out, which occurred two years ago. Far more handsome chaps than I were calling on her."

"There's nothing amiss with your features, Hollie. Why should looks matter anyway?"

"Easy enough for a beautiful woman to say."

"I believe I'm going to have a few scars, but I think they add character. So she's pretty, has a good dowry, and is timid. What else do you like about her?"

"She's kind, sweet." He studied her a moment. "I assume you were angry when you saw the announcement."

"Not angry. Surprised you hadn't told me about her." And a bit hurt.

"It seemed in bad form to discuss the woman I love with my mistress."

"But I always thought we were friends of a sort. Weren't we?"

"Yes. Which I suppose is the reason you aren't currently throwing things at me."

"Have you ever known me to throw something?"

He shook his head. "Although I do think you're a bit hasty in being done with me."

"It would prove awkward if we tried to carry on as we had been. You have someone now to whom you should owe your allegiance."

Letting that hang in the air between them for a minute, she wondered if he regretted having taught her how a woman could have power in a relationship. Not with all the sexual ploys she knew some mistresses used, but with a steel spine and steadfast gaze. She'd taken control from the beginning, vowing aloud that she wouldn't be the cause of his betrayal to a pledge. At the time, she'd meant a marriage oath but before the storm had tossed her about like a child's toy, she'd come to the conclusion that a betrothal was a commitment that meant just as much. At least to her.

And he'd shown her that her feelings were as important as his.

Eventually our time together will come to an end, and I don't want to worry that some gent is taking advantage of your good humor, he'd told her in the beginning. *When you leave me, you will do so with power to wield. You will be a queen, in a position to select your own lover. He will bend the knee, grateful to have been chosen as your consort.*

Hollie had always been flamboyant with his goals, and she suspected the timid Lady Euphemia would one day have more confidence and daring than most of the ladies of the *ton.*

"You learned your lessons well," he said with a bit of pique, and she suspected he'd been trying to get to London before the announcement landed on her doorstep because he was hoping for one more coming together. She might have gifted him with it if she hadn't fallen in love with Langdon.

That thought struck her so hard that she nearly doubled over. She did love him. It was the reason she couldn't be his mistress, the reason giving him over to another woman would tear her apart—and needle and thread would not repair the damage.

She realized those feelings were going to create a problem for her. He'd spoiled her, ruining not only Hollie, but any other man for her.

"I had a good teacher," she teased, determined not to let Hollie discern how much she was hurting. "When are you marrying?"

"December. She wants a Christmas wedding. I shall, of course, continue to pay the lease on this residence until the end of the Season. That should grant you plenty of time to find a replacement for me."

"No one could ever replace you, Hollie."

"That's kind of you to say, but then you always were kind, Marlowe. You were good for my pride. That I should have a beauty such as you . . ."

While she'd always suspected he'd valued her appearance above all else, she now had it confirmed. *You are more than your beauty*, Langdon had told her. And he'd made her feel whole, as though all of her mattered.

"I wish you every happiness, Hollie."

"You're not quite done with me, Marlowe. I intend to escort you about and ensure all these randy gents know you are still under my protection and guidance." He twisted his mouth. "We'll be a little more discreet, however, as I shouldn't like to make the gossip columns."

She didn't bother to ask if he'd introduce her to Euphemia, because she was aware that sort of thing simply wasn't done. She realized far too much of his life hadn't involved her. Living on the periphery was a price a mistress paid. It hadn't seemed so high with Hollie, but with Langdon—

Every time she thought perhaps she could be his mistress, she considered how much it would hurt when a night such as this came, when they spoke so politely to each other, without any fire or passion, when—

The knock interrupted her thoughts.

"That will be water for my bath," she told Hollie, hoping he could hear in her voice that he would soon be dismissed. There had been a time when he'd enjoyed watching her bathe and she'd enjoyed him watching, but not tonight. Tonight she would no doubt be thinking of pewter eyes watching her. "Come," she called out to the servant.

Her butler walked in, holding something white and folded on his outstretched hands, like someone presenting a crown on a pillow to a queen. "The maids were unrolling the balloon as you requested when one ran across this shirt, madam. We weren't quite sure what you would have us do with it."

He arrived at her side, and she took his offering as though it was made of handblown glass and might shatter if not treated with the utmost care. It was wrinkled from its journey. Still, she held it to her nose and inhaled. It wasn't the one she'd been wearing. It smelled not of her, but of him. When had he placed it in the folds of the balloon? How had he managed—

Why was she even questioning its placement? A man who had mastered sleight of hand when it came to cards could surely manipulate other things without being detected. Just as he'd manipulated her heart.

She didn't know whether to laugh or cry at his absurd gift, but her eyes took the choice from her as tears began to well. She pressed the shirt to her face in order to capture the tears and stifle the sob.

"Marlowe?" She was aware of Hollie's nearness, his hand on her knee. "Darling, whatever's wrong?"

Vigorously shaking her head, she knew he would think her mad if she explained that she'd be wearing this shirt to bed for the remainder of her life.

Chapter 25

"Sophie, do you ever think about giving up this way of living?"

Marlowe was sitting in her own parlor, sipping tea—even mistresses could appear civilized—with one of her dear friends who was also a mistress and lived on Mistress Row.

"It is the only life in which I have Sheridan." She and the earl had been together for several years now. "Why are you, of a sudden, discontent with what we have achieved?"

"It's not that I'm discontent with it. It's just that I wonder if I might find more satisfaction elsewhere. Hollie is getting married, so if I am ever going to begin anew, now is the time."

Sophie wasn't much older than Marlowe, and yet she had a tendency to look at the world through a vast array of experiences. "Who is it you want?"

Marlowe knew she shouldn't have been surprised that Sophie had managed to discern someone else occupied Marlowe's thoughts these days.

She shook her head. "It's moot. I couldn't be happy with only part of his life and it's all he'd offer."

Sophie gave her a melancholy smile. "I have found part to be better than none at all."

During the week that had passed since she'd seen Langdon, she'd debated that very question— was a portion better than nothing? She'd even written up a list outlining all the advantages and disadvantages to both part and nothing. Nothing always won.

Yesterday morning she'd almost decided she could be content with a little. Until she'd sat down to breakfast, opened the newspaper that her butler dutifully ironed and placed beside her plate each morning, and been greeted with gossip concerning Lord Langdon waltzing with one of this year's new crop of debutantes. She'd felt ill, feared she was going to cast up her accounts then and there. How could she possibly invite him into her bed, knowing a time would come when after he left her, he'd invite his wife into his bed. Or perhaps he'd go to hers. Marlowe knew jealousy would eat her alive.

But she had also come to the conclusion that she was entitled, deserving, of the whole of a man's heart, not merely a section of it. Although, truth be told, she didn't know if she held any of his.

"Can you afford to leave behind all that your hard-earned status as a man's fantasy has gained you?" Sophie asked. "You could have anyone you wanted, demand more of him."

Ah, there was the rub. She had yet to pay back all of her father's debts. Those who were owed would harass her mother if Marlowe didn't make monthly payments. With her scandalous reputation, who in London would hire her? She'd earn less than a pittance if she went elsewhere. And anyone who knew of her behavior was certain to take liberties.

She had followed this path because it solved so many of her problems. To walk away from what she had managed to accomplish would be foolish indeed.

*T*wo weeks. It had been two weeks since Langdon had enjoyed a peaceful sleep, since he'd dropped Marlowe off at her residence.

Sitting in a plush leather chair in the library of the Twin Dragons, he slowly sipped his scotch and wondered if she'd yet discovered the shirt he'd left for her hidden within the folds of the balloon. He didn't know why he'd done it.

Like an idiot, that night at the family estate, after she'd taken her bath and changed into a gown for dinner, he hadn't thought to ask a servant to bring him the shirt she'd been wearing. The next morning it would have been laundered and placed in his room, waiting for a future visit. He had nothing of hers to serve as a reminder of the time they'd been together. As though he needed any token when he could recall every minute.

With things truly over between her and Hollingsworth, she'd need a consort. While she had rejected his offers, now that some days—and nights—had passed, perhaps she'd reconsider.

He scoffed, louder than he'd intended, catching the attention of a gent who was sitting nearby reading a newspaper. Langdon gave him an apologetic nod before sipping more of his scotch.

Since his return to London, before tonight, he hadn't even stepped foot in the more respectable areas of the club because he'd recognized there was always a chance that he might pass Marlowe on a nearby street. Or that she could emerge out of the alleyway and cross his path as he bounded up the steps for the front door.

It was even possible she might be seen within the respectable portion of the establishment. Hollingsworth had spared no expense when it came to his mistress's wardrobe and Marlowe was clothed as finely as a queen. The gossip columnists had recently commented on her attire, noting that this Season's gown didn't seem quite as risqué as those of the past. But most of the ink devoted to her had revealed that London's most notorious courtesan was not in fact a brunette as everyone had been led to believe but was a blonde. Oh, the scandal of it all.

He'd been glad to learn that perhaps she was being more herself, that she wasn't catering to Hollingsworth's whims. However, he knew her well enough now to know that she never had. If she didn't want to do what he asked of her, she wouldn't.

Sipping his scotch, he contemplated his choices. Go to the main gaming area where he could flirt with spinsters, debutantes, and wives. And on the morrow he might see his name associated with someone, a hint of interest remarked on, but it would be all speculation and rumor. Just as had happened when he'd recently attended a ball.

Or he could go to the hidden-away portion of the establishment where he might cross paths with her.

But if she wanted more from Langdon, would she have not said, would she have not sent word? She might not know where he resided, but his parents' residence was no secret. She had to be aware that she could always get in touch with him there.

Did he ever cross her mind?

He couldn't stop thinking about her. He'd been home only two days when he'd sent her a copy of *Sense and Sensibility* with a note, *Happy Endings.* Even if they were not destined to find one together, he did wish she would have her own. He didn't identify who had sent it. She either knew or she didn't. Four days later, he'd had delivered to her a barometer. *For safer travels among clearer skies.* Again, no identifier. However, with it, he had included instructions regarding how she could use it to avoid storms in the future. It had been a selfish gift. He'd rather she not go up at all, but he had no desire to deny her any joy. Which was the reason he was keeping his distance. Because with him, she would no doubt eventually have regrets one way or—

A shadow loomed, the light from the chandeliers blocked. He looked up. Gave a brisk nod. "Hollingsworth."

The earl smiled slightly and dropped into the chair opposite him. "Langdon."

"I hear felicitations are in order."

"You heard that from my mistress, no doubt. She tells me you were instrumental in saving her from nature's fury."

"Having come to know her a little better, I very much doubt that nature is her equal, and hence my role in her rescue was minimal at best."

Hollingsworth tapped his fingers on the arm of the chair. "I suppose you're aware she and I will be ending our association."

"I've heard rumors."

"Even now she is searching in earnest to replace me. She's holding court here, auditioning men in the secret rooms that really aren't so secret."

The thought of other men touching her, performing for her, set Langdon's teeth on edge and caused his gut to tighten.

Hollingsworth shook his head. "Young swells are attempting to beguile her. However, I suspect, Langdon, she's yours if you want her."

He wondered what all she had told Hollingsworth. If Langdon was the jealous sort, he might resent her relationship with the earl. Hell, he was the jealous sort.

How could he not want her?

"I asked. She said no."

Perhaps she had sensed that he was broken.

He thought about how diligently she'd worked to repair her balloon, how she'd likened the patching up she'd done, the meticulous stitching, to creating scars and how she'd found no fault with them. He had scars that weren't visible but ran far more deeply.

Would she find fault with them?

"You never struck me as the sort to give up easily."

"I won't force her to take a path she doesn't truly want."

"You think she truly wants any of those swells who are presently trying to woo her?"

God, he hoped not. He could think of no one worthy of her.

"How did you manage it?"

Hollingsworth jerked a bit, like he'd been taken off guard. "Manage what precisely, old chap?"

"Spend so much time with her and not fall in love with her?"

The earl glanced around before leaning forward slightly and arching a brow. "Who says I didn't? At least some. But my heart has always been occupied elsewhere."

Which rankled. She deserved someone who would be devoted to her.

"You should have told her you were on the verge of becoming betrothed."

"I know. I have chastised myself repeatedly for any hurt I caused her. Tell her you will handle the matter better when the time comes. It might make a difference if you reassure her that you won't be a scapegrace like me." He slapped his thighs. "Well, I'd best get back to her," Hollingsworth said, coming to his feet. "Until she's replaced me, I'm still her protector. If you find yourself interested in a game of cards, come find me. I'll make the same wager as before. If you win, you'll have an opportunity to make your case. Only a fool would turn down such an offer. You've never struck me as a fool."

"As long as I have a face, you shall always have a place upon which to perch."

Marlowe fought to keep her features neutral and to swallow back the guffaw that desperately wanted to escape. She'd had far worse words—meant to entice—thrown her way this evening, but for some reason these suddenly seemed the most ridiculous.

The young man, who couldn't have been much older than her own twenty-two years, leaned forward expectantly. "You do know to what I am referring."

"What I know, my lord, is that we would not suit."

"But . . . but . . . shouldn't you at least invite me into your bed to be sure? I have a most impressive cock."

"I've no doubt. It seems to be the only kind present here tonight. Nevertheless, since I recommend you continue your search for a suitable bedmate elsewhere"—she wasn't the only woman in attendance tonight searching for a less fleeting arrangement that would be beneficial to two parties; she was however the most popular and well-known—"allow me to offer you a bit of advice. While bedding is a large part of having a mistress, it is not the most important part. Consider how you would get along when you're not in bed."

He blinked. Blinked. Blinked. Narrowed his eyes. Furrowed his brow. Tilted his head like a dog suddenly alert. "You like being taken against the wall, then?"

Oh, dear Lord. Hopeless. This one was utterly hopeless. She patted his cheek like he was an errant schoolboy. "Continue your search."

She whipped around and nearly ran into another prospective lover. It was so easy to tell because their eyes held such expectation. His were glittering with merriment. He was on the other side of thirty if he was a day.

"Your beauty is beyond compare

"Whether black or blond be your hair.

"I invite you into my lair

"Where I shall spoil you with utmost care."

Well, that was unexpected and almost lovely.

He flashed a broad, cocky grin, took her hand, and pressed his lips to her gloved knuckles. "Marlowe, I should like very much to replace Hollingsworth in your esteem."

At least he was a bit less flagrant and full of sexual innuendos than many of the scallywags who'd approached her tonight. "Lord Chadbourne. I should think your wife wouldn't be particularly pleased with that arrangement."

When it came to gathering information on men, the gossip sheets were her friend.

His smile faltered a bit. "Ours was not a love match."

"Regardless, it gives me pause to consider an intimate relationship with someone who has not yet mastered the art of keeping a vow. Nor do I fancy causing a wife distress when she reads her husband's name associated with mine in the gossip columns. As I'm sure you're aware, I'm quite often a favorite subject of the gossipmongers."

He leaned nearer. "I have found that keeping a relationship secret adds a thrill to the entire association. Sneaking about can be jolly good fun."

It was moments like this when she wished there were a universal law of mistresses that they all had to adhere to. She truly didn't believe that a marriage license should be required for a woman to engage in sexual relations but that didn't mean she lacked a moral code. She decided with this gent she needed to be blunt. "I don't take married men as lovers."

"Why limit yourself?"

Hadn't she already explained? Therefore, he was either a man who didn't listen or he believed a woman's words were of no consequence.

She felt a hand come to rest against her lower back. Hollingsworth. Strange how she'd never noticed before that his touch had a ghostlike quality to it. Barely there. A whisper. Gossamer.

Whereas Langdon could touch her with no more than a tip of his finger and it was as substantial as a branding. It left an invisible mark on her soul, her heart. A mark that ached anytime she thought of him. Since their parting, he'd sent her two gifts. She'd not written him an acknowledgment because she knew she shouldn't encourage him. She had to let him go. Their time together had been wondrous, but it was all she could allow without opening herself up to hurt. He had the power to break her heart, bring her to her knees, and cause her to caterwaul.

"Chadbourne," Hollie acknowledged with a bit of ire. "You're wasting your time, old chap. I believe I mentioned my mistress has no interest in married men."

"There is always a first time for everything."

"For you, to be rejected apparently."

"You're ending your association with her, Hollingsworth. I really don't see that you have any say in the matter."

"My association, not my protection. Did you know that I have a pair of dueling pistols I inherited from my father—who was kind enough to teach me how to use them?"

Marlowe was surprised Hollie didn't die then and there from the daggers Chadbourne was shooting with his eyes. Chadbourne turned his attention to her. "Should you change your mind, send word to the proper gaming area. That's where you'll find me."

He gave a curt bow and strode off.

She blew out a great huff of air.

"He's an arse, Marlowe. I would be most disappointed if you settled for him. When you trade, dear girl, always trade up."

She laughed, wrapped her arm around his, and pressed her head to his shoulder. "Oh, I'm going to miss you, Hollie."

"And I you."

Straightening she released her hold. "Where did you get off to?"

"Just did a bit of exploring."

"Why did you spread the word that I was looking for a new protector?"

"It seemed the most expedient way to ensure you no longer needed me. I don't want Effie hearing that we're still together, although I'm not sure if she is even aware we were ever a couple to begin with."

She shook her head. She did hope the young lady knew how fortunate she was to have his love. "Will you take me home?"

"I haven't had a chance to play cards yet."

"I'll hail a hansom cab, then." Perhaps she'd take out an advert for a lover because she certainly wasn't coming here again.

"Stay a while longer. Sit with me. For old times' sake."

"No wagers like you made before with Langdon."

He placed his hand over his heart. "On my honor."

Chapter 26

As Langdon ambled through the secret rooms, he couldn't help but reflect that they were as they always were. Hazy, thick with smoke. Loud. The din of conversation and the echo of ribald laughter. The clack of dice, the spin of a roulette wheel, the whisper of cards being shuffled. And the heavy odor of too much perfume.

This room was not the sort in which Marlowe belonged. She should never walk through it, much less be allowed into it. Because her fragrance was as light as the clouds through which she sailed.

"Langdon."

He recognized the voice coming from behind him. Hollingsworth. He was torn between praying that she would be standing beside the earl and that she wouldn't. Slowly, ever so slowly, he turned. And felt as if he'd taken a kick to the gut.

Because she was there. He detected the smallest scar at the corner of her mouth and another angled across the tip of her brow, near her temple. Wearing a mauve gown that seemed to bring out all the colors of which she was composed. The blue of her eyes. The moon shade of her hair. The pink highlighting her cheeks. And there, entirely out of place with the pearl earbobs and pearl combs, resting just above the part in her cleavage was his St. Christopher medallion.

He'd hoped after their time apart, he'd be immune to the sight of her.

Instead, all he wanted was to toss her over his shoulder as he had that first night of the storm and carry her to his bed.

"Hollingsworth," he said pointedly. And then a bit softer, gentler. "Marlowe."

"My lord." Her smile was small, almost bashful, much as it had appeared when she'd been on his island, when caution had been required so all her cuts and scrapes could heal. How it had been that night when he'd possessed her and she'd possessed him. Fully, completely.

He wanted her again, more powerfully than he had before. But not just the sexual aspect of her. He wanted to sit with her in a quiet corner and simply talk. He wanted to ask after her balloon, if it was repaired, if she had gone up in it again.

"We're heading off to play cards. Care to join us, Langdon?" Hollingsworth asked.

"Yes, I believe I will."

*S*omething was wrong. Marlowe had yet to determine exactly what it was, but she felt the tenseness in Langdon down to the marrow of her bones.

He sat across from her, Hollie beside her, just as they'd been that fateful night when he'd changed out his cards. But she didn't think that whatever was amiss had anything at all to do with the wagers being made.

Was he upset that she hadn't given him the smile that would invite him to kiss her? She didn't know why she hadn't. Her mouth was healed enough, and her entire body had fairly been singing with joy at the sight of him. She'd had to curb her delight to keep a smile from bursting forth, from showing her giddiness that he was so near she could detect his unique fragrance even in a room clouded with smoke.

Perhaps because she couldn't take her eyes from him, was aware of every move, she was able to perceive that he was not at all comfortable as cards were dealt, studied, cast aside, and replaced. His motions weren't lackadaisical as they'd been before, his posture not relaxed. He appeared brittle, as though at any moment something inside him could break off.

But more than that was the hesitancy, the uncertainty, every time he revealed his hand. And he was always revealing it because he never folded.

When he laid down his cards for all to see, he waited. Waited for someone else to scoop up the winnings from the center of the table. Waited for moans and groans and the winnings to remain untouched for several heartbeats before leaning forward to gather them up.

In the past, he'd toss down his cards with confidence, and a bit of cockiness, to be honest, before quickly claiming his winnings. Sometimes she'd thought he knew what everyone was holding before they exposed their hands.

When he'd lost, he'd shown his cards with the same confidence but a negligent shrug of a shoulder as if to say, *It's of no importance.*

None of that arrogance was visible tonight. There was almost a timidity about him.

"I say, Langdon, as it's only the two of us left, let's make this interesting, shall we?"

Hollie's words jerked her out of her reverie. She knew that tone. It never boded well.

"You wager all the money you have left, there"— Hollie nodded toward the far side of the table— "and I'll wager that you can spend the hours until dawn with my mistress."

Langdon's gaze sought out hers and held. She wanted to object, smack Hollie on the shoulder, remind him that he'd promised not to do this—and yet she desperately wanted those hours with Langdon. She was nearly frantic striving to determine why he was acting so differently. She wanted to give him that smile that would result in a kiss that would drop her to her knees. Why hadn't she given it to him before? Why had she felt bashful, like an untried debutante?

She was on the cusp of her world changing, but it could never be what she dreamed of with him. It couldn't be forever. A reworked version of Sophie's words echoed through her head. *The only way to have the man she loved.* She wished it were different but then her father had taught her that wishes had no value. As a result, she was a realist. She could look at a problem straight on and make the tough choices.

She could find *some* happiness, if not total joy.

For a while he could grace her life. But eventually they'd both have to move on.

"I accept your terms," Langdon said, his tone one of a man who'd already been defeated, a soldier on a battlefield drawing his sword, knowing it would be the last time.

She dropped her gaze to his cards, striving to catch sight of the sleight of hand that would result in his winning, because now was the moment when he could signal that he'd regretted climbing back into his carriage and leaving her alone at her residence. Now was the opportunity for him to be alone with her one more time. How often could they have *one more time*?

Hollie tossed down his cards, face up, even though she didn't think he was supposed to display his hand first. She'd never really paid much attention to the finer rules of this game.

She darted a quick look. A pair of jacks.

Holding her breath, she gave her attention back to Langdon and waited, his movements slowed as if he waded through treacle. Everyone except him seemed to blur into the background. Blood rushed through her ears until all the surrounding sounds faded into obscurity.

He never took his gaze from her as he set down his cards, one by one, and she struggled to make sense of them. Nothing matched. Nothing was in sequence. Nothing could beat Hollie's cards.

"Well, I wasn't expecting that," Hollie muttered as he began gathering up his winnings.

In Langdon's eyes, she read an apology. A great loss. A sorrow.

Why? Why? He had the skills to win and yet—

He shoved back his chair and stood. "Enjoy the remainder of your evening, Marlowe."

His tone said, *Enjoy the remainder of your life.*

Then he strode away as he had the other night when this stupid wager had been made. When she'd objected. But tonight she'd held her tongue. Should she have smiled so he'd have no doubt that she wanted him?

Reaching across, she snatched up the cards he'd shown and the ones he'd discarded. It was impossible to know what he'd held when he'd discarded those three—a five, a six, and an eight—but in the cards he'd shown were a four and a seven. Could he have possessed a straight?

Why didn't he play cards with his cheating family? Why did he have a maths primer?

Twisting around, she leaned over and kissed her former lover on the cheek. "Goodbye, Hollie."

His grin was small, as he nodded. "Be happy, Marlowe."

She knew he understood as well as she did that they were well and truly done.

She shoved herself out of her chair and began wending her way quickly through the crowd. A gentleman stepped into her path, and she skirted around him. He dogged her heels, waving a piece of paper at her side.

"I've written out all I would provide for you—"

"I'm not interested."

"I'll be very generous."

"No, thank you."

"Women praise my bed play skills."

"Leave me the hell alone."

She quickened her pace, going at a faster clip, almost a run. He was halfway to the door. "Langdon!"

He stopped, held still for three of her heartbeats, before finally turning around. Reaching him, she staggered to a stop. She had a thousand questions for him. But suddenly not a damned one mattered.

In spite of having just lost at the gaming table, he was looking at her with desire in his eyes. She wondered if he'd always have desire for her. She would for him. It was the reason tonight had been such torment. She could choose any man in this room. But her decision had been made before she'd ever arrived here tonight.

Her smile came slowly, almost bashfully, small at first until it bloomed full, brilliant, and, she dearly hoped, inviting. In spite of the dimness of the lighting—why were pleasurable pursuits always wrapped in shadows—she could see the fire of desire igniting over his features.

His hand cradled the side of her neck, his thumb stroking the underside of her jaw, tipping her head back slightly as he pulled her near and captured her mouth with a low growl that reverberated against the fingers she pressed to his chest and quietened all the other sounds surrounding her.

He was all that mattered. He'd always been all that mattered. From the moment she'd awakened to the sight of his bare backside—no, from the moment he'd sat down across from her at a gaming table all those months ago. She'd been restless since then, not certain why she was suddenly so discontent with her life.

Now she knew it was because he hadn't been part of it. Not for any length of time.

As he'd promised, the kiss wasn't gentle. It was hungry, starving in fact, his mouth feasting on hers as if in celebration of some magnificent discovery. She loved the taste of him, plaited through with scotch, a dark promise of desires to be fulfilled.

His arm came around her, crushed her against his chest. His mouth left hers to travel along her throat until he pressed his heated, moist mouth just below her ear. His breaths were coming in and out like heaving bellows. "I want to bloody audition."

As though he needed to, as though anyone could compare.

"Take me to your residence," she ordered.

She'd thought they'd separate and he'd offer his arm. Instead, he lifted her off her feet and cradled her against his chest. As he strode from the room, she wound her arms around his neck and settled her head into the curve of his shoulder. She cared not one whit that there was certain to be gossip on the morrow.

*I*n a far corner, at a card table where he had promised not to cheat, and had kept to that promise for three dealt hands, Stuart Langdon was sorry to see the most entertaining aspect of the evening come to a close as his brother carried Marlowe from the room where every gentleman had gone completely still and stared—most of them enviously, he was rather certain—the moment his brother's mouth had landed on Marlowe's.

"Now, gents," he began, hoping to snap them

back to attention, "at last you know why I didn't make a play for Marlowe. And for those of you silly enough to wager that you'd be going home with her tonight"—he snapped his fingers and held out his hands—"I'll collect what I am owed on the wagers I made with you that you wouldn't."

Groans echoed all around as he gathered up his winnings. Just as he'd known none of them would go home with her, he'd known she'd choose none of them. He'd seen the way she looked at his brother when they were at the estate in Cornwall. He was rather certain Ollie had ruined any other man for her.

He was also rather certain she'd ruined any other woman for Ollie.

What he didn't know, and wasn't yet ready to wager on, was what they were going to do about their fixation with each other in the long term.

As his carriage traveled through the London streets, Langdon paid no attention to anything other than the woman on his lap and the mouth moving so provocatively over his. As he had that night at the estate, he began locating and removing her hairpins until her tresses tumbled down around her shoulders. He knotted his fingers in the long strands, pulled her back slightly, and took his lips along a heated exploration of her throat.

"I am so grateful you didn't cut your hair when it was so tangled the night of the storm," he growled.

She laughed, and he thought he'd never tire of hearing her laugh.

Returning his mouth to hers, she gave his tongue permission to plunge deeply and to map the glorious confines. He loved the taste of her. Loved the way her tongue boldly parried with his. Loved the way her hands glided over him—through his hair, over his shoulders, along his chest—hurriedly, slowly, hurriedly again as if greedy for a time and then relishing.

He desperately wanted to undo laces, buttons, and ribbons. But they would be at his residence soon enough and he didn't want her struggling to hold herself together as they raced into his town house.

She tore her mouth from his and hungrily nibbled at his neck. "Oh, I have so longed for my mouth to heal so I could do this. You taste so good. Sweat, man, and . . . sandalwood, I think."

Kneading her breasts, he chuckled darkly. "I have decided you should only wear my shirts. All these layers of fabric put too much material between my skin and yours. I could have my shirt off you before you could blink."

"You should wear only your shirt. Your coat and waistcoat form unnecessary barriers to what I want to touch."

"And my trousers?"

"Especially your trousers. You should never wear them."

He took her lobe between his teeth and nipped. "I've missed you. No one challenges me as you do. The first time I saw you I was reminded of a lioness."

"Last summer at the card table."

"No, before that."

She drew back and held his gaze. He'd drawn

the curtains and the lantern was lit. Her brow wrinkled. "Earlier that night."

"No, about a couple of weeks before. I'd decided I wanted a mistress. I saw you with Hollingsworth and . . . even from a distance I decided you were rare. It wasn't your beauty. It was the manner in which you projected such power. I knew you would never cower, never surrender—and then when you landed on my island and I discovered how you'd gotten there . . . I knew everything I'd assumed about you was correct. You would never be conquered. You need someone who will rule beside you."

"What I need is another kiss."

She grabbed his lapels, jerked him back to her, and blanketed his mouth with hers, taking the kiss so deep it touched his soul. He wondered if his words had embarrassed her or if she wasn't quite certain what to make of them. She was no doubt accustomed to compliments on her beauty. How many men truly looked deeper than that?

She shifted her position and straddled him. Taking hold of her hips, he pressed her against his aching cock, needed her to know what she did to him. There was no aspect of his body that didn't want her, no part of her that he didn't want to lavish with devotion.

The carriage began to slow. Squeezing her hips, he stilled her, then slipped a finger beneath the curtain and peered out. "Thank God we're here."

$\mathcal{M}$arlowe caught glimpses of his residence as they made their way through a front parlor, into a hallway, up the stairs, and straight to his bedchamber. She'd never known clothes could come off so quickly or that people could laugh like naughty children while removing them.

But everything changed once they climbed into the bed. Nothing that was happening between them was childlike. He obviously enjoyed kissing very much, because that was where he began, with her mouth. While his tongue plundered there, his fingers explored the sensitive area between her thighs. She was already so wet that he could slide right into her with no trouble whatsoever.

Instead he taunted and teased and taught her that there was so much more than rushing to completion. That even a frenzied journey need not be quick. He lavished sensations over her breasts, kissing, licking, suckling. Not just her nipples but every portion of them.

She'd never known how sensitive the underside could be.

While he worked his magic, she worked hers. Stroking the inside of his thighs, going a little higher with each caress, noting the tension building in him, the groans and growls going deeper and deeper, more feral. Until she cupped him and gently massaged.

And then higher, wrapping her hand around the sturdy length of him, with her thumb gathering the dew.

When she could take no more, she shoved him onto his back, straddled him, and guided him home, groaning low and deep.

She rocked against him, meeting his powerful

thrusts. He cupped her breasts, flicking his thumbs over the hardened nipples. Then he sat up and took one into his mouth, sucking hard.

"Oh, God."

She was fairly bouncing, taking him deeper and deeper.

His arms came around her, holding her close, and he flipped them until she was on her back and his hips were pistoning. He laced his fingers through hers and carried her hands over her head, holding them there while he drove into her. She wrapped her legs around him, held him tightly.

When his mouth reclaimed hers, she captured his with equal fervor. All along, the sensations had been building and stretching out until there wasn't a single aspect of her that didn't feel touched, that wasn't sparking.

She was writhing beneath him, crying out—

Soaring, on a wind so strong it delivered her to the heavens.

He grunted, cursed, and struck with a final thrust that made her feel both conquered and like a conqueror.

Gently he lowered himself until his chest was a whisper's breath along hers. He kissed the once injured corner of her mouth. Slowly he freed her hands.

When he made a move to roll away from her, she stopped him by tightening her legs around him. "Not yet."

$\mathscr{S}$everal minutes later, resting on his side, Langdon watched as Marlowe slid out of bed, picked up his shirt from where he'd tossed it on the floor earlier, and slipped it on.

"You're welcome to take a fresh shirt from the wardrobe."

She smiled broadly. Damn, but he loved that smile. "It will be freshly laundered and won't carry your fragrance."

"If you want my fragrance, I'm carrying it right here." He waved his hand over his naked body, in demonstration.

She laughed. "I can never have too much."

She began sauntering sexily back toward the bed. His cock reacted. That shirt wasn't going to stay on her very long. "Did you find the shirt I placed in your balloon?"

"I did." She climbed onto the bed.

"Did you like the barometer?"

"I love the barometer." She lowered herself and snuggled up against him.

With one arm, he drew her more closely against him, while his other hand eased beneath the hem of his shirt and cupped her incredibly luscious arse. "Has your balloon been repaired?"

"Not yet. Can't afford the basket."

"You can now, sweetheart. Whatever you need, whatever you *want*, I'll provide." Because so very much of her was pressed up against so very much of him, he was incredibly aware of her going stiff and still.

"I . . . I don't want you providing for me."

They were not words that should have made him feel like a sword was piercing his chest. He looked down at the top of her head. "Did I not pass your audition?"

He kept his voice light, teasing, when so many awkward emotions were swirling through him. Confusion, hurt, jealousy.

Tilting her head back, she met his gaze. "You passed when we were on the island. I just . . . I don't want you paying for me."

"But it's all right for Hollingsworth to pay for you?" Apparently, anger was also slicing through him, and had taken up residence in his voice. She jerked as though he'd taken a lash to her back.

"It's different. You and I as opposed to me and him."

"How so?"

She shook her head. "If I try to explain it, it makes it all sound worse. Makes me appear . . . cheap. Can't we just be lovers tonight?"

"So you can fuck him tomorrow?"

Pushing away from him, she sat up. "I told you that it's over between him and me."

"How many were you planning to *audition* to-night?"

Her jaw taut, she glared at him, so much fire in her eyes that he wanted to take her then and there and feel the heat burning them both to cinders. "Twelve."

She leapt out of the bed, leaving him momentarily too stunned to move. How had bliss suddenly turned into hell?

She whipped off his shirt and began gathering up her clothes. "I'll need a maid to help me dress."

"I'll help you." He began to roll out—

"No."

Stilling at the sharp command, balancing half-way out of the bed, he looked over his shoulder at her. She stood there, straight and proud, the woman who beguiled half of London and infuriated the other half. A woman who could command a room of men and took no rubbish. A woman every man wanted to fuck, yet no man touched without permission. She had managed to become every man's ideal of what he wanted between the sheets, in the bedchamber. His equal when it came to carnal sin.

But few understood she carried all of that beyond the bed. It encompassed all of her, was part and parcel of the whole of her. She could command the wind, ride it through the sky. She could touch him and make him almost feel that he was once again whole.

"You're not to touch me. I want a maid. Call for one or I shall."

Slowly, as if she were a dangerous viper that would strike if he moved too quickly, he extricated himself from the bed and stood. "Marlowe, I apologize for my anger. I can't stand the thought of someone else touching you."

"Do you think it's what I want?" She shook her head. "Of course, it's what I want. I wouldn't do it otherwise. No one forced me into this life. But it comes at a cost. At nineteen, I was willing to pay it. I can't now begrudge or hate myself because I like having a nice residence. I like fancy clothes. I like having an abundance of food. I like being squired about. I like being given an allowance. I like that each month I can use a portion of that allowance to pay off a little bit more of my father's tremendous debt. It's not fair to the shop owners or tradesmen that they provided him with goods or services and they are the ones paying the price for it. That some may be going hungry or having things rough because he didn't pay what was owed. I'll be thirty-six and a half years old by the time I pay it off. I've calculated it down to the penny."

She took a deep, shuddering breath.

He wanted to cross over to her, take her in his arms, and hold her tightly. He wanted to find her father and beat him to a bloody pulp. He wanted to pay off that damned debt. He wanted to give her everything she *liked*. "Marlowe—"

Her hand flew up, palm out, stopping him. "I'm not done. My mother will not leave her house." She shook her head, visibly trembled. "Before I could return to London, I had to hire someone to care for her. To stay with her, to go to the shops for her.

"I know I was fortunate with Hollie. So many mistresses live in the area where I do. We visit with each other, chat, complain. I know some never go anywhere with their gents. They're wanted only for the bedchamber. It was never like that with Hollie. We've become good friends. And, yes, we . . . tumbled into bed on occasion. Was it like when I'm with you? God, no. It's a more quiet coming together. With you I feel like I'm being burned to a cinder and then I rise from the ashes and I feel so bloody marvelous and happy . . . outside of pleasure, I expect nothing from you and you expect nothing from me. And there's a beauty to that and what is between us which I think we will lose. Because I will feel I owe you what I am now giving you freely. I don't know what I'm going to do, Langdon. Perhaps I'll go back to being a seamstress, and it'll take me the rest of my life to pay off my father's debt." Another long, slow sigh. She held out her corset. "You can help me dress."

It felt like a victory, although he couldn't take it as her offering a white flag. He couldn't imagine her ever surrendering.

They didn't speak as he assisted her with her clothing. She'd given him a lot to contemplate, and he suspected she was worn out from all the emotions that had been roiling through her. It was never easy to face regrets, fear, or uncertainty.

Later, in the carriage, he sat across from her, giving her space, watching as the glow from the streetlamps washed over her and disappeared. Washed over her and disappeared. Again and again. He knew that at some point in the future, he'd watch it disappear for the final time. If he married, he wouldn't be unfaithful to his wife. And he knew Marlowe wouldn't expect him to be. But if he never married . . .

He supposed the audition, which he'd referred to as a joke, never thinking he was actually auditioning, wasn't over. He had to prove he could provide for her without making her feel like a whore.

The carriage came to a stop in front of her residence. He pushed open the door, leapt out, and reached back for her. He'd never grow tired of closing his fingers around her hand.

He escorted her along the short path and up the steps. He started to reach for the latch to open the door for her and stopped. He was angled toward her while she faced the building. "Lovers, then," he said quietly.

She turned slightly, and he read relief in her eyes.

"Until you say no more," he finished.

Her smile wasn't as brilliant as the one she'd given him at the club, but it was a smile nonetheless. "I'd like that but I don't know how long—"

"I'll take however long you're willing to give me."

She nodded. "I'll study my finances."

He truly didn't understand her reasoning for not accepting assistance from him when she had from Hollingsworth and would from someone else. It would kill him when she did.

"We can argue about it later," he told her, "but I want to cover the costs for the repairs needed on your balloon, including the basket—"

"The car."

He hitched up a corner of his mouth. "The car. Not in exchange for anything you've given me, but as a gift and because I want to take a ride in the bloody thing."

Another nod, a hint of a smile. "I appreciate the generosity and I won't be stubborn about it. Because I want to take you for a ride in the bloody thing."

Some of the tension he'd been carrying left him with her acquiescence. If he were patient and subtle, perhaps he could over time convince her there was no difference between him and Hollingsworth. And she would allow him to provide for her.

"I very much want to kiss you, Marlowe."

"I very much want you to kiss me."

He took her into his embrace, slashed his mouth across hers, and reveled in the eagerness with which she met his advance. He'd never have enough of her tongue parrying with his, of her sighs and moans, the manner in which her arms tightened around him, as if she'd cling to him forever, never relinquish her hold.

He considered following her into the residence, into her bed, awakening with her in the morning— the best way to begin a day—but he needed a little more time to determine what his relationship with her would entail. He suspected she needed a little more time as well.

Drawing away from her was hard, but he managed to do it and to place his thumb against her moist, swollen lips. Kissing was certainly going to be a large part of what they did when they were together. "I'll see you tomorrow."

He shoved on the door, ushered her through the opening. "Sleep well, Marlowe."

After closing her in, he bounded down the steps and clambered into his carriage. As it began rolling through the streets, he was struck by how lonely it was. He wondered if for the remainder of his life, he would feel as if a piece of him was missing when she wasn't with him.

Chapter 27

*W*ith their breaths still coming harsh and heavy, their bodies sweaty and cooling, following a session of mad lovemaking, Marlowe stared up at the deep purple canopy and decided she would never again look at purple in the same way. It would always remind her of these few nights of animalistic coupling. Sex was never tame with them, as though by knowing their time together was limited, they were determined to rejoice in each other's bodies and celebrate as if they were shooting off fireworks inside each other.

By silent mutual agreement, they never stayed within her residence. During the past week, with the arrival of dusk, they would be in his carriage heading through London toward his town house. If the street she lived on was surreptitiously referred to as Mistress Row rather than by its true name, she suspected his was known as Lords-a-Plenty Way because on more than one occasion she'd caught sight of a lord or two she recognized as they were entering or leaving their residence.

It had been funny to watch the manner in which their heads jerked back around once they realized whom they'd spotted. The widening of their eyes, the dropping of their jaws.

While ink had been devoted to reporting that "Marlowe" had been carried out of a notorious club by "Viscount L," she suspected the lords hadn't expected to see her on their street. Mistresses were visited upon within their lodging, not taken to the home of their benefactor. Perhaps that was the reason he brought her to the place where he lived—because she was his lover, not his mistress.

She was no doubt being silly to make such a distinction, and yet she found great comfort in knowing they were together simply because they wanted to be. She wasn't obligated to spread her legs because he'd provided her with an additional servant or purchased her a new piece of furniture or ensured she'd had a gown made using that red silk she'd been coveting at the dressmaker's.

She was welcoming him into her body because it was where she wanted him and where he wanted to be. The freedom she felt was almost as grand as what she experienced when she was floating high above the earth, queen of her domain.

"How many times do you think we've made love?" she asked, knowing it was seldom they did it only once a night.

"Haven't a bloody clue." His tone was almost mystified.

She turned her head to find him watching her. "Perhaps we should keep count."

"What does it matter?"

She couldn't quite identify his attitude, but it was like he really didn't care and wondered why she was carrying on so about it. "I suppose it doesn't. Hollie visited today."

They were lying on their backs, side by side, joined from shoulder to her ankle and his calf because of course his legs extended far beyond hers. Hence, she was very much aware of him visibly stiffening, like she'd punched her fist into his gut.

"For tea," she hastened to clarify, as she twisted onto her side so she could observe him more clearly.

He bent his head so his eyes could meet hers. She liked that they almost always held each other's gaze when they spoke, truly interested in what the other had to say.

"He was surprised you didn't ensure you won the last time you played cards, when he made another atrocious wager. He knows you have the ability to manipulate your hand." She didn't know why she was pushing on this, except it had bothered her that night and suspicions wouldn't leave her in peace. "Between what you held and what you discarded, you had the cards needed to form a straight."

"Did I?"

"You knew you did, surely. You looked at your cards before you discarded them, and then after you got new ones. You even rearranged them." She'd been watching him so closely she even knew how many times he'd clicked a finger against the back of one of his cards. "Did you not work your magic because I hadn't given you a proper smile?"

She'd never known his face to be so unreadable,

stony, as if he'd locked his thoughts within a castle keep and not even a fire-breathing dragon could set them free.

He studied her for the longest time, as if he was searching for something buried deeply within her . . . or within himself. When his response finally came, the words were slowly, torturously delivered, like he expected each one might explode or would lead him toward a destination he didn't want to reach. "No, that's not the reason I didn't manipulate the cards."

"Then why didn't you?" It wasn't that she necessarily had wanted him to win her, but it had been his chance to show Hollie and every man at that table that he truly wanted her.

He sighed. "What does it matter?"

He'd asked the same thing a few minutes ago regarding the number of times they'd made love. Suddenly she felt uncared for, as if *she* didn't matter, at least not to him, not with the same strength of conviction he mattered to her. She wanted to tell him that it did indeed matter, but it was only her pride, her heart, yearning for what she knew would never be hers to hold. His heart. Perhaps it was a good thing their time together would be short, the few memories accumulated, dear.

"I suppose it doesn't."

He rose up on an elbow and the shifting of the mattress caused her to roll onto her back. Cradling her face with one large hand, he looked at her with an abundance of tenderness. "That wasn't a very convincing lie. Why is it important that I should cheat to have you?"

"I suppose I wanted to feel that you yearned for me to such an extent that you'd do anything to have me." She shook her head as much as she was able with his grip on her. "It wouldn't have proven anything really." They'd have still ended up in bed, and she wanted him to want her without that. Or at least in addition to that.

"I do yearn for you. I burn for you. Have I failed at showing you that?"

"No." She smiled brightly. "You've shown me spectacularly well. You're right. It doesn't matter."

His mouth came down on hers, hard, almost punishingly, his tongue thrusting with the precision of the most finely honed rapier—one designed to pleasure, not hurt. There was fire. Need. Want.

How could she question his yearning for her when he always came to her with such hunger? It didn't matter if hours or only minutes had passed since he'd last tasted her. Always, always, he sipped and savored even as he plunged and stole.

Stole her ability to breathe, to reason, to think. To do anything except feel. Respond.

Her body heated as though he'd arranged wood in the most efficient way and set kindling alight within it. Slow to start until it was blazing with full force. The winds and rains of a tempest could not douse it. Instead they joined in the dance, fueling it. Every element responded and came alive.

And she knew, knew where they were headed, where he was going to take her. All the doubts she'd been giving voice to went silent. She was going to travel with him on this journey, as his equal, as his partner. It was the way he always treated her.

He dragged his mouth down the column of her throat, and then up. Along the soft underside of her jaw. Stopping at the sensitive spot just below her ear where he pressed the smallest of kisses.

"I didn't manipulate the cards because I couldn't determine what I was holding. I can't tell you how many times I've made love to you because I no longer possess the ability to count."

Saying the words aloud to her made him feel like a boulder being catapulted toward a stone fortress, and he hurled himself off the bed with such force and so quickly that her fingers barely grazed his hip when she reached for him. He stalked over to a table where he kept a bottle of scotch near for those nights when he awoke from a nightmare.

The only time he seemed guaranteed not to have one was when she was in his arms, in his bed.

He splashed scotch into a glass, tossed it back. He heard bare feet padding across the floor, a whisper of linen flowing over flesh, and when she stopped beside him, he knew without looking she was wearing his shirt.

"Would you like a nip?" he asked.

"*What* I would like is to understand exactly what it is you were telling me."

Words he'd uttered because he'd been able to see from the expressions shifting over her face, like storm clouds going from gray to black as they charged over the land, that she was beginning to think *she* didn't signify. When she mattered so much that it damned near ripped him apart whenever he considered how short their time together would be.

"I'm not sure there is an understanding to it."

"You went to Cambridge. You must have mastered maths."

"I could count to a hundred by the time I was five. Not only that, but I could also write the numerals. I always loved numbers. They were so much easier to understand than words. They had a purpose, could tell stories with precision. Then after the railway accident . . . they went away."

He poured scotch into a glass and slid it toward her. Filled another glass, picked it up, walked over to the sitting area before the fireplace, and set the glass on a nearby table. Feeling her eyes on him, he strode over, snatched up his trousers, and drew them on.

By the time he returned to his chair, she was already perched in the opposite one, her feet tucked up beneath her, her hands wrapped around the glass she held as if it was the buoy that would prevent the gigantic swells from taking her under.

"At your residence on the island," she began cautiously, "the room I went into, the one with the maths primer—"

"I was striving to relearn what I'd once known. You can probably guess from all the evidence of my frustration—and the temper I exhibited toward you, for which I apologize—I was having no success. I don't even know how much I paid for your barometer. As your father learned, when you are part of the aristocracy—or pretending that you are—you don't pay then and there. You're sent a statement at the end of the month or the end of the year. I send it to my man of affairs and that's that."

He could fairly see all the thoughts bombarding her brain. Her brow was furrowed so deeply, and she was gnawing her lower lip with such intensity she was going to create more scars.

"That night we had dinner with your family . . . you didn't play cards with them . . . because they don't know . . . that you are living with . . . this challenge."

"*This challenge*? Such a pleasant way to put it. I prefer to think of it as *this hell*. And you are correct. They do not know. My mother would only worry. When there is nothing to be done. At least according to my physician."

She brightened. "You've been to a doctor, then?"

He nodded. "Dr. William Graves. A friend of the family, and one of the more skilled surgeons in all of Great Britain. But even he is flummoxed. He identified it as railway spine. But in truth all that means is that I was in a railway accident and came away from it not quite right."

"How long will this go on?"

He took a swallow of scotch because this was the hardest part of all. "Graves said it might just miraculously go away. Probably not, though. Should I marry, I could line my children up and not tell you how many I have. When my father dies, how am I to effectively manage the estates? Stuart will no doubt help, but it shouldn't be his responsibility." He was weary of going through all this. Talking about it wasn't going to change it. He'd gotten lost in the dark depths when in truth she needed to understand only one thing.

He shoved himself to his feet, crossed over to

her, knelt beside her, and cradled her face with one hand. "I cannot tell you how many times we've made love, Marlowe, but I promise you that I remember each one."

*S*he felt the tears sting her eyes, and while she'd long ago learned to blink them back into submission, to never show any vulnerability, this time she gave them their freedom because she was so deeply touched by his words.

Her heart shouted, *I love you!*

Even as her voice refused to utter the words. Because just as nothing could be done for his struggle with numbers, nothing was to be done about her feelings—except to endure them in silence because she fully understood he had responsibilities as a lord.

"I'll keep track of the numbers for you. All of them. How long you've been married. How many children you have. How many dogs. We'll arrange a secret assignation where we simply pass each other on the street, and I'll tell you what you need to know so you can repeat it. Even if you can't fully appreciate the numbers, if they seem without context."

"You think your protector will be happy about that?"

"Hollie is often viewed as soft, but he knows what is needed to project power, and he ensured that when the time came, I could lay out my terms and if a gent wanted to serve as my benefactor, he had to accept them. We can remain friends, Langdon, even if we're not lovers."

Chapter 28

$\mathcal{S}$itting at her small desk in her tiny library, Marlowe studied her finances. Another week, two at the most and she would have to bring this respite from the trials of life to an end and become once more a *kept* woman.

Based on the number of men who had approached her that first night after Hollie let it be known she was on the hunt, she suspected it would take only a few days to find his replacement. She already had a list of the lords she wouldn't even bother to consider. She had yet to compile the names of those she would deem a possibility, because she didn't want images of other men she might like filling her head when she was with Langdon.

Not that any would outshine him.

At the sound of the hushed footfalls, she looked up as her butler approached.

"His lordship is here, madam. He has with him a rather large gentleman. They're waiting for you in the parlor."

His lordship. Hollie. The butler knew as well as

she did that she didn't have the option of not being at home when he called. Such was the life of a mistress. She really should write a book on the perils and pleasures of serving as a courtesan.

"Let him know I'll be right there." Shoving back her chair, she stood and fluffed out her skirt. On her way to the door, she stopped in front of a mirror and tidied her hair. Habit. It was habit to try to look her best for him. But the intimate part of their association had come to an end. She had no need to primp. Yet still she did it.

When she walked into the library, she was surprised to discover *his lordship* was in fact Langdon. Briefly she wondered if her servants thought he was her new defender.

Because she didn't know the older man— probably close to his father's age—standing beside him, she curtsied. "My lord, your presence is unexpected."

He offered her a slight smile and a bow. "My apologies for not sending word. Allow me to introduce Sir James Swindler, a longtime friend of my father's."

She curtsied deeply to the man of legend. "It is an honor to make your acquaintance, Sir James. I've read of your exploits in apprehending criminals for Scotland Yard. Although I don't remember precisely which case earned you your knighthood."

"Those were never reported on."

"As you know of his reputation," Langdon said, "then you comprehend he's very good at finding people."

Her stomach felt like it had the night of the storm

when her balloon had begun plummeting toward
the sea. She thought at any second it would hit the
floor with a resounding thud. "Someone like my
father."

Her words came out on a croak.

Langdon nodded. "I hope I didn't overstep when
I asked him to determine if he could learn anything
about his disappearance."

She swallowed hard. "I assume you're here because he did."

"Perhaps you'd like to sit down."

Throwing back her shoulders, she tossed her
head. "No, I'll take this news standing."

With her knees locked so she wouldn't sink to
the floor. She'd often wondered what would be
worse: to know with certainty he was dead or to
learn he was alive and well but had abandoned
them. She girded herself against the onslaught
of emotions waiting at the periphery of her heart
and soul.

Sir James's eyes held regret, sorrow, and sympathy. She knew before he even spoke the ending of
this tale.

"Around the time of your father's disappearance, in a remote area of Wales, a group of farmers
reported seeing a fire-breathing dragon fall from
the sky."

Her stomach concluded its drop to the floor. "My
father's balloon was decorated with dragons. Hy-
drogen is quite combustible. That balloon wouldn't
have been the first to suffer such a mishap."

Langdon appeared absolutely horrified, as if
he'd just realized the dangers of flight involved

more than encountering a storm. She wondered if perhaps the risk was part of its appeal.

"They were terrified, poor blighters," Sir James continued. "Were unfamiliar with hot-air balloons. Attacked it with pitchforks at first, apparently . . . until they saw the man. He hadn't survived the fall, I'm afraid."

She wondered how it was that those words managed to suck all the air out of the room, out of London. She couldn't seem to draw a breath. Still, she nodded jerkily in response to what he'd said. And she had the answer to her earlier debate. It was much worse to know he was truly gone.

"I visited the nearest constabulary. I don't suppose your father wore a signet ring."

"He did." He'd always said it proved he was a lord, as if only those among the nobility were allowed to wear such a thing.

"Do you recall what it looked like?"

"Why not just show it to her?" Langdon asked, and her entire body went stiff with the possibility of touching a reminder of her father. When she was younger, still small enough to sit nestled on his lap, he'd given it to her to wear for a few minutes. His hands and fingers were so much larger than hers she'd slid it onto her thumb, but still it had swallowed the digit and she'd had to close her hand into a fist to prevent it from falling off.

"Because the mind is unreliable when it comes to memories," Sir James said. "If I show it to her, the sight might replace the truth." He turned his attention to her, his expression one of patiently waiting.

She looked down at her thumb as if the jewelry

was still there. "It was gold. An elaborate *W* was carved into a flattened surface of onyx." She lifted her gaze. "It was the fanciest piece of jewelry I ever saw before coming to London. I suspect it was instrumental in convincing the shop owners it would be a privilege to extend credit to a man who wore such a thing."

Sir James dipped two fingers into a waistcoat pocket. When he withdrew them, he extended toward her the ring. Her gasp sounded more like a strangled sob.

"The authorities had kept it in hopes of using it someday to identify the poor chap. I convinced them to entrust it to my care. I promised to either return it to them or provide them with the identity of their daring mystery bloke."

Her father had been daring. He'd taught her the advantage of being unafraid to face the unknown. It was the reason she'd returned to London without her mother when she was seventeen, now lived a life of relative luxury, and her name was practically housed on the tip of every gossipmonger's tongue, readily accessible to be uttered. While she might be questioning the wisdom of some of the decisions she'd made in desperation, she couldn't deny they'd required bravery on her part.

Slowly, slowly, that bravery suddenly nowhere to be seen, she reached out and enfolded her hand around the ring. It fairly pulsed against her palm. She pressed her tightened fist to the center of her chest and laid her other hand over it. Closing her eyes, she envisioned her father's smile, heard his laughter, recalled how proud he'd always seemed of her achievements. How much he'd loved traveling with her in his balloon. How much she'd loved being so close to him.

When Langdon's arms came around her, she didn't push him away. Instead she absorbed his warmth and comfort, relished the steady pounding of his heart that was in direct contrast to her erratic one, forced her struggling breaths to match his calm ones. One of his hands stroked her back slowly. Had he spoken, had he offered words of condolences, she might have burst into tears. Hollie had plowed his way through any moments of emotional turmoil with constant monologues, battering her with words that prevented her from thinking clearly or processing what she was feeling. That Langdon knew her well enough to simply remain silent was a bit unnerving and something to think about later.

She wondered if her father had been afraid when his balloon had caught fire, if he'd been as terrified as she'd been when trapped in the storm. If he'd known his life was on the verge of ending. If he'd had regrets. Felt guilty for the lies. Felt sorrow at the thought of never seeing her or her mother again. Or had he believed he'd survive, been determined to brash it out, and have an adventure to share?

It wasn't unusual for aeronauts to don parachutes, even if they weren't always as effective as they might have been. But her father had viewed them as an unnecessary weight, and the lighter the basket, the higher the balloon would go. She wondered if he'd had a few seconds to recognize the foolishness of that attitude.

Opening her eyes, she gave Langdon a little nudge. Relaxing his hold, he tucked a finger beneath her chin. "Are you going to be all right?"

After she nodded, he swung around to stand beside her and placed his hand reassuringly at the small of her back. She met Sir William's gaze. "Robert Tittering—at least that's the name under which he married my mother. He was quite flawed by all accounts. But he loved deeply and without reservation, and I have often thought that to be his finest quality." Her chest was loosening a bit, her breaths coming more easily. "I'll be visiting my mother once the Season comes to a close. I'll share with her then what you've discovered. After all these years, a few more weeks of not knowing isn't going to cause any harm. But I very much appreciate you solving the mystery."

"I have found it's seldom easy to live with the not knowing. But sorting through the knowing is no easy task either. Therefore, I shall leave you to it and see myself out."

As he began to stride past, Langdon held out his hand. "Thank you, Uncle James."

"Not at all, lad." And he carried on.

When she heard the outer door close, she lowered herself into the nearest chair. "He's your uncle?"

Langdon studied her with the intensity of someone searching for cracks in a dam. "Not by blood. It's just what I grew up calling him."

He crouched before her, appearing almost afraid to touch her. Then, as if faced with a wild creature, he slowly, so very slowly, moved his hand toward her and gently wiped his thumb along her cheek. Only then did she become aware of the dampness, did she realize tears were rolling free like raindrops from a darkened cloud gliding over a windowpane. She wondered how long they had been doing so, if they'd begun their journey before Sir James took his leave.

"Would you have rather not known?" Langdon asked.

She shook her head. "I'd always suspected. I couldn't imagine if he still drew breath, he wouldn't have returned, even if it meant hiking the entire way . . . or crawling. I've shared with you the worst of him, but he wasn't all bad."

"Few ever are."

He had both hands cupped around her face now, his thumbs tenderly gathering up the dew that continued to accumulate.

"How were you able to tell him how long ago he disappeared?"

"You mentioned the length of time when you were recounting your tale. I can remember numbers when they are told to me. I can't tell you what they look like, I can't write them. I know not their value. But with the information I had, he was able to narrow his search."

"It makes me sad to think it might have been horrible for him. I know what it is to think you're going to die. I thought of all the things I meant to do. The dreams I abandoned. The ones I saw come true. Did the same thing happen to you, during the railway collision?"

He shook his head. "It happened too fast. I was

making up stories about my fellow passengers and in a blink I woke up on soaked grass and was being pelted by rain. For those who died, I very much doubt they knew Death was coming for them. I drew some comfort from that."

Sniffing, she squeezed her eyes shut, wrenching out the remainder of her tears. She took a deep, slow inhale, and an even slower exhale. He must have recognized she was coming back to herself, because his hands moved away from her face and he rocked back a little into his crouch.

Ten days, she almost blurted. *Ten days is all I can give you before the reality of my financial situation raises its ugly little head.*

She realized she could give him any number, a hundred, a thousand, and he would be unable to accurately judge the significance. Only she would be aware of the numbers ticking away, becoming smaller and smaller until there was one day left and then none.

Perhaps like Death arriving unexpectedly, there would be some mercy in his not being aware of their time slipping away. He could enjoy each hour without realizing how few remained. It was a gift she could offer him.

"I've had many moments of sadness through the years, missing him, wondering what happened. Now I know. And there is relief in that. The last time I saw my father, he was going up in his balloon, smiling broadly, waving, and the last thing I heard was his laugh. He had a wonderful, deep laugh. I'm going to imagine he arrived at Heaven's gate the same way: smiling, waving, and laughing. Thank you for finding the answer for me."

"*I* didn't actually find it."

"But you knew who would. Thank you for asking him."

"I didn't tell you because I didn't want to get your hopes up in case he didn't find out anything. But I also knew he wouldn't give up until he did discover something."

"Those poor farmers. I suppose it would be frightening if you'd never before seen a balloon."

With quiet contemplation, he studied her. "The sadness is going away."

She nodded. "As I said, it's been around over the years. It hit harder today, but it doesn't linger. I mourned him. And I remember him."

"I've been dragging you off to my residence every night. Perhaps tonight we should go to the Twin Dragons. Have a bit of fun."

"I'd like that."

He straightened. "I'll see you at dusk."

He never gave her an hour, a time. It was always dusk, dawn, midday, dark. He never looked at a watch or a clock, and she knew why now. "I'll be ready."

Bending over, placing his hands on either side of her chair, he leaned in and kissed her before striding from the residence.

Chapter 29

$\mathcal{A}$ few minutes later, as his carriage rumbled along, Langdon was grateful she'd agreed to go to the Twin Dragons tonight. He was on his way to an appointment with his father and when he was done with it, he wasn't certain he'd be fit company, and he was hoping the chaos of a gambling hell might distract her enough so she wouldn't notice his mood. Which he suspected was going to be quite dark indeed.

He'd awoken this morning feeling guilty that he'd shared his affliction with Marlowe and yet his family was still ignorant regarding his struggles. It seemed wrong that she should know what they did not.

And yet . . . nothing in his life had ever felt as right as telling her.

He hadn't given his father a time when he would arrive at the residence. He'd merely indicated *this afternoon* when he'd sent his missive. Clocks were controlled by numbers. So many ticks, so many minutes, so many hours.

When Langdon had reached his majority, his father had passed his timepiece on to him and he had cherished it. He'd felt the sting of tears the first time he'd tucked it away into his waistcoat pocket. On occasion, he took it out, studied its face, and tried to determine how he could still use it for its purpose.

He'd been six when his father had sat him on his lap and taught him how to read a watch, how to use it to measure time. He tried to recall the lessons, thought if he could do that, he could teach himself what he'd once known. But thus far he'd had no success.

Perhaps Marlowe could teach him how to unravel the mysteries of time.

When she had stopped silently weeping earlier, he'd been able to discern she was contemplating sharing something with him and had decided against it. He suspected it had to do with the time left to them. He wished he could place it in an hourglass. He could comprehend sand sifting through from the top to the bottom, marking the passage of time. He could see the amount left.

Perhaps he should have a huge hourglass built in his back garden, have her help him determine how much sand would be needed to accurately provide a way to measure the minutes remaining to them. Although he couldn't imagine not having her with him.

Why was she so opposed to his caring for her? He wasn't a pauper.

The carriage pulled into the circular drive of his parents' London residence, and he turned his attention to focusing on his meeting. Picking up the satchel resting beside him, he tapped it. He wasn't nervous or anxious. He was, however, dreading the disappointment that would cross his father's face when he learned the truth of his heir.

The vehicle rolled to a stop. He shoved open the door, leapt out, and headed up the steps.

The door opened wide, and the butler nodded. "My lord."

"Andrews. I assume my father is in the library."

"Yes, sir."

"See that we're not disturbed."

"Yes, sir."

Langdon continued on, his heels beating out a strong cadence. That of a man who possessed confidence, who knew his own mind—

Christ. Or at least what was left of it.

At the library, a footman standing at attention reached down and opened the door for him. Langdon gave a respectful nod as he swept through.

His father was sitting behind his desk, ledgers spread out before him, pen in hand as he made notions. While Langdon wasn't near enough to see them, he suspected most of them involved numbers.

The earl looked up, smiled, set aside his pen, and leaned back. "Oliver."

"Father."

He reached the desk. Ah, yes, the ledgers contained almost all numbers. Damn them to hell. Carefully he set his satchel on the corner of the desk that was free of any ledgers or clutter. He opened it and pulled out the sheafs of paper that contained words, words, words. So many words he'd written since he'd returned to London.

He held them out and hoped his father didn't notice the slight tremble of his hand.

Lucian Langdon, the Earl of Claybourne, was the sort of man that some found intimidating, that no one wanted to cross. Langdon suspected the love he held for his sire was equal to that which Marlowe held for hers. He couldn't fathom what he might have done had his father been taken from him when he was a young man. As a future lord of the realm, he wouldn't have found himself on the streets, but he would have inherited the responsibility of looking after his mother and siblings.

Would he have found the courage, determination, and fortitude to do whatever necessary to shelter and protect them—as Marlowe had done for her mother?

He watched as the papers slid from his hand with his father's tug.

"Have a seat," his father said, nodding toward a chair in front of the desk.

"I'd rather stand, if you don't mind."

His father lifted his gaze to him, studied him for what seemed an eternity, nodded, and gave his attention to what Langdon had written.

"It's my proposal for the estate steward that I was on my way to deliver to him last year when everything went ass over tit."

"Yes, I can see that."

He waited as his father's gaze slid over each page. When he reached the last, he said, "You haven't included your figures, indicating how these changes will benefit us financially."

"No." Because those figures had been lost in a

torn apart railway car. Lost in a mind that couldn't find them.

His sire was studying him, and all the while Langdon was striving to determine how to explain what needed to be told. He'd practiced a few different ways to say it, but looking at his father now, none seemed quite right.

"Well, they were only speculation," the earl said. "If you believe these plans are the direction we should go in, they should be implemented."

"They are more impressive with the numbers."

The man he'd loved and admired from the moment he'd been old enough to understand love and admiration shrugged. "They're impressive enough without them." He held out the papers, his hand so much steadier than Langdon's had been. "Go forth, my son, make your vision happen."

Langdon stared into eyes the same pewter gray as his. The same shade as his grandfather's, he'd been told, although he'd never met him because he'd been murdered when Langdon's father was a lad. The same shade as his great-grandfather's, the man who had rescued Langdon's father from the gallows.

"Graves told you."

His father set the papers down. "Told me what, precisely?"

Langdon felt a tilting of his world. Why was his father playing coy? There was no other explanation possible. "That I've lost my ability to recognize or decipher numbers."

A shake of his head. "He told me nothing. I have watched you since shortly after you took your first breath. I knew something was amiss. I didn't know exactly what it entailed. Your mother has watched you *since* you took your first breath. She, too, is worried about you. I assume this situation is a result of the two trains colliding."

He felt the tears burning his eyes. Christ, he was too old to cry. "Father, I feel as though I've lost half my mind."

The Earl of Claybourne came out of the chair, around the desk, and was embracing his son so quickly that Langdon barely had time to register his actions. But he slumped against his father and welcomed his tight hold.

"There now, you don't have to face this alone any longer."

Strange, but after telling Marlowe, he'd stopped feeling as though he was.

He wriggled out of his father's arms. "You could go to Parliament, bring a motion, a bill, to have me declared unfit to serve as heir and have Stuart named in my place."

His father gave him a pointed glare. "Oliver, you are my heir. I suspect Stuart won't mind helping. He's a bit of an irresponsible scamp but he loves you."

"There are times when I feel as though I'm going mad."

"I think when we survive something horrific that our mind tries to find a way to protect us. I was there when my parents were murdered. In an alley, here in London. And yet I had no memory of it, not for more than a quarter of a century. When the memories finally returned, it was like being bludgeoned. I don't know why you've lost numbers, but I *do* know you have always been a sharp lad. You will find a way through all this." A corner of his mouth hitched up. "For me, that way was your mother."

Langdon thought of Marlowe, but then she was mostly what he thought about these days.

The door opened and the Countess of Claybourne glided in. She abruptly came to a stop. "My God, you both look . . . unwell. What's happened?"

The earl held out his hand. "He's finally told me what challenge he is facing. It's not as bad as we surmised."

One of her hands joined with her husband's while the other was flattened against Langdon's cheek.

"What could be worse?" he asked.

"We thought you were dying," his father said.

Langdon grimaced. "God, I'm sorry. I should have told you sooner."

His mother, being the woman she was, took control, poured them each a glass of scotch, sat them down in a sitting area near the window, and announced, "You can tell us all the details now."

Chapter 30

"*I* told my parents about this wretched condition I have," Langdon said quietly once he and Marlowe were settled into his carriage.

He'd arrived right on time. Marlowe wasn't at all surprised. He seemed to have no trouble at all reading the passage of time in the shadows. She supposed ancient man had done the same before clocks were invented. "Having met them, albeit briefly, and seeing how much they love you, I suspect they were extremely supportive."

He looked out the window. "They were actually relieved. They'd already surmised something was amiss. They thought I was dying."

"Oh, my God! Poor things. They certainly hid their fears well."

"It's what aristocrats do, Marlowe. We don't show our emotions. Didn't Hollingsworth teach you that?"

"He wasn't expecting me to go out among the nobility. At least not among the proper nobles. What he expected me to know of the aristocracy, what he thought I needed to understand, was the way of the unfaithful husbands and the randy young swells. How to tell if a man would treat me with kindness or . . . misuse. That's the reason he stayed close after we ended our association. He didn't want me to choose poorly."

"I don't want you to choose poorly either, but I don't know that I have it within me to stand by and watch while you choose at all. You might have to seek his guidance again."

"I know. I've considered that. You and I haven't many nights left. I know it will mean nothing if I tell you how many, but it will be soon. I have enjoyed being naughty and taking some time away from responsibilities."

"I think some might argue regarding your definition of *naughty*."

"Not if they saw what you and I get up to."

He laughed. Oh, she was going to miss that sound.

The carriage came to a stop and a footman wearing the Twin Dragons livery stepped up and opened the door for them. Langdon climbed out and then reached back and assisted her. With a smile, she wound her arm around his.

She took a step.

Felt the pull as he took a step as well, only in the opposite direction.

They both stopped, looked at each other. With his brow furrowed, he appeared as confused as she felt.

"Why are you headed toward the front steps?" she asked. "The entrance to the secret rooms is around this way."

"We're not going to the secret rooms. We're going to the main area."

Her bubble of laughter cut off into a scoff. Because people were rushing past to get to their destination, she dragged him off to the side. "I can't go in there."

"Why not?"

"It's for proper people."

"You're proper."

"No, I'm not. I'm a courtesan."

No one wanted mistresses in the respectable part of the Dragons for fear that if associating with them, wives would begin having affairs and daughters would decide to become paramours instead of wives. It was ridiculous, of course. No one was going to change their ways because they looked upon a mistress or stood near one. It wasn't as though they were a disease to be caught.

"You're not tonight. Not mine. You refuse to be mine. You're my lover." He leaned near and whispered sotto voce, "But no one need know that."

"They're all going to believe I'm your mistress. Just as those who were in the secret rooms the night we left together are convinced that I've chosen you." She sighed. "Let's just go to the area where the clientele is more accepting of sinners."

It was where she belonged. Why was he being stubborn about this?

"Have you ever been inside the more acceptable area?"

"Of course not."

"I should think a woman who is daring enough to go up in a balloon would at least be curious."

She was dying to take a peek. "I hate you," she muttered under her breath, which only caused the rapscallion to laugh.

He offered his arm. "Come on, Marlowe. Let's go have some fun."

"Are you going to attempt to play cards?"

"Roulette. I don't have to know the numbers to place my tokens on them. If I've lost the croupier takes them away. If I've won, he adds to the stack. I'll even give you tokens to play with."

She placed her hand on his arm. "If things go pear-shaped, don't say I didn't warn you."

"Everything is going to be fine."

She wished she didn't feel so much excitement as they ascended the steps.

At the top of the stairs, a footman opened the door. "M'lord."

Langdon gave a curt nod and ushered her into the massive, elegant chamber with its gigantic chandeliers. So many tables of various games. The gentlemen weren't attired so differently from those in the questionable areas of the club, but the women . . .

They were all so stylish, with glittering jewels at their throats. They didn't bray, talk loudly, or seek attention. They were graceful and sophisticated, projecting an image similar to hers. She understood now that Hollie had done her a favor when he'd taught her to act demurely. It was what would appeal to these men of rank, what they were accustomed to.

And Langdon was correct. She didn't feel at all out of place. In truth, she felt she belonged here more than she did within the secretive walls. She looked up to find Langdon watching her with the air of a man whose horse had just crossed the finish line first.

"Still hate me?" he asked.

"I may have misspoken earlier."

"I thought perhaps that was the case. There is a room for dancing, a room for dinner. A library if you want to sit and talk. Perhaps we'll explore those later. For now, shall we get some tokens and play a little roulette?"

Langdon decided he wanted to experience with Marlowe everything there was to experience in the world. He'd seen her at the card table with Hollie where she'd only watched.

But when she was engaged in play—good Lord, but her excitement was intoxicating. She was so animated: giving a little hop, clapping, and issuing the tiniest of squeals when she won. Even when she lost, she continued to smile, and he could see in her eyes her determination and belief that the next spin of the wheel would be hers to own.

If she played cards with the same enthusiasm, his family would have had no trouble at all determining when she was holding something of worth, when to best her. If he could convince her to become his mistress, he'd teach her how to manipulate the cards so she could hold her own against his family.

Although he suspected she'd done that anyway. Held her own against them.

While she wore a gown of striking crimson that caught the eye, made her more visible than the other ladies, none could hold a candle to her when it came to beauty or elegance.

While their time together was coming to a close, he didn't want to let her go. He'd already begun compiling a list of all he'd offer her if she would but stay with him. Mistress, lover, friend. Why she parsed words when applying any of them to their relationship was beyond him. Why define what they had together? He possessed the means to provide for her. He just had to convince her to allow him to do it, to reassure her that his doing so would change nothing between them.

She looked up at him, her smile so bright, the sort of smile that demanded a kiss. "I think I should quit while I'm ahead."

"Always a wise move." He slid her tokens into his hat. "Let's exchange these."

"And then?"

"You decide."

With his hand on the small of her back, he began guiding her toward the corner where a man behind a cage would handle the transaction.

"I say, Langdon—"

He turned to face the Earl of Chadbourne.

"—I don't believe whores are allowed in this part of the building."

Unfortunately, the crowd was thick tonight, and he was aware of a few gasps as others heard the vile words uttered. He'd never much liked the earl, a man who had broken off his engagement to the daughter of a duke when the duke had been convicted of treason. "Apologize or name your second."

This time the gasp came from Marlowe. She placed her hand on his arm. "It's not important. Let's just leave."

"Not until I have satisfaction." He held Chadbourne's gaze. "Apologize to the lady."

"She's not a lady. She spreads her legs—"

He struck quick and hard, his fist slamming into Chadbourne's jaw, closing his vile mouth and sending him sprawling to the floor. Glaring, Langdon stood over him. "Name. Your. Second."

He felt Marlowe's hand on his arm again, noted the trembling of her fingers, and his anger went up several notches because she had been exposed to this.

"You're not going to engage in a duel," she said. "It's against the law."

"Not for the nobility. Exceptions are made for us all the time." He didn't take his gaze from Chadbourne.

"Please, Langdon. Let's just—"

"What's this, then?"

He recognized the voice of Drake Darling, owner of the establishment. Chadbourne scrambled to his feet, obviously of the belief that help had arrived.

"Chadbourne insulted Marlowe. I can't let it stand. I demand he apologize to her or face me at dawn."

"I suppose I'll serve as your second, then."

"If you'd be so kind."

Chadbourne's eyes bulged. "You can't be serious."

"I don't allow insults in my place," Darling said. "Although you should know, I've gone hunting with Langdon. I know him to be a damned good shot."

Chadbourne looked on the verge of bringing up his accounts. He turned his attention to Marlowe. "I apologize. I may have imbibed a bit too much this evening and uttered what I ought not."

"Thank you, my lord," Marlowe said. "I accept your apology."

Darling clapped his hands. "All right. We're done here. Chadbourne, I suggest you go home to your wife."

The man scurried away.

"What an arse," Darling muttered. "I halfway wish he'd let you shoot him."

Langdon placed his hand on the small of Marlowe's back, acutely aware of her trembling. "I regret you had to endure that. However, allow me to introduce Drake Darling, my cousin."

She gave a small curtsy. "Sir, it's an honor to make your acquaintance. Thank you for your assistance with the matter."

"My pleasure. My family would never forgive me if I allowed Langdon to do something reckless. Although he is a damned good shot."

"I wouldn't have liked him dueling."

"Don't blame you."

"You're the second family member I've met today."

"Oh?"

"She met Uncle James earlier," Langdon explained.

"Ah. You'll find we're rather a large family. Lot of different branches on our family tree. My adoptive father, the Duke of Greystone, is Langdon's mother's brother. Now if you'll both excuse me, I have some other pressing matters to which I must attend." He patted Langdon on the shoulder. "See you at Grace's ball." With that, he strode off.

Langdon turned to Marlowe. "Grace is his sister, the Duchess of Lovingdon."

She didn't look as though she cared for a genealogy lesson.

"I suppose you'd like to leave now," he said.

She didn't look at him when she responded. "Yes."

*M*arlowe was still shaking as she climbed into the carriage. While exchanging their tokens, Langdon had sent someone to alert his driver they'd be leaving, so the conveyance was waiting for them when they stepped out of the club.

As the carriage rumbled away, she didn't know if she'd ever experienced such anger. She was mad at Langdon for convincing her to go into the club; mad at herself for agreeing; mad at Chadbourne, certain his coarse words were a result of his upset that she'd not become his mistress after the awful poem he'd recited. But most of all she was furious with Langdon for putting himself at risk.

"Did you give any consideration to the fact that numbers are involved in dueling?" she asked the shadow sitting across from her. "Would you have recognized that ten comes after nine and been at the ready to quickly turn in order to fire your pistol at your opponent before he got off a shot at you?"

His answer was to look out the window.

"I thought not." She imagined him getting confused as the numbers were called out, his hesitating, the echo of gunfire, and him crumpling to the ground. The prospect of his death was more terrifying than that of her own.

"I'd have worked out a signal with my second," he stated succinctly.

"Oh, well, nothing to go wrong there." She took several deep breaths to calm her temper because other matters needed to be addressed.

"All that aside, I tried to tell you what would happen," she finally said. "That I wouldn't be welcomed."

"I didn't notice anyone else not welcoming you, and as Darling pointed out, Chadbourne is an arse. I won't be at all surprised if at some point, he does face a pistol at dawn."

He was trying to appease her, and she wasn't in the mood to be appeased. "There were a few raised eyebrows, a few narrowed gazes."

"Has it happened before? An insult?"

"Of course it has. Whenever Hollie took me to a lecture or the theater or even the horse races. Sometimes the slights were muttered behind my back, sometimes to my face."

"What did he do about them?"

"Ignored them. Told me to ignore them as well. So those who issued them wouldn't know they'd hit their mark. It would have drawn much less attention and caused less embarrassment if you'd simply ignored Chadbourne."

"I protect what is mine, Marlowe."

"But I am not yours."

He crossed over to her so quickly she barely had time to note what he was doing before he was sitting beside her, his hand cupping her face. "Are you not?"

He trailed his lips along her throat, the heat from his mouth turning her anger into an emotion far hotter, far more dangerous to them both. "Tell me to stop and I will," he growled.

Squeezing her eyes shut, she searched for the words to end this madness. Why with him did it always feel like a storm was swirling around her? Why did she want so desperately what she knew she should deny?

She grabbed the lapels of his coat, intending to shove him away from her, and instead she pulled him nearer. His mouth traveled down to an upper swell of a breast, and molten fire poured through her, unleashing a torrent of desire and need that she couldn't have denied if her life depended on it.

Cradling his head, she lifted it and took his mouth with urgency, as if it provided all the sustenance she needed to live. Their tongues tangled, their breaths clashed. Their hands became greedy to touch forbidden skin.

He was dragging down her bodice. She was unbuttoning his trousers. When he sprung free, she knew triumph. He groaned low, a tormented keen as she wrapped her fingers around him. She whimpered when he latched onto her breast and suckled hard.

She felt they were trying to punish each other for the reality of their situation. They were not a couple who could go into proper places. They were meant for the shadows. For secret doors. For sin.

Tonight had brought the reminder home. He wasn't one to ignore a slight, and she knew they could come as fast as the arrows slung by archers during a battle.

At that moment she hated her father, hated that his actions had denied her the very life he'd promised. She was angry at her mother for not being stronger. Mad at her younger self for choosing a path that had seemed to be easier but in the end was all the harder to traverse.

And worst of all, she was furious at this man for making her want everything she could never have. For making her squirm with need. For forcing her not to want to let him go.

He skimmed his fingers up her leg, drawing little circles over the sensitive flesh of her thigh, going higher and higher, until the circles became strokes where she was damp and ready for him.

He plunged into her and she cried out from the pure ecstasy of taking him into her body and holding him close. As he rocked against her, she grabbed his buttocks and urged him on, his thrusts hard and forceful, his grunts and groans echoing around her as the pleasure built to almost unbearable heights.

"Tell me you're mine," he ground out.

"I'm . . . not yours."

His tempo increased, his thrusts more powerful. A storm to be reckoned with. But she'd faced storms before. She moved her hips in rhythm to his, taking and giving, until all the sensations converged, and she bit down on his shoulder to stop her cries from competing with Big Ben for volume. Her body spasmed and shook as a million stars erupted within it.

He released a tortured growl as he slammed into her one last time.

They both lay there on the bench, cramped and awkwardly positioned, their clothing askew as their rough breathing slowed. Finally, they began to extricate themselves from each other. Without a word, he helped her to put herself back together. Then he saw to himself.

She couldn't look at him. She had no words. All she'd needed to utter was "stop." Only, she hadn't wanted him to cease his attentions. She would never want him to stop. Always she would want him to continue. Always she would want him. And therein resided the danger of obtaining a broken heart.

The carriage came to a halt. He shoved open the door, leapt out, reached back for her, and handed her down. He walked with her up the steps. She placed her hand on the latch before turning to him.

"We're done," she said quietly but with conviction.

"Marlowe—"

"We're. Done."

She went inside, leaving him there, and almost doubled over from the pain of doing so.

Chapter 31

Sitting in her front parlor, Marlowe looked over the design for her new car that the builder she'd hired had sent over. She wanted something a little larger, a little sturdier. She was contemplating hiring out, giving people rides. She doubted she'd make enough to feed herself, much less to care for her mother and pay off her father's debts. But it would fill her days and perhaps eventually set her on a new path. Mistresses were seldom bothered during the day.

Two nights had passed since the calamitous affair at the Dragons. Of course it had made the gossip columns. Naturally the lords were offered some protection, only their initials used—Lord L and Lord C. She, however, was on full display. Marlowe. There was a time when it had pleased her to be so well-known. Now she wished only for anonymity.

She did an awful lot of wishing. Her father had taught her that. *Wish for anything you want. You never know which wish will come true.*

She also wished she'd not been quite so curt with Langdon when he'd brought her home that night. He was obviously honoring her hasty announcement that they were done because she hadn't seen or heard from him since. Oh, how she missed him.

Especially as she studied the design of the car he'd offered to pay for. Or when she crawled into bed at night wearing his shirt. Or when she looked at the barometer upon first awakening in order to determine if the day would be brilliant.

So many lovely days when she missed having her balloon. But it should be repaired in another week, maybe two. While she and Langdon were no longer together, she could still offer to take him up. She wanted to share that experience with him, show him the joy of being above it all. Troubles and strife always seemed to remain on the ground, too heavy to float above the clouds.

She heard the resounding knock on the door, but ignored it, knowing her butler would see to it. Only a few minutes passed before he was walking into the room, holding what appeared to be an ivory envelope.

"This was just delivered by a young man dressed in livery," he said. "I'm afraid I didn't catch the design of the coat of arms on the coach well enough to identify whom he might be serving."

She took the envelope. Her name was written on it in elegant script. She turned it over. Within the wax resided the outline of the coat of arms. She'd never memorized them all, so she hadn't a clue as to whom this one belonged. Was a duke extending her an invitation to become his mistress? It seemed possible. Perhaps Hollie had enjoyed dinner with said duke and put a word in his ear about his former mistress needing a protector. Yesterday she'd sent him a note alerting him that she and Langdon were over and she would begin in earnest the hunt for someone to provide for her all she required.

Oh, how she hated that. She wanted a different way to take care of herself. But she'd grown so accustomed to the life she now led that it would be hard to give it up, to go without. And unfair to ask the shop owners in Vexham to be more patient than they'd already been when it came to being paid what was owed to them.

Knowing for certain that her father was dead, and how he had died, her anger with him had dissipated somewhat. Perhaps she should take a few days to visit her mother now, before she gained a new lover who might not be thrilled with her going away once the Season ended. She'd have to learn all his various quirks. How he liked his tea. His favorite alcoholic beverage. Which side of the bed he preferred.

She waited a few minutes after her butler left to pluck off the wax seal and take the vellum card from the envelope. As she read the inscribed words, her heart began to pound in a frantic rhythm.

The Duke and Duchess of Lovingdon
Request the honor of your presence . . .

"Are you responsible for this?"

Sitting at his desk, Langdon looked up from the possible future plans he'd been outlining for the estate. He wasn't yet certain of their viability, but it thrilled him to consider how he might improve what he would one day inherit.

Waving an ivory card, Marlowe was marching toward him. He'd not slept since she'd slammed the door on him, he missed her so. He'd barely eaten. He didn't like the way things had gone the last time they were together. She might be ready to end things, but he wasn't.

He stood and fought against going around the desk, taking her in his arms, and capturing her mouth with his own. "And what would that be?"

She slapped the card down on his desk. He didn't bother to look. He couldn't tear his gaze away from the fire in her eyes. So much passion in this woman.

"The Duke and Duchess of Lovingdon have invited me to the ball they are hosting tomorrow night."

"Yes."

She appeared flummoxed. "Yes, what?"

He wondered if being so close to him, so near, her thoughts had drifted to them doing something a good deal more fun than sorting out an invitation. "Yes, I asked them to invite you to their ball."

"Did you learn nothing from our night at the Twin Dragons?"

"I was reminded that you are not mine . . . and I am not yours. However, I spoke with them before our trek to the club and as they've gone to the trouble to invite you, it seems you could at least go to the trouble to attend. I am more than willing to provide escort."

She shook her head. "My presence would only serve to ruin their affair."

"I very much doubt it. The Duke and Duchess are powerful in their own right. Add to that the influence of their families—Lovingdon's stepfather is Jack Dodger, one of the wealthiest men in Britain, and you already know the duchess's father is the Duke of Greystone—and the fact that those three families are very near and dear to my family and none of their guests are going to want to cause any unpleasantness. Especially toward a woman on my arm."

"And the duchess is your cousin."

"Yes. Drake Darling and his wife will be there. As will Uncle James and his family. Uncle William and his."

"Uncle William?"

"Dr. Graves."

"You're related to him as well?"

"Not by blood. But as you can see, unlike at the Dragons, should I have a need to defend you, I'll have an army at my back. One that plays dirty."

She released a caustic laugh. "We're done."

"Attending the ball doesn't change that. I can escort you without being your lover."

She began pacing. "This is madness."

"Have you ever been to an aristocrat's ball?"

Coming to a stop, she glared at him. "Of course not."

"Wouldn't you like to attend one?"

Her glare intensified just before she looked away. He knew it was because she didn't want him to see the yearning.

"What I want has no bearing on the matter. I refuse to be the cause of bringing mayhem to their ballroom."

And people deemed her selfish. Fools all.

"An invitation to the Lovingdon ball is coveted. And here you have received one. I certainly don't wish to influence your decision, but I think if you don't go, a day will come when you'll regret your lack of courage."

He was surprised the arrows her eyes shot his way didn't mortally wound him.

"It's not cowardice. As I've said, I don't want to ruin things for them."

"As I've been trying to convey . . . that's unlikely to happen. It'll be a much friendlier gathering than we had the other night. And Chadbourne won't be in attendance. His invitation was rescinded after he demonstrated such atrocious behavior."

"I suppose you were responsible for that as well."

I protect what is mine.

"He needed a lesson on when to open his mouth and when to keep it shut. I was more than happy to oblige when it came to his education."

She began pacing again. "I don't have anything to wear on such short notice."

"I've never known you to wear anything that wasn't appropriate. Except for my shirt. I would advise against wearing my shirt."

He felt a tightness in his chest begin to relax when he caught sight of her mouth twitching as though she was trying not to smile. Not to give him a smile very similar to one he'd imagined her smiling every night after he crawled into bed and watched the shadows cavorting over the ceiling, wondering if they'd moved in that manner for her when he'd been buried inside her. Thrusting, gyrating his hips. Entranced by the tightness of her.

And there was the slightest teasing sparkle in her lovely blue eyes.

"If you truly feel you have nothing suitable in your wardrobe, I'm certain Poppy wouldn't mind loaning you a frock."

"I can find something. I just don't want to be a distraction."

She would always be a distraction. It couldn't be helped. Even if she'd never been written up in a gossip column, she was the sort to be noticed. Her beauty might snag someone's attention, but it was her intriguing and confident mien that would hold them enthralled.

"Trust me, Marlowe, Lovingdon and Grace can hold their own against any distraction."

She sighed deeply. "You speak of them as though they are nothing special. Because that is your world. Whereas I am in awe. A duke and duchess, for God's sake. A duke. And duchess."

"They're just people. Fancier house. More servants. But they face challenges just like everyone else. I'm certain Grace, at least, is curious to meet you. Poppy has probably told her all about you. Imagine the stories you'll have on hand to tell your mother when you visit her." He moved around his desk and perched himself on one of its corners. "Attend the ball, allow me to escort you. The minute you experience the slightest bit of unease, we leave.

We won't argue. I won't try to change your mind. As soon as you say, 'Let's go,' we go."

Shaking her head, she released a low groan. "Our night is going to end as it did at the Dragons."

"I promise you it will not."

She studied him for several ticks of a clock. "Also promise me that you will not challenge anyone to a duel. No matter what insult they may direct at me."

"I am a good shot."

Her eyes widened with intensity. "No duel."

He nodded. "No duel." A fist, however, would not be out of place.

"All right, then, I'll go, and hope this isn't another lesson for you."

"I'll pick you up near the end of dusk."

She looked as if she might come over and kiss him. Instead, she gave a curt nod and walked out.

Chapter 32

$\mathcal{M}$arlowe was accustomed to feeling eyes on her. Normally she wasn't bothered by it. It was only that tonight there were so damned many all at once.

Standing at the top of the stairs with Langdon, waiting to be announced, she felt as though she had a thousand balloons flying around, caught in a storm in her stomach. It was madness to have come and yet—

The grandeur of the ballroom fairly took her breath. Large gilded and crystal chandeliers. A mirrored wall that reflected the room and made it seem like it went on forever. The gowns, the jewelry.

While she had selected a mauve gown with a fairly modest neckline, she had opted to forgo the pearl necklace Hollie had once given her in favor of the medallion Langdon had gifted to her. She never took it off and tonight she thought she might need it traveling through the ballroom.

When she glanced over at her escort, her breath left her completely. In evening attire, Langdon was simply too deuced gorgeous. Looking at him heated her to the point of combustion, made her want him so desperately, that she yearned to sneak off somewhere with him, take off his clothes, and lift her skirts—

Yes, madness, absolute madness.

The couple in front of them were announced. She and Langdon were next. She swallowed hard. His hand came to rest on hers where it clung to his arm.

"Remember, we'll leave whenever you're ready."

"There are so many people here, I don't think the duke and duchess would have noticed if I didn't come."

"They'd have noticed. No one would have been on my arm."

"I imagine at least half the unmarried ladies in this room are not going to be happy to see someone on your arm."

"Only half?"

She laughed. "Your ego doesn't need stroking."

"Something else does."

She gave him a pointed look. "Behave."

He touched her chin, his eyes serious. "I care about the happiness of only one. Yours."

Don't don't don't make me want you more than I already do.

Before she could come up with a witty comeback, a deep voice was filling the ballroom.

"Marlowe and Lord Langdon!"

She didn't know why she hadn't considered how it might sound to have their names linked together. She'd never gone anywhere with Hollie where they'd been announced. The gossips had always referred to him as Lord H. Certainly there were those who saw them together, knew to whom she owed her allegiance but for the vast majority he was offered some protection, the focus on her, not him.

As Langdon began escorting her down the stairs, she said, "We should have been announced separately, to give you some distance from me."

"I don't want distance from you."

"Langdon—"

"You're worrying about things that don't matter. I'm perfectly capable of navigating my way through the briar patch. Relax and enjoy your evening."

They took the last step together and he walked over to a stunning couple, their hosts.

"Langdon," the duke said sharply.

"Lovingdon." He took the hand of the lady and pressed a light kiss against her knuckles. "Grace. Allow me the privilege of introducing Marlowe."

Marlowe dropped into a deep curtsy. "Your Graces. I am incredibly honored by your invitation."

"We're glad you could join us this evening," the duchess said. "We've heard so much about you."

She forced a smile. "I hope you don't believe all of it."

"My husband was once a favorite among the gossips. It can be quite the burden. We take all rumors with a grain of salt. Langdon tells us you're an aeronaut."

She jerked her gaze over to him. He was watching her, with something akin to pride reflected in his eyes. It was an odd sensation to be associated with flight rather than sin.

"Yes, Your Grace, it's a hobby of mine."

"You must come for tea, when I won't have so many guests to greet, so you can take your time telling me about it. I'm most curious."

"My wife enjoys adventures," the duke said, and the way he looked at the woman at his side told Marlowe that he loved her deeply.

"It would be an honor to answer any of your questions about ballooning."

"I look forward to our spending more time together. Enjoy your evening."

Marlowe curtsied again and then took the arm that Langdon was offering to her. As they walked away, he asked, "That wasn't so bad, was it?"

"It was rather pleasant, although I don't think she really expects me to come for tea."

"Oh, I expect she does."

When they were a good distance away, he stopped, reached into his coat pocket, and withdrew the dance card he'd been given when they arrived. She had a much smaller one in the shape of a fan attached to her wrist.

"I'd like to waltz with you. Which is your favorite tune?" he asked.

She looked over the list. "'Greensleeves.'"

"'Greensleeves' it is." He wrote her name on his card, his on hers, in the appropriate places.

"Langdon."

He looked up at the young woman with red hair. At her side was a tall, handsome man. "Minerva. Ashebury. Allow me the honor of introducing Marlowe."

She'd always rather fancied that she was known

by one name, but tonight she was wishing she was Miss Tittering. Even if it wasn't particularly elegant.

"Marlowe, the Duke and Duchess of Ashebury."

Another curtsy. "An honor."

"It's lovely to meet you," Minerva said. "It's such a crush here tonight. But then it always is. I don't think anyone declines an invitation from them." She turned her attention to Langdon. "Our latest investment is paying off quite nicely. I have an idea for another. I'll send the numbers round next week so you can let me know if you agree it's viable."

Langdon looked at Marlowe. "Minerva enjoys finding investment opportunities. Gambling with greater risks."

The lady smiled brightly. "I am my father's daughter."

"And your father is . . ."

"Jack Dodger. Ah, there's Rexton. I need to have a word with him as well."

"After our dance," the duke said and led her away.

Marlowe studied Langdon, had sensed the stillness coming over him as though preparing for a blow when Minerva had mentioned numbers. "What will you do when you receive her calculations?"

"Pretend to study them and then tell her they're viable. She's seldom wrong."

"Did you forget that I offered to help you with numbers?"

"There are a lot of numbers in my life, Marlowe."

"Still . . ." Averting her gaze, she saw Hollie standing nearby, staring at her. Beside him was a small woman, with black hair and unremarkable features. So easy to be overlooked. Marlowe was glad, not because the lady offered no competition physically but because she knew that Hollie—so obsessed with beauty—truly loved the woman, had looked beneath the surface, something he rarely did.

She gave him a small smile, a subtle nod, striving to communicate that it was all right for him to give her a cut direct, to walk away without acknowledgment. His gaze shifted to her left, to where Langdon stood, and whatever he saw there had him escorting the lady toward them.

He stopped before her. "Marlowe, I'm surprised to see you here."

"The duke and duchess were kind enough to invite me."

"Of course they were." He looked at Langdon, nodded as though coming to some conclusion. "Effie, darling, allow me to introduce Marlowe, a dear friend of Lord Langdon's here."

"It's a pleasure," Effie, blushing, said so quietly that Marlowe almost didn't hear her over the din of the conversations surrounding them.

"I saw your announcement in the *Times*. What a fortunate lady you are to hold Lord Hollingsworth's heart. I wish you naught but happiness in the years to come."

"That's very kind of you to say."

"Not at all. I don't know him well, but I have on occasion seen the goodness in him."

Effie smiled as though Marlowe had placed a crown on his head. The young woman turned her attention to Langdon. "I suppose Poppy is here."

"I have yet to see her, but I do know she is coming. If you will both be kind enough to excuse us, I promised Marlowe this dance." Langdon offered his arm and she wrapped hers around it, grateful when he led her away from one of the most awkward situations in her life.

As he guided her over the dance floor, Langdon wasn't certain—that under similar circumstances—he could have exhibited the same grace that Marlowe had. Before the couple had come over, he'd been able to tell from Hollingsworth's posture that he was considering ignoring her, or worse, giving her a cut direct. Langdon had managed to signal that if he did either of those things, there would be hell to pay.

He'd been able to promise Marlowe there wouldn't be a repeat of the incident at the Dragons because he was well aware the tale of it had made the rounds, embellished here and there, growing to epic proportions until most realized she was under his protection and that he was damned serious about safeguarding her. She might not be pleased to realize that, but he would do all in his power to ensure she never suffered such an insult again.

How dare anyone judge her! How dare anyone not properly assess the worth of her!

A young woman taking care of her mother, striving to undo damage done by her father. Taking on burdens that weren't hers to carry.

"He truly loves her," Marlowe said. "Thank goodness, I don't think Lady Effie knows about my role in his life."

"Few do. The gossip focused on you, not him."

"That's the way of it, isn't it? A woman puts a foot wrong, and everyone is aghast and eager to point fingers at her. A man, however, his transgressions are overlooked. A man of the nobility . . . if his misbehavior is bad enough, suddenly he is an initial, not a name. That's the reason you can duel. You're all forgiven. Although tonight might do some damage to your reputation. With the exception of Chadbourne, I believe every noble in Christendom must be here."

"I suspect you're correct. Are you glad you came?" he asked.

"So far, but you don't have to watch over me. I'm certain a goodly number of ladies would like to dance with you."

"But it is you, alone, with whom I wish to dance."

"Don't get accustomed to this. I won't be attending any more balls with you. This isn't where I belong."

"You belong in the sky, chasing after rainbows."

"I'll be back at it soon. My basket should be ready in two weeks." She grimaced. "I'm sorry. That time frame probably means nothing to you."

"You can come to my residence and mark it in my diary. I've discovered when I turn the pages, I create a visual image of the day getting nearer. It gives me an idea of how time passes."

"I can't accept your offer to pay for it, though."

"I give gifts to my friends."

"Tonight is the last gift I'll accept. And it is a gift. Growing up, I always dreamed of attending a ball as glamorous as this one."

"Eventually your father would have had to tell you the truth."

She nodded. "I've often wondered when he might have done it. What other lies he might have spun. But here I am where I always thought I would be. I'm trying to memorize everything so I can share it with my mother. She still believes I'm a seamstress. I'm not ashamed of what I do, Langdon, but I don't know how she would take it."

"I should think she'd be proud of you."

He caught the sight of a tear glistening in her eye before she blinked it away.

She'd worked hard to increase her value, not realizing she'd been valuable all along.

"I did have a nefarious reason for bringing you tonight."

She arched a brow. "Oh?"

"Mmm. All of my immediate and most of my extended family are here. It seemed the appropriate place."

"For what?"

"To ask you to marry me."

*M*arlowe wasn't certain which one of them had stopped first, but suddenly they were standing in the middle of the dance floor, people waltzing around them.

She was certain she'd not heard correctly. In addition to the orchestra playing, a cornucopia of noises echoed around the room, loud enough to affect a person's hearing. Many kept a hand cupped around an ear in an effort to hear more clearly. Or perhaps it was simply that in her more recent fantasies, he'd asked for her hand—and she was presently dreaming. She would soon awaken with an emptiness in her soul.

Still, whether dream or reality, she asked, "I beg your pardon?"

His grin was small, tender, and very nearly apologetic. "I don't want doubt regarding how precious you are. How deserving you are of any dream you've ever dreamt. I want you for my wife."

She nearly released a sharp bark of laughter. "Have you forgotten *what* I am? The portrait the newspapers have painted of me? If you married me, you'd be shunned, cast out of this upper tier of Society. Langdon, I've nurtured my reputation. I'm fit to be a man's mistress, not his wife."

He studied her for what seemed eons before nodding, as though acknowledging to himself a decision made. "Then be my mistress."

She shook her head. "I can't. You don't understand."

"Then explain it."

She looked around frantically, not certain if she was searching for the answer or an escape. She loved him too much to burden him with any of this. Her reputation. The gossip. And she loved him too much to be with him when he married. "I can't share you. I won't share you. Therefore it would be only until you marry, but it would be too hard, too hard to see you walking away from me into another's arms."

"I'll never marry."

He said the words with such finality that she was taken aback. "Of course you'll marry."

"And be unfaithful to you? I think not."

What was he on about? It was to his wife he'd be unfaithful. "Once you marry, I'll move on."

With one hand, he cupped her face in that gentle way he had and touched his thumb to her healed mouth. "Would you be able to abandon me with such ease?"

The pain of watching him live out his life with another would force her to leave not only him but London. Still it was imperative he not know how she would be torn asunder when he married.

"Because I could never leave you," he added before she came up with a rejoinder. "I want to be with you until I draw my last breath."

"And what of your family?" she asked succinctly, returning to his first question. "Could they survive the embarrassment if I married you?"

"You've met them. When all is said and done, do you believe they give a tinker's curse what Society thinks?"

"Langdon—"

"You don't deserve to live in shadows, Marlowe. You don't deserve to spend evenings hidden away. You got caught in a maelstrom of bad decisions that were chosen by others. You made the best of the situation. But if you could shake off the past, what would you want for your future?"

Not fair. Not fair. Because he was what she wanted. He was what she would always want. But she was tainted. However, the thought of being with this man for the remainder of her days . . .

Even if they only spent them in bed, the days would fill her to bursting with contentment.

His hand fell away from her face and she was bereft at the absence of his touch. She dearly wanted to grab his hand and return it to where it had been.

"Perhaps I've gone about this all wrong," he said somberly. "Certainly I could have come to your residence with my proposal, but I wanted witnesses, I wanted you to see that I'm not ashamed or embarrassed to be with you. I love you, Marlowe. I love how courageous you are. To go up in the sky. I love how compassionate you are. To offer me solace when locked in the throes of a nightmare. I love how you see a problem and search for solutions. You're going to keep track of numbers for me. I love the kindness you showed my sister when she was embarrassed at her reaction when she looks down from on high. I love you for your loyalty to Hollingsworth. I love everything about you."

He lowered himself to one knee. "So I ask again, with everything that I am, with everything that I will ever be, with a heart that will forever be only yours, regardless of your answer . . . will you marry me? Will you be my wife, my viscountess, one day my countess, my keeper of secrets, and my lover?"

She was acutely aware of the din fading away and eyes coming to rest on him and her. Looking into Langdon's pewter eyes, she saw all the love he held for her, all the promises he'd make over the years, promises he would keep. She saw in her arms a little boy with eyes the same shade as his.

"Are you sure?"

"I've never been more sure of anything in my life."

She felt very much as she'd felt when she'd been caught in the tempest, clinging to the gondola for dear life, not certain what fate awaited her. Terrified.

She still didn't know what fate awaited her—and it was frightening to leave behind a life she knew how to navigate, in order to travel through one that had yet to be mapped out—but she knew that together nothing could defeat them.

"I love you," she told him. "And because I do, so very much, I know I should decline your proposal, I should say no, but there is nothing I want more than to be your wife, to share your life."

He was a blur as he shot to his feet, took her in his arms, and latched his mouth onto hers. She heard claps and cheers. From his family no doubt, from all the members he'd told her would stand at his back in defense of her.

Hence it was that the following morning several gossip sheets reported the most infamous courtesan in London had received what was certain to be the most romantic marriage proposal of the Season.

Chapter 33

*T*wo weeks later, in St. James Park, Marlowe stood in front of her repaired ballon. It was to be its maiden voyage. If she looked closely enough, she could see a few of the mended tears. She thought the colorful strips of cloth had never looked more beautiful.

There had been a downpour that morning, but now the skies were clear and the sun bright.

Beside her, Langdon opened the door she'd had added to the wicker basket so it was easier to get in and out of. Stepping into the gondola, taking a deep breath, she felt as though she'd come home.

"Come along, Vicar," Langdon said.

The older gentleman, clutching his Bible, looked askance at her beloved contraption. "Are you quite certain it's safe?"

"For the ceremony, we're only ascending a few feet. It'll stay tethered to the ground. Perfectly harmless." He looked at her, an eyebrow arched. He was so handsome in his gray trousers, waist-coat, and neckcloth, white shirt, blue frockcoat, and top hat. She could hardly believe he was going to be hers forever.

"Perfectly safe," she assured him and the vicar, as well as those who'd be joining them.

With a bit more grumbling, the vicar finally boarded. The gondola rocked slightly. He grabbed onto the edge of the basket and uttered a prayer. She suspected her wedding was going to contain more prayers than any other in England.

Langdon assisted Poppy in coming on board. She was going to serve as Marlowe's attendant. Stuart, as best man, followed.

"Anyone else?" Langdon asked.

His entire family—parents, aunts, uncles, cousins, by heart or by blood—were gathered around them. Marlowe's mother had decided not to join them. She had no fond memories of balloons.

"As there is room," the Countess of Claybourne said, taking her husband's hand and dragging him after her.

Before Marlowe had left for the park, she'd studied her reflection in the cheval glass and felt a bit like she was wearing a lie. Her gown was ivory and looked so pure and innocent, when she was anything but. Sophie had assisted her when she went to the modiste, had convinced her that it was perfectly acceptable for her to wear a gown such as the one she now wore.

"You're leaving the old life behind, starting afresh. Let your wedding gown announce that loud and clear."

She'd asked Sophie to stand with her, but her

friend had declined and reminded her, "You're leaving the old life behind."

"But not you, Sophie. Not my friend."

Sophie had given her a sad smile. "I've known women who have left this life. They all promise to stay in touch but eventually they stop coming to call. You will as well. And I don't blame you. Nor do I hold it against you. But it's less painful if we make a clean break."

Therefore, they'd hugged and wept and said their goodbyes.

After his parents were situated, Langdon stepped onto the car, closed, and bolted the door. She'd already explained what he would need to do. He took hold of a bag of sand and dropped it over the side. Then another and another.

The balloon began to slowly rise. Poppy squealed. The vicar prayed. Some in the crowd gasped. Others released exclamations of awe.

Edging around Stuart, Langdon came to stand beside her and took her hands. "Whenever you're ready, Vicar. I'm incredibly anxious to take this remarkable woman as my wife."

Much to her surprise, the vicar's voice rang out loud and clear and she suspected it traveled through the entire park. While he spoke about the sanctity of marriage, she never took her gaze from her soon-to-be husband. She was certain life would deal them some challenges, but she also knew together they could weather any storm.

As he placed the diamond-encrusted band on her finger, Langdon repeated his vows so passionately that she thought she might find them emblazoned on her skin somewhere. They most certainly found a home in her heart.

When the vicar pronounced them man and wife, Langdon took her in his arms and kissed her—not with the passion he would later that night—but she was well aware of the heat simmering below the surface.

Several men, who'd remained on the ground, came forward and grabbed hold of the tethers, bringing the balloon back to earth. The vicar was the first to disembark . . . quite hastily in fact.

While everyone else departed from the car, Marlowe waited, happy and content and in love. And loved.

While the path she'd traveled to get here might not have been the one she would have chosen had circumstances been different, she neither resented nor regretted the journey.

Her husband leaned toward her and whispered in her ear, "Are you ready for our grand exit?"

She nodded, smiled.

He turned to face his family. "My bride and I want to thank you all for sharing these moments with us. As you know, a luncheon has been prepared for you at my parents' residence, but we shan't be joining you. It is time for us to make our departure."

She touched his arm. "I have something to say."

He stepped back slightly. "Of course."

She looked out over the smiling crowd. "I want to add my thanks to my husband's but not only for your being here, but for accepting me, faults and all. While I have known you for hardly any time at all, I do know that you already hold a place in my heart, and I shall endeavor to ensure I earn a place in yours."

"You already have, sweetheart," the Earl of Claybourne said. "Just take care of each other."

"Oh, we shall." She looked up, gasped, and wrapped her hand around Langdon's arm. "Oh, look, a rainbow."

"I ordered it just for you."

She laughed lightly. "You command nature now, do you?"

He grinned, put an arm around her, and drew her in close.

"Where are the two of you going for your wedding trip?" Poppy asked.

"We're going to the other side of that rainbow," he said. When he looked at Marlowe, his eyes were twinkling with mischief. "Are you ready for an adventure, Lady Langdon?"

"I'm ready for anything, as long as we're together."

Epilogue

From the Journal of Lord & Lady Langdon

We have been married 10 years. We have 4 children. 2 boys. 2 girls.

I look at the sentences my beautiful and beloved wife wrote in our journal, and I cannot interpret everything. I see the numbers. I know they are numbers. Do they represent a few or many? I still cannot recall their name without being told or comprehend their value.

No, that is not true. Because what I do understand about the above numbers is that each one is composed of an abundance of love. Love that is equal to every star in the sky. Stars I cannot count but I can determine go on forever, into infinity.

And that is the depth of my love for my wife and my children.

Marlowe and I created quite the stir with our marriage. But it didn't take long for the name Marlowe to fade from the public consciousness altogether because "Marlowe" was no longer written about. Not in gossip columns, gossip rags, or gossip sheets.

Lady Langdon, however . . . she fills the Society pages with her balls, dinners, and good works.

She visits orphanages and carries the children up in a tethered balloon. She does the same thing in the slums and rookeries. She takes little scamps with nothing and gives them what few possess: the confidence of knowing that anything is possible.

She even believes in the impossible, my wife does. She is certain that in the very near future, a machine will be invented that will soar through the heavens with such speed that it will replace the railway as a means of transporting people. When it comes to pass, she intends to fly it.

The unhappy wives of lords come for tea and confide in her regarding their straying husbands or their discontent, and she advises them on how to bring their men into line without them even realizing they are being tamed.

I suspect in some ways she may have even brought me to heel. Not that I mind. I want only for her to be happy.

She allowed me to pay off her father's debts. It took some doing, but we convinced her mother to come live with us. Eventually she met an aging lord she liked immensely, married him, and became what her first husband promised her she would be: a countess.

Marlowe has kept to her vow of keeping track of numbers for me. Sometimes I can almost snag one and then it dissipates like fog before the sun. It is such a strange affliction. Numerous doctors have studied me but are no closer to determining what the hell is going on in my brain. Perhaps numbers will return one day, but I am no longer bothered by their absence.

Marlowe and I even devised a series of signals that provides me with the information I need so I can cheat when playing cards with my family.

We are a team, Marlowe and I. Together we can weather any storm, survive any tempest. We are unconquerable.

That is the strength and power of our love. It is immeasurable. Where it is concerned, numbers are moot.

I still am unable to tell her how many times we have made love, but I have yet to forget a single moment of loving her madly.

Author's Note

When I came up with the notion for a story about a woman being marooned on a grouch's island, I struggled with how to do it so I wouldn't have to deal with a lot of casualties, and thus sadness, from a shipwreck.

Hence, when I ran across *Balloonomania Belles: Daredevil Divas Who First Took to the Sky* by Sharon Wright, I was intrigued, especially as the cover artwork showed women wearing Regency attire. The book was a fascinating study of not only the history of ballooning, but women's instrumental roles in making it a fad. From an interesting hobby to daredevil escapades, ballooning enabled them to find freedom in the skies they seldom found on land.

And I had the answer to my dilemma: my heroine would be an aeronaut.

I wanted her to land at night, during a storm. Would readers believe she would be that reckless? Then *The Early History of Ballooning* by Fraser Simons revealed that many balloonists went up at night because the winds were calmer. It also included an account about a group of balloonists who got caught in a storm, crashed into the sea, and were rescued by a passing ship.

As for the fate of Marlowe's father . . . that was based on an incident that happened in the late 1700s, when a balloon caught fire while flying over a remote area and the locals, unfamiliar with such a contraption, did indeed believe it was a monster and attacked it with pitchforks. Fortunately, it was an unmanned balloon.

Regarding the dye Marlowe used on her hair— during the Victorian era, for a period of time, dark hair was treasured, and women used such concoctions to darken the shade. Like Langdon, I was horrified by the waste of good wine.

As for my hero . . . I mentioned to my younger son, a history major, that my hero had such a charmed life, I wanted something to happen that created a challenge for him. Maybe he would be injured in a railway accident because they were so common at the time. To which he replied, "You should research railway spine. It was quite the thing during the Victorian era."

I found a series of lectures John E. Erichsen delivered at the University College Hospital in London in 1866. He didn't believe enough attention was being given to injuries that occurred during railway accidents. Some injuries could be traced to a physical cause such as a concussion and some seemed to have no physical origin (possibly the patient was suffering from what we now know as PTSD). But any injury sustained during a train wreck was often classified as railway spine, regardless of its underlying cause. Erichsen shared numerous case studies but one involved a man who, after being involved in a horrific railway accident, lost his ability to comprehend numbers.

While Langdon's situation doesn't exactly mirror the patient Erichsen referenced, I decided it would cause him to doubt his ability to handle all the responsibilities he would one day inherit—and might be the sort of condition he'd strive to keep hidden. Being as proud as he was.

Dear reader, I do hope you enjoyed Langdon and Marlowe's story, as well as the trials they faced alone and together. Writing the children of beloved characters is always a challenge because I don't want them to have awful parents, nor do I want them to become orphans. So how do I develop their character?

But I thoroughly enjoy searching for a way to keep you entertained, and I hope I didn't disappoint.

The next story will also take place in the world of the Scandalous Gentlemen of St. James. I believe I know whose it will be, but as I've discovered, sometimes when I sit down to write, the story doesn't belong to the characters I thought it did.

Warmest wishes for hours of joyous reading,
Lorraine

READ MORE BY LORRAINE HEATH

THE CHESSMEN: MASTERS OF SEDUCTION SERIES

THE COUNTERFEIT SCOUNDREL   **THE NOTORIOUS LORD KNIGHTLY**   **IN WANT OF A VISCOUNT**

—— ONCE UPON A DUKEDOM SERIES ——

SCOUNDREL OF MY HEART   **THE DUCHESS HUNT**   **THE RETURN OF THE DUKE**

—— SINS FOR ALL SEASONS ——

—— THE TEXAS TRILOGY ——

BEYOND SCANDAL AND DESIRE   **WHEN A DUKE LOVES A WOMAN**   **THE SCOUNDREL IN HER BED**   **TEXAS GLORY**   **TEXAS SPLENDOR**

THE DUCHESS IN HIS BED   **THE EARL TAKES A FANCY**   **BEAUTY TEMPTS THE BEAST**   **TEXAS DESTINY**

DISCOVER GREAT AUTHORS, EXCLUSIVE OFFERS, AND MORE AT HC.COM